Gemutations

Mercenaries and Angels

By

Denise Randall

authorHOUSE™

1663 LIBERTY DRIVE, SUITE 200
BLOOMINGTON, INDIANA 47403
(800) 839-8640
WWW.AUTHORHOUSE.COM

First published by AuthorHouse 04/14/05

ISBN: 1-4208-3307-3 (sc)

Printed in the United States of America
Bloomington, Indiana

This book is printed on acid-free paper.

Table of Contents

Prologue:
Underhanded Dealings

An older gentleman sat on a simple redwood bench near the water, looking very out of place. This park was a newly refurbished section of Old Fresno, a belated attempt to return prestige to the once powerful agricultural town. He looked around, still able to see the creases in the grass that marked where each section of living carpet had been laid, even after being settled into its new home for a month. He glanced over his shoulder seeing the scrawny trees that one day would actually be able to provide shade for the visitors to this newest park.

His name was Glenn Thompson and he was a very high-ranking executive of Blue Collar Subsidiaries. That added even more mystery to why he would risk being in this section of town so late at night. He shivered involuntarily, his thin arms fluttering at his sides, as a chill born of nerves ran through him. Bad elements still lingered here, even after the facelift of the park, and he was making himself a target in his three-piece suit and his well-groomed appearance. Reflexively he ran a hand through his neatly cut but thinning white hair, smoothing it down only long enough for the next gust of wind to muss it again.

"Where is he?" the man muttered nervously, his dark blue eyes darting back and forth along the walk in front of him. He slowly stood and turned back toward the darkened park behind him, wondering if Cortez was going to materialize from the darkness instead. "He's late."

Glenn looked down at his watch and then back up to the heavily shadowed park, butted up against steep hills that used to be the tops of mountains. This whole area had been created by one huge fill, taking just a small portion of the Sea of San Joaquin back. Large cement blocks, like a giant's version of jacks, lined the perimeter of the artificial plateau in an effort to prevent the water from stealing back the sand and dirt. He glumly questioned the effectiveness of the devices, and wondered just how long it would take for the hastily built refuge to erode back to its mother. Just before him was a section of artificial beach, for the amusement of visitors to the place in the hot summer days to come.

His cynical thoughts turned back to his purpose here. His company and Marlin Incorporated were in the process of a business merger, and a mighty nasty merger it was turning out to be. Cortez's proposal would have nearly seventy five percent of the workers in the company thrown out on their ear. He also had managed to make BCS stock worth nearly nothing, and now the stockholders were complaining.

BCS's board was about to back out of the whole deal, even knowing that it would cost them billions of credits to do so, so sour was the deal to them. On the eve of their negotiations Glenn had received a call. Cortez promised that he had a proposal that would benefit both sides and clear the bad taste left in the mouth of the board. That was if Glenn could sway the board to see it Cortez's way. It had sounded good enough to get Glenn out here, especially when Cortez had spoken of ample compensation for his troubles.

Glenn looked down at his watch yet again, anxious about the tardiness of his compatriot in this deal. He widened his eyes, trying to gather more light in them to make something out through the dark blanket shrouding the park and thinking that he had seen something or someone moving.

As he continued to stare toward the land, the placid surface of the sea was disturbed by something moving very close to the surface. The dark inky ripples lapped onto the shore, slightly louder than the light surge. Glenn's head twitched a little toward the water, but he did not look, used to the sounds of the ocean at night. He had grown up here in this valley and spent most of his teenage years either on the water or by it. He was convinced that it was just some kind of fish, perhaps even a small shark, swimming into the murky shallows to feed. Glenn squinted again, sure he saw movement toward the hill behind them, and anxiously hoped Cortez would soon appear.

The water's smooth contours split as the creature eased its nose above the surface. Predator eyes glinted in the soft florescent light centered over and illuminating the bench and the glowing orbs seemed to flash as their owner blinked several times. Their colors changed as the eyes shifted, one moment stark, full moon white, the next red, and again to a blue green as the angle of light reflected differently into them. There was another disturbance as the creature hunched its back and a dorsal fin broke the surface, pale and luminescent and just barely visible through a brighter shock of brilliantly white hair. It rose steadily higher out of the water, strong legs freeing it from the possessive grip of the ocean. Long slim arms dangled, oversized webbed hands lax at its sides, as the creature slowly and quietly straightened to its full height. When it stood upright, it was six feet tall, and there could be no doubt that it was nothing born of the sea. The light glistened in textured brilliance off of the creature's skin.

As it stepped out of the surf onto the raised boardwalk, its webbed and clawed foot made a wet slapping sound. This did get Glenn's attention and he turned back curious about what kind of fish had jumped clear onto the concrete. He was looking down expecting to see a fish flopping helplessly on the sidewalk; he took a shocked step backward as he came face to face with an abomination.

The creature seemed oddly amused by Glenn's discomfiture, smiling widely and exposing multiple rows of triangular teeth that an elongated, very shark-like, snout housed. Before Glenn could realize he was horrified enough to scream, the creature was leaping toward him, his clawed hands outstretched. With a quick swipe the creature slashed his throat deeply, severing artery, tendon, and larynx. The sound that Glenn tried to push out became an airy sigh.

The man stumbled back, hands to his ruined throat in a vain attempt to staunch the massive hemorrhage that was now staining his expensive suit. His consciousness faded in and out, coming into focus long enough to see the creature stepping toward him.

The creature grabbed his lapel and with a strength that seemed odd in such a thin humanoid, threw him easily into the cold water of the inland sea. Glenn barely felt the impact, sputtering as water and blood mixed around him. He made a weak attempt to reach shore, but the creature, smiling again, splashed back into the ocean, and, grabbing his jacket, dragged him further away from the thin hope that was the shoreline.

"No!" he mouthed, knowing he had been unable to make himself clear. Slowly his consciousness ebbed again. He was only barely aware when the thing pulled him beneath the black surface.

Chapter One:
The Mercenary, the
Businessman, and the Angel

"Well done, Tigershark," Marlin purred as I came upon the shore, and catching deftly the proof of my successful hunt. He looked at the ring finger I had freed from my victim momentarily, and then casually flicked it toward a pile of rocks to one side of him. Several small, brownish red crabs scuttled out of hiding, descending on the fleshy feast.

I was rather surprised to see him actually, especially down here in the cold dank cavern that somehow managed not to collapse under the weight of the skyscraper above. It was a large cavern, here and there pierced with thick girders that helped hold the infrastructure of the said same building. Along the stalactite dotted ceiling, were incandescent bulbs scattered haphazardly, providing almost a permanent sunset where we stood. There was a broad flat shelf that gradually climbed out of the sea, becoming almost a landing as it reached further in. Towards the back of the immense cavern were networks of cubbies and tunnels and chimneys in the rock. Marlin Cortez kept a lot of secrets down here. Even I didn't know them all...honestly, I didn't want to. I was only his mercenary after all.

I glanced back up at the man's broadly smiling face. He was a short man, stout, and well muscled. He was a man who took great pains to keep his already thick look from turning into a berry of some nature. That was a compliment considering half his contemporaries were rotund from the opulent lifestyle they lived. Marlin Cortez had a broad flat face, milk chocolate colored skin, with light almost sand colored eyes flecked with green. His hair and mustache were black slowly fading with age, now peppered with gray.

"He was right where you said he'd be," I remarked as I stepped past him. "Idiot, you'd think he would learn that cheaters never prosper." I shook my head. "You should have seen the look on his face!"

"Yes," Marlin said, looking not the least bit interested in the details of my foray "As agreed your bonus has been posted. And my negotiations will go much easier in acquiring BCS, now that Glenn is no longer around to stir trouble for me."

Just about then my wrist band beeped and, looking at it, I could see that he was as good as his word the agreed upon funds instantly made their way into my account. "Outstanding," I answered, plopping down on a flat topped stalagmite near the water's edge. Marlin tossed me a towel and I proceeded to dry my hair.

"I have another assignment for you," Marlin said without any more pleasantries. I looked up as he handed me a file about 3/4" thick.

Setting the towel aside I leaned back, balancing the now open folder on my overlarge hand. I flipped through the paperwork getting a general idea of what kind of assignment he was giving me, pausing as I took a good look at the picture of my next victim.

"What the hell happened to her?" said I, my lip curling in disgust.

It was a woman of fine features staring blindly out of the photograph. I said blindly because her eyes had the white filmy look of someone who had been blind their whole life. That was not all; her eyes exactly matched the milky shade of her skin and the wild stand of hair on her head. "She's an albino? I thought that didn't happen any more."

Marlin didn't answer my question and instead said, "This woman has gained access to some very sensitive information regarding our contracts and trade overseas."

"Oh?" I said, looking up from my reading of the file to the man's face, absently pulling the pheromone swath out of the attached bag and running it under my nose.

"She is looking to sell that information to the highest bidder."

"That bitch," I said in mock indignation.

The look I received for my humor was scolding, to put it mildly "I don't need to tell you that if this information gets out Marlin Inc. will end up bankrupt."

"I understand," I added, bristling slightly at the tone in which he used on me.

"Good," he said shortly, turning slightly away from me and cleaning his nails in indifference.

I stood, nodding. "I'll get started tracking her first thing in the morning."

"Of course," Marlin said amiably, and then looked me in the face again. "By the way, I'm having some...contributors over tomorrow."

3

My gut sank and my previous happy expression drew down into a frown. He had done this to me before.

"I want them to see you," Marlin said carefully. "You are after all the best. It could earn you some extra assignments."

The thought of more and varied bonuses did not clear the grimace from my face. "You mean to showcase me in the cage," it was a statement, my voice icy, I did not like when he did that. There were other ways to go about impressing his business partners, "Don't you think I could just...mingle for once?"

"That would lessen the impact of your presence," he answered smoothly.

I raised my eye ridges to let him know I didn't believe him for a second. "Look, Marlin, I'm not some dog and pony show for you to trot out every time your billionaire buddies come to visit, you know."

"Need I remind you of the clause in your contract?"

I couldn't help the growl that escaped my throat. "When I read that I would be involved in 'promotional meetings,' I did not think that it meant being a zoo attraction."

His smile grew wider. "I could compensate you for the trouble."

My brows furrowed now, knowing his meaning of "compensation" did not always mean credits. After all, I was Mr. Thompson's "compensation," and he was none to happy with the deal.

"How much?" I asked gruffly, crossing my arms and looking aloof.

"How about 150,000 credits," he said almost too quickly, as if expecting my question.

My eyebrows rose again and then flattened back out. Knowing that I was backed into a corner with no escape, I conceded "All right," That I had gotten him to offer me money was a boon too.

I'll be damned if that smile didn't grow even wider across his broad face.

*****

I stood, leaning into the corner of the silver barred shark cage (of all things), staring at the cloth that kept me out of view of my audience. I shook my head; surely I was getting too greedy to do something of this nature, and it was nothing short of demoralizing.

That thought slipped quickly out of my head when the soft click sounded at the top of the cage. I stood straighter, trying not to look like I was either bored or a strip club parlor trick, as the cloth quietly slithered over the bars to fall into the water well below where I was suspended.

Below and immediately in front of my position was a group of about seven people, all of them executives, or at least trying to pretend that they were. They each wore suits much like the others, bland gray of varying shades and textures, each with either a gray or black casual top underneath. One of the suited gentlemen at the water's edge was practically bouncing off the balls of his feet as he got a good look at my features. The others simply stared at me as if I was a circus animal they had seen all too many times before.

"How do you think I feel?" I thought sullenly.

The one who was so enthusiastic whispered that I was a perfect weapon. I couldn't help thinking that the man needed to get away from his desk a little more. The others turned to the younger executive as well with looks of disdain for his uncouth performance.

I guess I was unusual to them, so insulated from the world that went on around them. Seven years ago I traded my humanity to better survive in this world, a world that had been forever transformed by the rising ocean levels caused by global warming. I had been genetically enhanced, given the ability to operate as a sea dweller, with the added advantage of retaining enough humanity to still function on land. They must think that fairly amazing.

I chanced a look at Cortez who was puffed up and proud to show his friends just what enough money could buy. He caught me looking and smiled just a little, then glanced away and nodded. The cage jerked as the cable brake abruptly released its hold. The sudden motion unbalanced me, and I jammed my shoulder hard against one of the bars. I glared at the operator as I rubbed the sting away against sandpaper rough skin.

"This is definitely the last time," I muttered as I leaned forward, forgetting myself and bumping my elongated muzzle on the bar in front of me. "Damn it," I swore softly, blinking back tears of pain.

I turned my face slightly sideways, succeeding at looking through the bars and watching the water rise to greet me. Soon I could start to trail my mark, and get away from this stage. I could still smell the scent of the woman, lingering in my sensitive olfactory canal. Marlin had learned early on that I was preternaturally good at tracking down scents. He provided me with pheromone markers of each of my contracts, and it was one way to guarantee that I would not lose my assigned hit. I was a great deal more reliant on my smell than my eyesight. My sight even under water was not the best, having a range of only thirty feet. I have accommodated for it well in the last seven years, having no problems maneuvering with just my hearing and my smell. Even the blurred images I see now translate to a perfect picture in my head.

I watched intently as the water began to lap into my enclosure, preparing myself for the hunt. I tensed in anticipation as it engulfed my ankles and my leathery skin bristled at the chill of the area waters. I found myself taking an unconscious breath as the water closed over my head, though I couldn't tell myself why. I was calm at first, ready to get away from the atmosphere of a three-ring circus above the surface, but something snapped to life inside my head and a black wash of inexplicable and instinctive panic overtook my body. Before I could rationalize the feeling, I leapt for the top of the cage, ramming my head and shoulder into the suddenly very solid bars at the top of the enclosure. Some part of me was convinced I was about to drown, and the impact only served to intensify my panic. I twisted and writhed as I felt the oxygen in my lungs burn off. Polluted air escaped from between my clenched teeth, and I regretted its loss. As was inevitable, I had to take that next breath, even if it would mean a mouthful of saltwater and therefore my death. I drew it in, waiting for the painful collapse of my throat at rejecting the ill suited substitute, and was therefore surprised when the only thing I felt was relief in the demand of my body for oxygen. I stopped all motion; occasionally bumping into one set of bars or another, wondering what the hell all that had been about.

There were times when switching from air to water overwhelmed me with anxiety, for there was about fifteen seconds of time where I was getting oxygen from neither lungs nor gills. To this day, some seven years after my change, I still panic on occasion, thinking that the autonomic function would not switch like it was supposed to and leave me to suffocate. That had to be the explanation for the panic attack that had overtaken me just then. But, what was with the sudden disassociation? It was like there was a period of moments where I had forgotten completely that I was able to "breathe" water. That was not like me.

I shook off that feeling and moved out the now open gate in the bars toward deeper water searching for the pheromone scent I was after. Luckily the girl had made her escape by the cove to open ocean, making her that much easier to track. Though, I wondered vaguely how she knew where the cavern was in the first place.

As I cleared the entrance I pivoted in the water until I was facing the way I had come. From here the mouth looked just the same as the rest of the cliff face. The entrance was hidden now by a cleverly programmed hologram and did its deceptive job all too well. Only the web set Cortez had provided me, would give me access to the entrance, in coordinates and an access code that would prevent me from being shocked by the security interweaved into the façade.

Cortez was definitely a man with a lot of resources; that kind of gear was rare and expensive. But he had the contacts and he most definitely had the money to get the job done. I pivoted back around, sampling the air about me to pick up the faint trail still in the air after all this time. And with that I set off in search of my latest assignment.

*****

Angelina Linda Cortez sat at the counter of the "Bar Topical," cursing her ever-increasing bad luck, and trying to drown in liquor a pain which was unwilling to fade from her heart and mind.

She swallowed hard as the images came unbidden again. They were visions of pain, of torturous processes, and humiliation. Screams echoed in her head. Some were hers but most were bodiless, echoing out of the darkness. She glanced over, catching her own image in the mirror, and quickly glanced away again, sickened by what they had done to her.

She forced herself to look again, pushing back the hood of her dirty sweatshirt, and noting every detail of the damage Cortez's mad scientists had done to her once proudly Mexican beauty. No longer did she possess her raven black hair, her darkly tanned skin or her almond brown eyes. She was now as pale as a snow-capped peak. Her eyes were white and pupil-less, and how she was still able to see baffled her. Her stark white hair was coarse, thick, and frizzy, standing out like more of a mane. She shivered when she thought of what might have been intended for her.

She looked away from the mirror, staring back at the shot that stood in front of her. She quickly downed it and ordered another, as her mind did another loop through the events leading up to her current condition.

She had come to New Fresno originally to attend college, four years of political science on Mom and Dad's dime. She had broken away from them shortly after graduating, unable to cope with Dad's loss of the family business to her uncle, Marlin Cortez, and her mom's total denial that anything had changed.

Twisting the small napkin in front of her glass, Angelina grimaced at the thought of her uncle. Marlin Cortez headed one of the largest companies in the United States, one so big her friends referred to it as a 'megaglomerate.' Not even relatives were safe from Marlin's appetite for power, as was proven by his hostile takeover of his brother's business. He had used it and many other small companies, molding them into something huge. He now owned all needed processes cradle to grave for the multiple lines of products and services that supported his livelihood.

He had been one of the reasons she had used her degree and had joined an anti-monopoly watchdog called The Movement. And it was her involvement with them that had gotten her into this predicament and had taken David away from her.

She felt the pain well up again and bit her lip, blinking heavily to keep the tears from falling. She closed her eyes, seeing his smiling face in her mind, his light blue eyes sparkling. They had been so happy together, just returning from a vacation in Mexico where David had taken her...to propose.

Then this had to happen.

He had looked so good in Playa Nueva; the sun had bleached his blond hair nearly white and darkened his fair skin. She wished she could go back in time and tell The Movement to shove their little mission into Cortez's Labyrinth up their asses. The consequences of that decision had been nothing but misery for her.

She smiled through her tears at how she had despised David at one point in her life, owing to the fact that he had been her chief rival while they had both been in college. They had been in competition for the best grades and for Valedictorian. He had gotten both, damn him.

It had not been until she had run into him a year later that she had become attracted to him. He had been the one to convince her to join The Movement. They had made a great team, and had been responsible for bringing some very crooked businessmen to their knees.

Cortez's home had been their latest assignment. There were some shady dealings that were beginning to come to light within his organization, red flagged already because of the size of the man's business. She had been originally slated to go alone, but David had insisted on accompanying her, if for nothing else to provide a plausible cover for their visit.

They had been caught in their attempt to spy, separated, and she had never seen him again. They had interrogated her, ensuring no sensitive information had been leaked from the premises. When they had finished they blindfolded and transported her to a place where there had been the incessant sound of water and moans from the distance echoing through the place. Several times she would have sworn she had heard David's tortured screams. After what she estimated was a month of suffering through strange experiments, she was able to free herself and escape, but she had already been turned into the thing she saw in the mirror. She had escaped the laboratory, but she had never found out what had happened to David. She felt hot tears streak down her cheeks at the thought of losing him forever. "I should have gone back for him..." she whispered to empty air.

After her escape, Marlin had sent his personal army to retrieve her and she had found herself hopping from one slum bar to another, trying her best to blend in with the rest of the flotsam to avoid detection. That was hard, considering her appearance. Albinism stood out, even among these dregs of society.

At first she had feared the police would be involved in the chase. She had since realized that Marlin would not inform them about her, or about David. That was due to the laws regarding illegal experimentation set into place to prevent procedures such as the one that he had used on the two of them. No, no police would bother her, or help her for that matter, so she was forced to this, hiding in plain sight and hoping they would think her too stuck up to consider a bar on the water.

Wiping her eyes quickly, lest she lose what little control she had left on her emotions, Angelina gulped the last of her drink and glanced around the slum bar she was sitting in. It was exactly what she had expected of a water-town bar. It was filthy looking, smoky, and dimly lit. She turned toward the other end of the building, watching with glazed eyes as the water pushed the mud back and forth where the building was submerged.

She focused as she caught movement in that area, watching as the Wanderer entered the bar, her eyes starting to be affected by the alcohol that she had consumed to this point. The Wanderers...they were water born and nomadic humans, traveling around in little flotillas scavenging the ocean for their livelihood. They moved from port to port selling seaweed tonics and fresh fish and other treasures culled from the now submerged city under their feet. Some of them even resorted to piracy - or so the story went.

He stepped slowly into the bar, emerging from the dock provided for them to tie their boats long enough to get smashed before they moved on. His face was weather worn and dark, his eyes stuck in a constant squint, another perfect match to the picture she had built in her head for their appearance.

Her eyes moved slowly over to several gemue patrons sitting near the sloping floor that allowed them entrance to these establishments, staring vacant eyed into the amber liquid in their glasses.

"Abominations," she thought in disgust, shaking her head. She couldn't shake that impression even now. She had grown up disliking them and what they represented. gemues were genetically altered humans who in a panic had dropped themselves into the pit of hell. Angelina just could not comprehend how someone could just willingly give over their humanity to scrape out the kind of existence gemues were forced into.

Angelina sighed, looking back to her empty glass. She waved to the bartender, ordering another, knowing she was going to have to leave soon. She cast another glance around the room, looking for the telltale looks of unease from the other patrons of the bar. It was her appearance she knew, odd even for this crowd. She could not delude herself from the knowledge that her uncle had put the word out about her "defection;" surely there would be a bounty hunter or two after her hide. Some of these patrons certainly had similar problems with the bounty hunters.

There were no outward signs of unease, but the fear in the room was nearly palpable to her. Angelina could feel it oozing from their thoughts. That had been her other gift from her uncle, however unwanted it was. The tinkering they had done on her had awakened some kind of latent telepathic talent. She found herself picking up everything from long forgotten memories to active thoughts from those around her. She had no control over it and it made her feel like a voyeur. The thought of raping minds without knowledge disgusted her, and daily that ability grew stronger. All the voices in her head constantly had given her a splitting headache, and she wished for enough control to shut her reception down. In another meager attempt to drown them and her sorrow she ordered another shot, sinking into despair.

Chapter Two:
Recent History

I nosed out of the water near Old Fresno, a city that had been mostly underwater since the Meltdown sixty years ago. That was the brilliant catch phrase the media used at the peak of global warming, when all but the thickest glaciers gave up their moisture to the seas of the world.

I took a whiff of the air knowing my quarry was close. Surfacing near one of the better bars on the water, I struggled to read the glaring, ugly, puke green neon sign hanging in the window. Paddling a bit closer the sign came into focus. "Bar Topical," I muttered, shaking my head. Leave it to a bar on the water to come up with a name like that.

I snorted and slipped back under the surge, heading for the building's north wall. Most bars in this area had entrances to accommodate their seafaring patrons, which made up the bulk of their business. All said entrances were located on the north side of the building so that no matter how drunk you got you could still find your way into the next bar.

It is written somewhere that at one time the Sea of San Joaquin had been a lush fertile valley reclaimed from the desert. Fresno, as the city had been called then, had been a bustling hub of agriculture. It had provided a central point for all the produce in the area to be distributed to the rest of California and the nation.

Sea levels had been rising for some time, and those who lived on the coasts of the world adjusted as the oceans grew. No one in the Central California Valley was prepared when the Pacific overcame the small range of mountains at the mouth of the San Francisco Bay. The damage was greater than it might have been, because of the dam erected in an attempt to preserve the valley, the livelihood of the farmers, and buoy the economy. The resulting torrent tore loose much of the mouth of the bay as it gave new life to its long lost sister the Sea of San Joaquin.

What remained of Old Fresno were the slum bars and hooker joints that catered to the Wanderers and gemues like me. I really despised that term, but it was convenient; easier to say than "gene-spliced mutated beings."

Most gemues fell into three categories and were easily defined: mech-splice, whamue, and dolphimue - or if you wanted to be politically correct, Porpoise. Dolphimue had sounded better so it stuck.

Mech-splices were the half-baked brainchild of a scientist alive near the beginning of the Meltdown. Mechs were humans who surgically had themselves altered with regulators in their throats, and lenses implanted to cover their eyes. Some had even had their tank housings fused to their spine, ribs, and shoulders. They seemed more cyborgs than gemues to my mind.

Mech-splices were the least versatile of the gemues and only in the category because of their radical appearance.

Their requirement to have tanks of compressed air to survive underwater severely limited them. Mechs wasted what little money they could scrounge on their supply of tanks, their refills and maintenance required on their units. Mech-splices constantly stole from each other and squabbled over rights to other's stashes when one of their numbers died. If there was anything good to be said about them, it was that they were a dying breed in a very limited number, and would soon be extinct.

Whamues were a step in the right direction, however awkward they seemed on land. The splicing was crude, leaving them with little or no leg, stubby paddle like hands and a load of blubber that would have shamed a true whale. Underwater was another story; they could dive as deep as 200 feet on one breath of air with little or no complications in surfacing, and they could stay down for an hour or more.

Dolphimues were much the same in most respects. They looked slightly more humanoid, and carried less blubber on their bodies. They were faster in the water, although their air reserves were much less for the higher metabolism.

Another disadvantage to the transformation was that the subjects for the dolphin program lost their ability to speak as humans, their mutation taking on the more dominant genes for dolphin and recreating their vocal cords as such. Some of the more ambitious of them had practiced long and hard to recreate passable human speech from the whistles and clicks they were restricted to. Most however were lost on how to learn it, and most other gemues and humans did not care to take the time to learn the conglomerate language.

Most Dolphimues either kept an interpreter by their side or spent their life savings on a translator box that they could strap to their blowhole. If they could not afford either, they were shunned. I was one of those who could understand Dolphispeak, though I found speaking it impossible. I have found that they are excellent sources of information.

Dolphimues and whamues were the most populous of the new breed of human, and though I use the term "human" loosely, I mean it. Homo-aquaticus, I suppose those stuffy old scientists who study these things might dub us. The last I had heard they were reproducing, and rumor was that the population was large enough to start its own nation. That scared a lot of humans, already threatened by the gemue's existence and probably a little worried for their souls should the dolphimues and whamues decide to join forces and exact revenge for their current treatment.

My particular genus of gemue is based on a tigershark; hence my name. I cannot explain why my process turned me into more . . . graceful a gemue than my brethren, except to say that it was an experiment of the most radical kind. I found that there are no other gemues like me. I often wondered if I was some sort of prototype that my creator never followed up on.

I thought it a pity, for in my form lies the least in the way of disadvantages. With my gills I have no need of atmosphere, no problems with decompression, hypoxia, nitrogen narcosis, or any other malady that befalls each of the other forms of gemue. On the reverse side, I was left my lungs, allowing me to function on land equally as well.

When I had heard about the experimental process, I had been a loner, looking for a kick. I had nothing to lose, and easily ignored the scorn my acquaintances and family looked upon me with.

I have no recollection now of what I had looked like before my transformation. Oddly, I can't even remember the names of my family, where I went to school, or even what I did prior to my submittal. They explained it as a side effect of the transformation; a sort of trauma induced amnesia, explaining also the fact that I don't recall processing.

Gemues were created from a panic, when popular opinion held that the Earth was going completely under and the human race driven to extinction in the process. Scientists also spurned by that thought developed a coalition to research ways to adapt humans for the coming apocalyptic change in the Earth. Gene-splicing had been around for decades and seemed to scientists to be the easiest way around the problem. They made passable beings that could survive well in a watery world, though they never really perfected the technique. Four years later they uncovered evidence that the rise was slowing and projected that it would stop in about three years, putting the time and money they had used in their research to waste.

Dry land was still present, though many millions of square acres smaller than it had been, and overcrowding was prominent.

To defray the cost of their research, the scientific community offered their miraculous gene-splice procedure to the public, at least those who could come up with the 500,000 credits a procedure price they were asking, without informing them of the newest information regarding the seas. People flocked to the centers by the hundreds, mostly those from coastal towns, and they sold everything they owned to come up with the money.

When those dirty little secrets became public knowledge, nearly two million people had already been transformed into one of the other aquatic forms, and the scientists had hell to pay. Once the criminal proceedings were conducted most found themselves safely incarcerated, trying in penitentiary labs to come up with some sort of counter-process. In addition, they were made to pay all who had undergone the process a restitution of money paid plus additional costs for pain and suffering, if the knowledge was withheld about the oceans' rise. If the recipient was no longer alive it was paid to the nearest living relative. Of course, all gemues, happy with their life or not, claimed hardship over the issue, as well as swearing they had never been informed about the end to the rising waters. This drove the scientists into bankruptcy and took a better part of four more years to straighten out.

All the money and apologies in the world could not make up for the environment the new gemues found themselves trapped in. Those who did not give in to popular opinion, no matter the probable cost of their lives, felt vindicated. In their gloating they began to equate gemues as stupid, at first for their unfounded panic and later that they were just dumb in general.

The general population used it as an excuse to exclude them from even the most trivial things that humans enjoy in life. Many found themselves unable to live with that scorn and slews of them turned up dead on the beaches of the world, and not by any natural causes. Still others found themselves ill prepared to live in the ocean. Many sharks and other predators had followed the trail of carnage the floods had caused in creating the Sea of San Joaquin, and seemed unwilling to move on for fear of missing another feast. That meant high dangers for the new gemues, still acclimatizing to their new bodies as well as the strange surroundings. Sharks and other predators found easy pickings from those out of their element. Those who had survived were those who were too independent, ornery, or downright happy being what they were to just roll over.

Meanwhile, the richer, better informed residents of the valley moved their businesses and homes to higher ground, renaming it New Fresno, leaving those too poor or unenlightened to fend off the deluge to come. Only a few got off their high horses to lend a hand. Marlin Cortez was one such, at the time a small town politician and businessman.

But even with their help, which was stopgap at best, the poorer folks sank quickly to scrounging an existence out of the seaweed and stilted buildings that existed at the fringes of the city. The decrepit remains of Fresno were a perfect refuge for ruffians, scoundrels, and anyone trying to avoid detection. It was exactly the kind of place where I would find my quarry.

*****

Angelina was on her tenth shot of tequila, feeling quite numb and wondering distantly when it would be safe to move on. She heard someone coming in through the water entrance, followed by silence from the other patrons of the bar. She turned around, curious as to what could have caused such a jaded group of people to stop their oh-so-important conversations. Expecting to see another scuba man, or the bloated carcass of a Whamue, she was unprepared for what her eyes encountered and an involuntarily squeak of fright escaped her lips.

It was humanoid, definitely gemue, but the quality of the work surpassed anything she had previously encountered. The creature stood about six feet tall, and had clearly been a human male at one point. It was gracefully muscled, hovering handsomely between bulky and wiry. Its skin was a pale grayish tan fading to ivory on its chest, stomach, and around its mouth. The face was elongated, stretched down and out at the chin and nose, coming to what looked like a shark's snout.

Its eyes scanned the room quickly, small yellow gray slitted orbs that were barely visible from the sunken sockets. Its head sloped back sharply to meet a stark white shock of stiff hair. She caught a glimpse of working gills hidden by that mane, and she wondered if they were real or just elaborate mock-ups for added effect. The last she had heard was that gills were impossible to replicate on humanoids.

The gemue ran its hands through its hair, and she noticed that it was almost immediately dry. She gasped at the proportion of those extremities. They were half again as long as the average human hand, webbed with a thin elastic membrane, and each finger was tipped with a long lethal looking claw. At each elbow there was a small fin moving independantly of its arm movements.

Various items hung from its utility belt, including a stunner and a Wet-Net set, speaking of at least tool-using intelligence. It made itself decent with a pair of cropped, neon yellow dive pants.

She watched as the creature glanced over the last of the patrons before turning its attention to her. She made the hasty conclusion that this was one of her uncle's hapless creations, for only her uncle would insist on a gemue with a shark template. That would mean that this thing was here for her.

No sooner had she thought it than the creature, locking its eyes on her, snarled. Several rows of serrated teeth were exposed, completing the shark effect. She felt the black wash of the creature's dreadful thoughts, of what it was here to do. The images clouded her mind with fear and dread. "Oh, shit!" Angelina whispered, sobering quickly despite her condition. She started to rise, darting a glance around her, and repositioned so that she had a better chance of escape should the creature make a mistake. Somehow she doubted that opportunity would arise. It struck her as a very efficient killer.

The creature moved fluidly through the bar as it approached her. The gemue wasted not an ounce of extra effort, she could tell that of it immediately. However, it wasn't as if anyone was getting in the creature's way. Even the whamues showed exceptional speed in moving their bulks free of its path. Angelina brought out the only weapon she had, an out of date hydro-gun. It was useful, no doubt, but unless the user was a crack shot it was not lethal, and Angelina was anything but a crack shot. It was a moot point however, for without hesitation and with quickness she had not credited the creature with, it lunged forward, knocking the gun from her grip. Angelina grabbed her stinging wrist, backing away from the creature.

The gemue followed her, a smile of superiority stretching his face. That grin faded, leaving its face a grim mask as she ran out of room, back to the bar. The creature snarled, "You're meat, bitch!" as one elongated hand closed on her throat.

Angelina had been relatively calm to that point. In the back of her mind she had convinced herself that this creature was an animal, albeit a smart one. When it spoke so fluidly, without a hint of difficulty in rolling his tongue around the English language, it broke that delusion and became something much more deadly. She had instinctively grabbed the wrist of the creature, trying to free herself from his grip.

"Leave me alone!" Angelina heard herself scream, struggling vainly against his strength.

He grabbed her long white hair with his free hand and yanked her head back. "It's a pity too," she heard him rumble, his voice a deep throaty baritone; "you're a pretty one, despite your dead eyes. Ah, well."

The gemue then took its hand from her throat and captured both her wrists, pulling them down toward her waist. The thing snarled wickedly, baring teeth as he descended for her exposed windpipe.

Her world started to blacken as segments of her life flashed before her eyes. She knew that she was going to die, and what a way to go, in a stinking shit hole of a bar and at the hands of a gemue.

As Angelina watched, the snarl faded from the creature's face. Slowly, his eyes widened and lost focus, his head whipping back sharply. Without warning, and seemingly without reason, he screamed in pain, a throaty growl of torment. Quickly, his hand freed itself from her hair, and he stumbled back, clapping both hands over his ears as if to ward off some offensive sound she could not hear.

His agony lasted several more seconds, leaving him in a half-crouched position, panting and wheezing. Angelina should have taken advantage of his distraction and run, but she was too frozen with fear to even step away.

"Nnngh!" he grunted, his eyes flashing open. Slowly and shakily he straightened. The tormented look had not faded from his face; his hands were still glued to the sides of his skull. Yet, he seemed to control the effect as he closed the gap between them. She saw hatred glaze over those foreign eyes.

"GET OUTTA MY HEAD!" he bellowed, even as a balled fist lashed out, catching Angelina squarely across the cheek.

Angelina reeled into the bar, winded as she struck hard bones on to an equally hard surface, and pain lanced up her side. She whirled to face him, sure that she was in for another attack. Angelina stared at the shark-man, still a little shell-shocked at the whole chain of events. She straightened, rubbing the sore spot on her ribs from her abrupt meeting with the counter, and the other massaging her cheek and throat.

The gemue looked severely rattled to her eyes; much different from the swaggering self-confidence she had seen it come in here with. The creature did not approach her and instead backed away, shaking its head as if to clear it of some fog. The creature glared at her hotly one last time before turning and slipping into the water without leaving so much as a ripple.

The patrons of the bar were quicker than she to recover and returned to their drinks and their own conversations. The bartender came up to her then. "I thought you were dead there, lady."

"So did I," she replied to him honestly. She noticed that he had set a drink in front of her, and without hesitation or question, she downed it to calm her edgy nerves.

"So, what exactly did you do to make him stop? He looked like you put him through some serious pain there."

"Yeah . . ." She shook her head. "I couldn't tell you, I've never done that before."

It was several hours before Angelina could talk herself into venturing outside the bar. She was afraid that the shark-man was waiting just outside to take her down, without so much as a word of warning. Even when she did leave she made sure to insert herself into a group of human patrons on their way to the next bar down the waterway.

*****

My head was still splitting seven hours after encountering my mark. "A Tepe! A freaking Tepe," I muttered to myself. Cortez had mentioned nothing to me about this girl being a telepath, much less one strong enough to cripple my attack. It had caught me off guard and even had overrun my peak pain tolerance. I had been hard put to pull myself together long enough to stop her assault. I didn't like being blind-sided like that. Pausing a moment, I thought perhaps Cortez did not know himself about the girl's abilities. After all, she was a minor worker in his company, and he can't know personal histories on everyone he has working for him.

Either way this was turning into a whole new ball of wax.

I had been swimming circles since the incident, trying to figure out exactly what had happened. I could not go back to Cortez without some plausible reason for my failure. The operation had been so smooth, until that white witch had pulled some mental whammy that short-circuited my brain. It was a defense I had never dreamed of, much less heard about. She had left a memory behind, surely not my own, some fabrication to throw me off.

In that vision was a bar, not a slum town bar, but a very fancy dryworld one. No . . . It was a restaurant. It was one of those really upscale restaurants where the prices were high and the servings were small. Every detail was now eloquently etched into my head. It was decorated in wood and iron with large tinted windows that allowed the patrons to watch the world go by in SPF110 protection. I was sitting at one of the tables with the remnants of a light noon meal scattered about. Art deco filled every unused corner and the plates were dainty china, and before me, stood a cappuccino steaming from an equally pretty cup. Looking across the table I found a vision of loveliness smiling warmly at me. She was of Mexican heritage with a finely chiseled face; raven black hair, dark brown eyes, and she looked as if she was hanging on every word. I suddenly realized that the sound I had been thinking of as background noise was my own voice, lacking the depth and gruffness it possessed now. It had been beautiful...

Then pain had cleaved the memory and my concentration in two like an ax buried into my skull.

I had never been in a restaurant like that, much less bought lunch for a beautiful woman. There was also that the woman in my vision would look exactly like my mark would, if she had possessed any coloration. And that was what brought me enough control to fight off the attack and knock her on her ass. But I had been in too much pain to try and complete the job then. So she got a reprieve.

But how do I explain that to Cortez? I could not bring myself to tell him the truth. He'd lock me up in an asylum, rip up my contract, and blacklist me for the rest of my life. How could he believe it? I didn't believe it, and I had been the one it had happened to.

Chapter Three:
Back From the Dead

Angelina nervously approached the drab looking apartment complex on the outskirts of New Fresno, pulling her hood tighter about her pale face. This was considered fringe and some said that it even surpassed the vileness of Old Fresno. She glanced around at the burned out husks of cars and the shadowy people who preyed off each other for their daily survival. Quickly, Angelina climbed the stairs to the third floor and knocked on the door only identified by the darker spot of paint that was vaguely readable as 310. Glancing around, she ensured she wasn't being followed or sized up as a potential victim.

After a moment, the door before her opened up a hair and a brilliant green eye looked over the security chain. "What is it?" a higher pitched male voice said. "What do you want?"

"Max," she said, relieved that she had found him. She had been in hiding on the streets since she had run into that shark creature, trying to be sure that she had eluded his pursuit. She had finally admitted to herself that she was in over her head on this problem. She had not wanted to involve Max or The Movement in this, because of what had been done to her, and the possible response she might receive. That was why she had kept running for two months. Everyone she knew probably thought she was dead and David with her. But now she felt that she needed help and that it was time to call in her favors with The Movement.

"Do I know you?" Max queried suspiciously.

"It's me!" she insisted. "Angelina."

"Nice try, gemue. Good research though. Go panhandle somewhere else." He tried to close the door but Angelina put a shoulder into it to keep it ajar. Max looked at her with shock and anger through the crack.

She leaned close to his face, her expression ugly with fury. "Three and a half months ago, The Movement sent out an operative to the Marlin Cortez estate in an attempt to root out evidence of illegal mutations and other questionable business practices. I was chosen because of my relation to him, giving me easy access to the grounds. David Scott volunteered to come along with me as a reasonable cover for our visit.

"You disapproved of sending two operatives into the same situation, citing the dangers that had been hinted at by operatives outside. David convinced you after some time that it was even more dangerous for me to go alone. Do you remember that? Who else would have that information, Max? That was a private meeting between us three. It's me . . . you have to believe that. I need your help." She relaxed her pressure on the door, stepping back and allowing him to look her over again.

The eye gazed into her face, searching it back and forth for her sincerity. She could not tell what he was thinking, for that one feature she could see revealed no hint of emotion. The door abruptly shut, leaving her staring in shock at the ugly faded blue surface. Angelina's shoulders sagged visibly; he hadn't believed her, and now she had nowhere to turn. She pivoted slowly and began walking away when she heard the chain being removed and the door opening again. Angelina peered over her shoulder, seeing Max take a step out of the doorway to get a better view of her. There was a mixture of emotions on his face, ranging from disgust to sympathy to horror. When he did not immediately retreat into the apartment, Angelina swiveled her body around.

Suddenly, he reached out and embraced her. "Oh my God, I was so worried about you!" He released her, and stood back to look at her again, uncomfortable about her appearance. "C . . . Come inside."

Angelina stepped past Max and into the small apartment. "I see your tastes haven't changed," she said as she took in his place, wanting to smile but unable to muster up any humor.

"What . . . What did those bastards do to you?" he asked as he seated himself on a billowy couch. He appeared as if he still was unsure whether to believe that it was actually she.

Angelina shrugged as she sat down on a very straight, high-backed chair across from him. "I'm not sure. I know it was painful and you see the results, but what exactly they did, I couldn't tell you."

"And . . . David?" he asked tentatively.

She stared at him with a blank expression that decayed into a tearful sob. "I . . . I don't know, Max. They separated us . . . and, I never saw him again. Max, it was so horrible! I tried so hard to find out what happened to him . . . there was nothing! I tried to find him . . . I really did!" She was openly crying now, all the guilt and helplessness that she felt came to a head and she had to let it out. Max closed the space between them to comfort her. She sobbed heavily for long minutes before she was able to recover from her anguish.

When she was no longer hiccupping and sniffling she continued, "Marlin has his army out after me. He wants me back, he wants to finish whatever it is he started with me. I have been able to keep out of their reach, but now they have this . . . thing . . . this gemue, after me. He's deadly Max, I just know it. I barely escaped him, but I know he won't stop. I need help." She sat up and gazed dead into his green eyes. "I can't evade that thing alone! It's smart, and vicious. Talk to The Movement, I need their help hiding from this thing."

Max sat back, thinking, obviously disturbed by the account she had just given him. After a moment, he shook his head. "I don't know that they'd even let you plead your case, Angelina. You know the rules - no mutants. They are going to put that label on you the moment they see you."

"Those bastards owe me protection, damn it!" she shouted, rising and glaring down on Max, "Their 'plan' is the reason I'm like this and David may be dead! You had better convince them of it, Max, or I will. They knew spying was not within my realm of expertise!"

"I know Angelina . . . we'll see what I can do for you. But you know that I can't guarantee anything." He went silent again, and then he nodded his head minutely. "I think we should first find out what Cortez did to you."

*****

The next day, Max allowed Angelina to sleep long into the morning, knowing that she had gotten little or none in the last several weeks. When she finally woke, Max took Angelina to a local clinic, one that he had made

30

arrangements with the night before. They had gotten there about one, and had been instructed to find a seat in the overcrowded waiting room. They were there for nearly two hours constantly getting passed over for more urgent cases. That was the way of clinics such as this one. It was one of the few in the area that would see to the needs of the gemue population. Angelina was about ready to give it up and tell Max to forget it when a nurse finally called her name. Reluctantly, she rose and followed the lady to one of the rooms, Max close in her shadow.

The nurse was indifferent to Angelina's appearance, exposing just how jaded she had become to the gemues that she surely saw every day. "Please have a seat," she stated in monotone and, sitting across from her, began to take her vitals. When she had finished she simply got up and said, "The doctor will be with you shortly."

Max and Angelina sat for another seeming eternity when the doctor finally arrived. Angelina turned her gaze toward the man as he came in and her heart leapt anxiously at the sight of him. He was a man in his fifties, portly and paternal looking, with a horseshoe of white hair ringing the bright bald spot on the crown of his head. His dark blue eyes were lined with age and laughter, and an easygoing smile graced his face.

Angelina found herself even more self conscious and embarrassed, because she knew this man. His name was Doctor Chris Thomas, and he had been her family's physician for nearly thirty years. He had been providing her with care since she had been born. She wondered what he would be doing here and then she remembered that he had taken a volunteer position with the clinic when he was not working at his job with the New Fresno Medical Center.

He did not look at her as he came in, but instead peered over her chart, and Angelina began to fidget, becoming more nervous the longer she sat in the room with Doc Thomas.

Finally he turned his attention to them and Angelina had to avert her eyes for fear of being caught staring.

"Now what can I do for you today?" he said, focusing on her. She stayed stoically silent.

Max cleared his throat then. "My friend here wants a check up. She seems to think that she is changing still, and I can't seem to convince her otherwise."

The doctor looked over at Max. "And you are?"

"Max," he replied, smiling. "Max Groden."

"Max? Aren't you Angelina's friend?" the Doc queried.

Angelina swallowed hard.

"Yes," Max answered honestly.

"How is she these days? I haven't seen a whole lot of her in the past few months."

Max cast a sidelong glance at Angelina; she in return shook her head emphatically yet minutely in the negative, her eyes wide. "She's fine," he answered instead.

"Good," he said. Then he looked from Max to Angelina and back again, frowning. "That's strange. I would have sworn that she mentioned you to have an aversion to gemues?"

Max cleared his throat again. "I did . . . at one point, but I met someone who changed my mind."

"Good, I'm glad for that. They are, after all, as human as we are," Doc said. Then he turned to his work on Angelina. "Let's see if what you suspect is true, shall we?"

Angelina nodded, still unwilling to speak for fear of giving herself away.

*****

The next hour and a half were spent determining just how far the mutation of Angelina's body went. He not only examined her for any signs of continued mutation, he used his considerable arsenal of state of the art equipment to determine what was going on inside her body on a cellular level. Studying the charts he began to notice a familiarity in the medical facts to someone he had treated before. When he had gathered all of the needed information, he turned back to look into her expectant face. Even that was familiar despite the pale complexion and dead eyes. "Well," he started, "Where should I begin? At the beginning, I suppose . . . An expert, someone who has been making gemues a very long time, did whatever was done to you. The biology is very advanced. There are foreign cells in your body, cells that are not human. They look like mutated carrier cells, but they are dormant. How long they will remain that way I cannot tell you. The cells are not being attacked by your system." He turned away a moment, jotting another note in her folder. When he returned his attention to her it was with keen interest. "What was your template?"

She just shook her head.

"Look, if you refuse to talk to me, how can you expect me to help you?"

She looked up at him angrily, finally giving voice. "I don't know."

"How could you not know? Did you not specify when you submitted . . . didn't you tell them what you wanted for your templated creature?"

Angelina jumped up, upset by the question and the proximity to the man she knew so well. "I've had enough, Max. Let's get the hell out of here."

When she finally spoke, it brought all of the clues together for Doctor Thomas. Now he did know who this angry young woman was.

"Angelina?" the doctor said, freezing her in her tracks. There were tears in her eyes as she twisted back around to face him. He stepped up to her and tenderly lifted her chin up so that he could look at her features. "My God, what did they do to you, child?"

She shook her head again, tears running freely now. "I told you . . . I don't know," she said, shaking her head, her eyes fixed on him for the first time since coming in. She then began to explain what had happened, in more detail than she had even given Max. Before long the doctor was holding her as she sobbed and shook with her pent up frustration and anger.

*****

"Your mercenary has yet to return, Mr. Cortez," the young man at the door said upon entering, his distaste for gemues evident in his tone. He was the newest executive to join the staff, and he had great potential. The boy was smart and highly committed to his job, but had yet to learn not to state the obvious. Cortez was not in the mood to be reminded that his most prized employee was still out there somewhere.

"He'll return . . . I didn't spend all that money on him just to have him go absent without leave on this assignment," he replied, leaning back in his chair. "Besides, he agreed to an underwater tracking implant. We know where he is at all times."

"But it works only if he's in the water, and the tracking net is only set up in the Sea of San Joaquin. What if he decides to stay ashore, or worse, swims out of range?"

"He won't. He can't . . . I've read up on his particular abilities. The procedure he underwent left him very little lung tissue, and that is atrophied by his heavy reliance on his water-bound ways. Combined, it has left him with approximately ten percent of his former capacity. He'll head back to water as soon as is possible. As to swimming out of range . . . I think that is just highly unlikely."

"Does he know he can't survive in atmosphere?" the young executive asked. "I mean, there is a possibility that he may overtax himself and end up dying somewhere on shore, and we would never know where."

"I don't give a damn if he knows or not. I didn't ask him. His instinct should keep him near water. He's more comfortable there."

"But if he does desert . . ."

"He won't, damn it! Give your brain a rest; I didn't hire you to ponder the chaos theory . . . Ah . . . here he is now," Marlin said, watching a screen that was focused on the pool hidden in the basement of the complex.

*****

I practically had to drag myself ashore, my whole body spent of energy. It was certainly a result of my exertion combined with consternation over the incident with my mark. I was more than ready for a rest. I barely noticed the jump-suited goons beginning to ooze out of the wall as I moved further onto the shoreline. All too soon they were encroaching on my space, each with a stunner trained at my body. It wasn't long before I had had enough, my temper being rather short after the night's events.

"You stooges don't get those pea shooters away from me, you're going to find out first hand just how nasty I can get." I turned slowly, eyeing each of them. They all were scared. "You can see that I am already headed for my quarters," I growled at them with a glare. "I have one splitting headache, and if you insist on escorting me, I would be more than happy to take out my frustration on you. . ." That stopped them dead in their tracks.

I couldn't help grinning at how intimidated they appeared. The humor passed quickly and was replaced almost immediately by fatigue. I trudged on to my "room," a shallow cave located in the very back of the Cortez cavern, to try to sleep off my headache. I guess it was the best that they could do for someone with my needs. There was a depression about a foot and a half deep that held a measured amount of heated saltwater. I was much more comfortable in the water, for gravity weighed oddly on my body since my transformation.

I had no personal effects save what was clipped to my web belt. In my profession that was a burden that could mean the difference between making the hit or not, and I never took that kind of chance with my livelihood.

Illumination came from a naked bulb suspended precariously in the doorway. I ducked the light and stripped off my web belt and pants before settling into the small pool. I sighed heavily, feeling my bundled muscles begin to relax. I caught out of the corner of my eye movement and whipped my head around to see who it was. It was one of Marlin's goons and he did something that made my hackles rise. He swung a creaking hinged and barred door, closing me into my hole, and with a ringing click locked the gate.

"What the hell are you doing?" I growled and threw my web belt at the bars in frustration, listening to the clang echo off the subterranean walls. He smiled cruelly, turned, and walked away.

What was going on? I was an employee, not a prisoner, and I hadn't done anything wrong. There was no necessity to lock me up. I furrowed my brow as the anger was slow to dissipate, and I mentally told myself that Cortez and I were going to have a talk about this. Then I shrugged and rolled over onto my stomach.

It was a position I suddenly found uncomfortable, as an overwhelming urge to lay on my back welled up in me. I knew that it was physically impossible; the three cartilaginous fins grown from my spine would be injurious if I even attempted it. I shook my head, thinking that I was reminiscing about what it had been like before, and drifted off to sleep.

Chapter Four:
Complications

Angelina was ushered into a dark room by a nervous young woman not much older than she was.

"Wait here, please," she whispered, not meeting Angelina's dead eyes. Angelina had not enjoyed the drive over here, where she had been blindfolded, and the thoughts of her escorts, telling her just how disgusted they were to have to even consider transporting a gemue to conference, washed over her brain like ice water. The woman disappeared quickly and shut the door behind her, leaving Angelina standing in the pitch.

Slowly her panic wore off and she began to filter several thought patterns at the other end of the room. She shuffled that direction, intent not to trip in the dark. She was sure that they could see her, even if she herself could not see at all. When she came to the other side she found that there was no one actually in the room. The thoughts came from just the other side of the wall.

"Welcome back, Ms. Cortez," a distorted voice said. "We are sorry to hear of your misfortune, and the loss of your companion is also ours."

The thoughts did not match the greeting, however, and Angelina scowled. She backed several steps away from the wall. "Thank you," she replied anyway, turning darkness blinded eyes up at where she felt the thoughts.

"It has been brought to our attention that the butchers involved have made attempts to recover you. Our source has also apprised us that a gemue, possibly a mercenary, has been hired to track you down."

"Yes."

"You have come here asking our aid to avoid this beast and remain hidden until their interest in you fades."

"It would be most appreciated."

There was a long silence and Angelina guessed that they had cut audio and were discussing her request. She felt the disbelief beat at her, as well as mistrust in her intentions here. But she waited patiently for them to speak again. She was not about to add fuel to her pyre by letting them in on her other secret.

"After some consideration and for matters beyond our scope of authority, we must deny your request."

"What?" she blurted, sounding more surprised than she really was.

"If you are discovered here it will draw unwanted attention to our operations . . . You understand the political factions that would see this organization closed down for such impropriety." The voice paused. "There is also the matter of the bylaws of this organization."

Angelina laughed tersely. "I am not a gemue! This look . . . this curse of their experimentation on me is due to the spying that I was doing for you . . . something I told you I was not capable of, yet you insisted! You have no basis on which to deny my request." Having gotten her anger back under control, she continued, "I have served this organization for three years without incident. Yet you now question my loyalty?"

"We cannot blindly trust that the physical changes are the only damages that Cortez's butchers have done to you. Consider that you may have been implanted with a surveillance chip. Or worse, that you have been psychologically programmed to betray us to them. We cannot allow that to happen."

Angelina sighed in frustration. "All I am asking is for a place to stay, somewhere that this merc will not be able to follow me. I don't want reinstatement, but you owe me this much and I will have it."

The pause was short. "I'm sorry, but we cannot even take that small risk."

"I don't believe this!" Angelina sputtered, anger beginning to well up in her again.

Just then, another distorted voice chimed in. "Consider this . . . how are we to maintain loyalty in our junior members if we are not willing to provide protection for them in the course of their duties?" A long silence followed, and the voice went on to say, "The place does not need to be near here, it can be Old Fresno or Fringe. But she should have our protection from this persecution, until such time that this can be resolved."

The silence fell again. She realized that they had cut audio and were discussing the new statement by one of their own members. She waited silently, feeling the anger and accusation at the new voice for airing a dissenting opinion in front of the subject of the debate. It went on for a very long time, before the rebellious voice was able to convince them that the risk was worth taking.

The voice sounded like thunder after such a long silence. "Upon further consideration, we are agreed . . . we will grant you asylum and you will contact Maximillion tomorrow for an address where we will house you. This grace will only be for three months. After which time, if the matter is not resolved to satisfaction, you will be on your own."

"Agreed," Angelina said.

"Bother us no further unless we contact you first."

"Of course," she said quietly.

*****

"Get up you miserable gemue!" was what I heard just as a size twelve boot was planted into my largest dorsal fin. That area was very sensitive, and with a growl of pain I jumped up, spoiling for a fight.

It was one of Cortez's flunkies, an aging man named Tony Karr, one of the oldest soldiers in Marlin Inc.'s employ and the general of his private army. He was from the Old School and fully believed there was no place on Earth that was meant to accommodate gemues. Tony was a gaunt wiry man nearing his fifties, but like Cortez he took special pains to keep himself fit. His skin was deeply tanned from a life of constant sun exposure, and loose on his thinning frame. That was in no way to imply that Tony was weak minded or lacking in strength. The man's mind was cruelly keen; he remembered everything and held grudges longer than anyone I have previously met. Lord knew he hated me in particular; I seemed to pose some sort of threat to him. What exactly it was, I had yet to figure out.

Tony's face was heavily scarred from some wound he had suffered in a war that I had never heard of. I had been told, by one of the friendlier of the guards here, that a grenade had gone off next to where he lay unconscious during a battle. The scarring extended to his left eye, looking out from its socket unseeing. He had refused prosthesis for it, preferring to keep the reminder of his pain. The other intact eye was a brilliant sea blue and it shone with a maliciousness that made most men cower at his very presence. His hair was thinning and white and he always wore an immaculate, crisply pressed uniform that was reminiscent of the late Twentieth's Army.

He sneered at my startled form, seeming to know what was on my mind. "Try it and you'll be dead before you take your first step."

"You ever do that again, you'll need more than that toy to stop me, Tony." I stretched, never letting my eyes leave him. His hatred for my kind was well known by the logbook he kept of his gemue hunts. It was a book that he had been constantly waving in my face since hiring on here as he tried to get some sort of rise out of me. What he didn't seem to realize, was that I didn't care spit about the other gemues in the world. If I had been hired to track and down one, I would have no qualms about doing it. Hell, if he invited me to, I'd tag along on his hunts. Slowly, I moved to where my pants were and pulled them on so as not to offend the gentry we might pass in the hallways. Tony's visits only meant one thing.

"Yeah, right. The boss wants to see you," he sneered again, motioning toward the door.

I stepped past him, gnashing my teeth just in front of his face. Despite his bravado, he ducked. He shoved the barrel of his weapon into the small of my back in retaliation and I whirled, nearly shredding his face in a purely reactionary response. I straightened and smirked as I said to him, "Gee, Tony, I get the impression that you don't like me very much."

"Shut up and walk, freak," was his reply, belying the look of fear in his one good eye.

Tony herded me up the stairs to the first floor offices. This building's organization and the man who ran it were different from any other firm that I had encountered. Most businesses held to the credo that the higher up the executive ladder you climbed the better your view on the world, until you were vying with God for position in the heavens. Not Marlin Cortez. If there was a God to compare him to, it would have to be Poseidon, ruler of the oceans. He had made his money from the sea when he had volunteered his services at the height of the deluge, his generosity to those in need had made him very rich indeed, but donations to his company were not the only thing to keep it buoyant. Marlin Cortez was a shrewd businessman and knew how to manipulate things to benefit him. He reminded himself and his workers daily of the company's connection to the sea by the surf that pounded three hundred feet from their door.

We reached the intricately carved doors of Marlin Cortez's office, and I opened them, stepped inside, and blew Tony a kiss as I shut them quietly behind me. "Marlin, you have got yourself some serious assholes working for you," I said as I sauntered up to his desk.

"You are including yourself on that list, I presume," he replied blandly. But there was an underlying tone that warned me that this was not a social visit.

I slowed my step, looking at him oddly. "So, to what do I owe the pleasure of being in your audience?" I said, bowing deeply to cover my delay, before sitting on the stool he kept for my audiences.

"Cut the shit. What happened yesterday?"

Oh crap, he was angry.

"I . . . really don't know," I replied evenly. That much, at least, was true; now would he press for details? I knew the answer before the question had fully run through my head.

"You found her . . . didn't you?" he growled

"Of course. I am worth my fee, you know."

One corner of his mouth turned up as if he thought it was funny. "Yes . . . Yes you are. But you didn't kill her?"

"No." I felt a snarl start to curl my lip and forced myself to smooth it out. I'm not stupid - a man with this much power was dangerous. I learned long ago that corporate types in high positions were the most ruthless of people; otherwise they wouldn't be where they are.

"Why not?" he bit out.

Now I was in a stew, for just how do I explain my trouble with her?

"It's hard to explain," I started, not looking at him. "I suddenly developed a migraine. I couldn't concentrate, I couldn't even think." It sounded lame to me, but I was not ready to tell him that I had encountered a telepath with more talent than I have ever heard of.

Cortez slammed a fist down on the table. "I don't want excuses, damn it! I want that bitch dead! That's what you're here for!"

I stood up and leaned across the desk, using every bit of willpower to maintain my composure. "Look, there is no need for threats. You hired me for a job and it will get done." I stood straight, letting my nails drag along the expensive finish of his desk.

"You had better, or you won't see the next full moon," he growled angrily.

"That's okay, I can't see it now. Bad eyesight, you know." I turned and left.

As I walked down the hall toward the stairwell, I wondered silently if it was wise to provoke him. But something about him just led me to be rebellious. He treated me with an air of someone who feels they are superior, not because of their status, but because they have some information in their possession that they know can hurt. A quick mental review turned up no incriminating evidence that he could possibly use. I was licensed for my job and no one had crossed me yet that had lived to hold a grudge. The feeling of irritation was something I could not shake and I found myself trying to rub him wrong if only to lessen that air about him.

*****

Angelina stared at her reflection in the mirror without really seeing it. She was staying in a seedy motel room on the fringes of New Fresno; a safe house provided her by The Movement. They had stated that it would only be until they found something more suitable, but she doubted that would happen not in the short three months that they had promised her protection.

Angelina's thoughts had turned to the night she had been taken to The Movement's local council. Only one person out of those five minds was open to her request. They had denied her even before she had pled her case. Max . . . he was the only reason that they had changed their minds, and that had come reluctantly. Yes, she knew that it was him that had been the dissenting opinion that night, and she could not thank him without letting him know about her "gift." She was unsure that he could be forgiving about something like that. She would have to tell him someday, but now was not the time.

They were not ready to give in and support her, and it all stemmed from the fact that The Movement was an organization for humans only. Its membership considered gemues abominations, no matter the circumstance. Scientists had done away with the gene that causes albinism, and that only meant that her appearance was manmade. That relegated her to the gemue level in the eyes of most of her friends, and it did not matter that she did not sign a consent form to allow it. It made her realize, being on the outside looking in, just how shallow that view of the world was.

Each time she replayed that chain of events she became madder.

She shook her head, wishing that was what was really bothering her, wishing that it was as simple as being abandoned by her friends and coworkers. But the thought that lingered in her mind was like a barb. Even after the several weeks since, the drinks in between and her vocalization of her ordeal with both Max and Doc, she was still perplexed about her encounter with the shark-man. She had been under the impression that she had crippled him mentally, with some kind of mental defense mechanism that had ensured her survival.

Try as she might, however, with the people below on the street, she was not able to duplicate the defense. The only result she got out of the mind probes, no matter how forcefully accomplished, was exactly what was on their minds at the time and much of that was distasteful, to put it mildly. Rarely, she would get one who shook their head as they moved under her perch, showing that they had at least been aware of her presence in their minds. But the probe had not been enough to slow them, much less drop them to their knees.

So the question arose, how had she crippled the gemue? What had been different?

Stress may have played a role in the sudden ability to short out another's synapses, but she doubted even under extreme duress that she would be able to do it again. It also bothered her about the timing of the defense. She had been having a flashback to when she and David had begun dating, and it had made her certain that she was going to die. So just how was she able to mount such a formidable weapon against her assailant? She was sure there was a logical reason for his reaction, but she was unable to puzzle what that might be.

Chapter Five:
Privacy

I was more than glad to be free of Cortez's scrutiny after two weeks holed up in my "room" because the businessman didn't trust me enough to go hunting. My complaints about my treatment of late fell on Cortez and Tony's deaf ears. When they had finally opened the creaking gate, I found myself determined to find a place where I could have some privacy and work at my own pace. I needed to get out from under Marlin's microscope and away from Tony's mouth, which had only gotten more acerbic while I was held captive. I guess he felt he was safe from my reaction on the other side of the bars; it gave him bravado he didn't normally show toward me.

It took me more than two days to find a place both suited to my needs and out of the way enough not to be immediately detected. Open water was always a freedom for me. I never felt better than when I was on my own and left to my own thoughts. Unfortunately, I couldn't just swim forever. Eventually, even I had to sleep. I did not feel comfortable about staying in open water during my rest periods. It would leave me vulnerable to attack from not only the natural predators in the sea, but also wandering scavengers and gemue pirates who were always on the lookout for an easy payoff.

I needed a place I could fortify if the need arose, a place out of sight and protected from the elements so I could rest without disruption. And with that in mind I searched every cranny that held a promise of a possible cavern. As afternoon neared I began to get discouraged, and that is when I happened on a gold mine. I had investigated what I was sure was one more dead end tunnel, just one more disappointment, and was therefore surprised when it proved to be a chimney in the rock that rose sharply toward the unseen surface. Cautiously I followed it up, sure that it was too good to be true, and waited for it to narrow and leave me stuck backing out. It again proved me wrong when it opened into a small pocket of air. I could barely make out a narrow ledge in the pitch of the place and found myself cursing my ill preparedness. Reluctantly I returned to open water, discretely flagging the entrance as I headed back to Cortez's.

I came back the next day, bowing out of yet another one of Tony's chastising lectures about the kind of scum I was and just how worthless I was turning out to be. The whole way to my find I contemplated the several different ways I wanted to dissect him the next time he decided to do that. Before, I knew it I was back at the entrance and my anger turned to anticipation of what this place might hold. Treading water, I unlatched the lantern that I had filched from one of Cortez's emergency lockers. I frowned in disappointment at what the lantern illuminated for me. The ledge stood just out of the water and was only several feet wide; at either end it tapered off and appeared to burrow into the rock. Not willing to give up so close to success, I pulled myself up and headed first to the right, curious about the appearance of the landing. I was right in that there was a narrow wedge of a passage there, but after a few dozen feet it narrowed so much that it was impassable for my frame. With a sigh I backed out and headed for the left end of the landing. As I started in, the passage narrowed just as the one on the right had, but not nearly so much, and I pushed through the neck of it to practically fall into an underground cavern. It was not nearly as big as Cortez's hidden cavern but it was impressive in its own right. Stalactites were thick across the ceiling in an array of colors; several were thicker than my leg and met with equally stunning stalagmites on the floor. Arranged across the rocky surface were six pools of condensed water. Most were small, but one or two looked promising enough to accommodate me. I stepped up to the largest and dipped a hand in it. Luck was smiling on me today it seemed, for the water was warm. And tasting it, I found the water to be brackish. That was suitable as well. Salt water, ocean water, was what I wanted, though brackish was not bad for the periods that I needed to use it. I would recover enough in transit to Cortez's or to the city. Fresh water would do in a pinch, but long exposure to it tended to make me sick. That would be osmosis at its finest.

I nodded absently, pleased with my find, and breathed a sigh of relief that I would finally get the privacy I needed.

*****

Marlin Cortez was in the middle of a conference call with some clients overseas when his assistant barged into the room. Cortez looked up momentarily, glaring at the young man. The assistant stopped dead in his tracks and Cortez continued for twenty minutes with his call before acknowledging his presence. When he had said his farewells he returned his gaze to the nervous young man, an eyebrow raised in silent question.

"Sir?"

"Yes, what is it?" Cortez growled in irritation. The boy was being dense today. "This had better be good. You know I don't like to be disturbed during business negotiations."

The young man swallowed. "I am sorry, sir, but this is important or I would not have bothered you." He paused again before going on. "I reviewed the logs of our employees, as you asked, and I have found that the merc has not checked back with us in nearly a week."

"Well, what do you want me to do about it? He does need some time to track his mark."

"But sir . . . his signal disappeared four days ago and has not reappeared. I thought it odd, especially after your trouble with his last attempt at completing his contract."

"Where was his signal last?"

"Around Dreco. There is a series of caverns in that area, all of which open to the sea. We think he may have found one to hole up in."

"Again I ask you, what do you want me to do about it?"

"Y . . . You're not going to retrieve him…even after his last failure?"

He shook his head. "No. Let him think he's getting away with something. If he works better that way, so be it. Now go away. I have more pressing matters to attend to."

"Y . . . yes, sir."

*****

I began to filch small things from Cortez's stockpile, and buy others on my credit rating, to stock my new lair. I had been filling every nook I could with non-perishable foods, emergency supplies, first aid kits, towels and anything else I thought I might need during my stays away from Cortez.

This move would probably piss him off, but at the moment I didn't care, so long as I got a little freedom and a lot of privacy.

I was stacking some of the smaller boxes into an alcove when I got a whiff of a smell I shouldn't be able to get here, the smell of dry land. Following my highest developed sense, I trailed the scent deeper into the alcove, following a narrow passage in the rock, and after several minutes it surprised me by opening into the sunlight.

I found myself standing on the edge of a marshy meadow cupped between several small hills, and it was just beginning to bloom. There was no evidence of any buildings in the area or even that it was in use. I stepped out into the sea of yellow flowers, turning to face the hill from which I had emerged. In contrast to the valley, the hills were covered in yellowing summer grasses that made the hillside look smooth and featureless. They swayed with the gentle early summer breeze rippling up the face like waves on the ocean. Here and there grew some of the dune grasses typically found near the beach, showing the gradual adjustment the valley was still making to its new state of being. It was beautiful and serene, a total contrast to what I was used to in and around New Fresno. Actually, the silence was making me feel uncomfortable, like an intruder on something sacred.

I faintly smelled the ocean, surely on the other side of the ridge. Curious about just where I was in relation to New Fresno, I climbed the hill. I found myself panting heavily when I reached the summit, and was crouched over for some time before I could consider taking a look about me. My breathlessness worried me, because I knew I was not out of shape. Rationalizing the weakness, I convinced myself that my body was just unused to those particular groups of muscles anymore. I was more of a swimmer lately, not a walker, and it was certain that my body was favoring a different set of muscles. When I had recovered a bit, I straightened and searched hard for the shadowy gray outline that would mark the city in my poor vision. I surely must have looked over it four times before finally spotting it some ways south and a bit east of my position. I nodded. At least they would be a while trying to find me, if they were even worried about my disappearance. Satisfied, I climbed down and reentered the cavern. I also had another mark in favor of this place; if things got ugly I had a second escape route.

Nearly a week passed as I contacted my group of dryworld informants, trying to ferret out what I needed to find the albino witch. I returned to my den, intent on resting before going the final ways to my target and the completion of my mission.

I kicked strongly, gliding easily up the narrow shaft leading to my entry pool. I broke surface with enough momentum to clear the water and land lightly on the outcropping. I shook the water out of my hair as I snorted to clear my sinuses and forced the last of the water through my gills, before taking a breath.

I strode through the nearly invisible passage in the wall that connected the landing to the cavern beyond. I stopped abruptly, appalled by the condition of my new home. The lights I had meticulously set up in the bare cave were already on and the cavern looked as if someone had ransacked it. Things were haphazardly strewn about the room. Listening intently, I stepped through the mess, hearing noises echoing through the cavern from the area where all of my electronics and the more valuable of my possessions were kept.

In the back of my mind it occurred to me that Cortez might have found my hiding place, and had sent a contingent to reclaim his errant child. I peered around the corner, assessing the intruder, prepared to fight tooth and nail to keep from going back to that dingy cell where they felt I needed to spend my off time.

I was deeply surprised therefore when my gaze moved over the profile of a tall woman, who was busily stuffing my things into a salvage locker specially designed for deep-sea hauls. Her height exceeded my own and her head was completely bald, the skin pasty and white. On her back was an expensive rebreather set up. Those were units humans used to maximize their air usage, they took only small bits of pure oxygen, mixed them for breathing with standard atmosphere, then reclaimed the unused oxygen. and as she moved I caught glimpses of the trachea implants that she had. She was a gemue! Not just gemue, but mech-splice, and her skin tone told of a long life under the waves. Her arms and legs were sinewy with muscles and spoke of strength uncommon in women.

Her obviously burly build did not daunt me, as incensed as I was that she would have enough nerve to steal from me so shortly after my getting settled in. "Hey!" I boomed as I cut the distance between us in half, striding quickly to close the rest before she could bring to bear any defense she might have. By the time she reacted to my voice, I was on her, and despite her size I lifted her off of her feet. "What the hell do you think you're doing?"

"Holy shit," I heard her whisper in panic. "What the hell are you?"

I couldn't help grinning as she looked as if about to pee on herself.

She struggled for a moment, knowing she was in trouble. "I . . . I'm sorry mister . . . I thought it was deserted. See, I've been casing it for nearly a week."

"I've been out," I growled menacingly. "Now give me a reason not to kill you."

"I . . . I'll put it back," she said lamely. "If I broke anything I swear I'll replace it, just don't kill me."

Shaking my head, I set her down. "Pathetic," I muttered under my breath, then motioned to my stuff. "Well, get started, I got to sleep here tonight you know."

"Th . . . Thank you, mister."

"Don't thank me. You're not yet out of this cavern," I said flatly.

Her brow ridges rose in fear over the bright green lenses that covered her eyes. The comment set her to a faster pace and she diligently began replacing everything where she had found it. Several hours later she was near completion. I had napped unexpectedly and woke to find her still present, surprisingly, as I had half expected her to make a break for it the moment my eyes closed. My opinion of her went up a notch.

"You must not think I have the guts to kill you," I said as I approached her.

"I just wanted you to know that I'm not a thief, and that I am worth trusting," she replied. "You still have every right to kill me. I just hope that you won't."

My brow furrowed as I leaned on the nearest stalagmite. "What's your name?"

"Scud," she replied. "And you are?"

"They call me Tiger."

She went silent and I watched as she worked on putting the last of my things back. She continued, however to look back at me, but there was no hint of fear in her eyes; rather, she looked curious. Finally, she paused and turned toward me. "You haven't been around long, have you?" she said unabashedly.

"Why do you ask that?"

"I've seen a lot of gemues in my time and have never come across one like you."

"Well, for your information I have been a gemue for seven years."

54

"Seven?" she laughed, shaking her head. "I don't think so. You're much too pretty to be from that lot in gemue tech."

"Believe what you want. It's true," I replied.

"What are you saying...that you were some sort of Super Secret project with tech ahead of the time?"

"Something like that." I noticed that her whole attitude during the last hour had changed dramatically, exposing a more self-assured personality. That led me to believe that her previous show of timidity had been just that, a show. Taking a deep breath, I rose to my feet, and Scud turned to face me. "Well," I started, "I've decided to let you off the hook."

"Really?" she said, as if it was no surprise to her.

"On the condition . . . that no one else finds out about this place. I find any more visitors I will find you in turn."

"What? You on the run or something?"

"No, I just want my privacy intact. I haven't had much lately," I said testily. "Now get out of here before I change my mind."

She only nodded and, retrieving her now empty salvage locker, she disappeared into the pool of my home.

Chapter Six:
Take Two

One of my leads had led me to a run down motel on the edge of the water. I had been here nearly two hours trying to ensure that the information I had received was accurate. Dryworld tended to confuse tracking for me. There were so many smells that mingled and mixed until it was too difficult to pinpoint any one. I had established a fairly trustworthy group of land based informants that kept me enlightened when forays Dryworld were required. They had told me that the porcelain woman had checked in here several days ago and had yet to move on. They had also said that a front company had funded the place for The Movement. So that told me just who she had stolen her secrets for. The Movement was about the lowest, vilest group of anti-monopoly enforcers there was. They had Corporate America so tied up that it couldn't breathe without being monitored.

I listened carefully for any information coming to me over the 'net or any recall that Cortez might send to get me to do another short-term job. At the moment, however, it was just feeding me static and annoying me. I ripped it off my head and hung it absently on my belt as I continued to stare at the door of the motel. Several minutes later I was rewarded to see her leaving the motel; she was definitely hard to miss. I leaned forward watching intently as she looked up and down the cross street and moved to the other side.

Cautiously I followed her, not wanting to give away my advantage by having her see me. I moved from shadow to shadow, never losing sight of her. When she stopped at a local store I retreated into the shadows of the alley, willing to observe some more before taking her out. If she was a worker for The Movement, it might behoove me to follow her to some bigger fish.

I tried to melt into the wall so as not to be seen as a curious look crossed the girl's face, and I wondered what she possibly had heard or sensed to give her pause.

My brain answered that question as every neuron lit afire. My vision began to blur and I felt my knees buckle as another unfamiliar vision assaulted me.

In my mind I looked out from a raised hardwood stage with a podium before me. I was in an auditorium that was dusky, and those assembled were barely visible but for the first five rows. By the noise I would have to say that the assembly was full. Those I could see were dressed in maroon caps and gowns, and several of them were playing with the maroon and gold tassels hanging from their caps out of sheer boredom. I heard a voice I suddenly recognized as my own, speaking of prosperity and hard work. It was a long speech.

A familiar pain began in my head as I finished and the crowd of students rose to their feet and began to cheer. The sound rose in decible as more and more of the audience joined in, and synchronous with its volume the pain intensified until I thought my head would split open. Through the haze of pain I saw the raven-haired beauty. She was sitting four rows back from the front, approximately middle of the row so that she was sure to be seen. She was scowling at me, looking jealous and hurt for a reason I could not fathom.

I heard my own scream of pain, which broke through the vision that had clouded my mind, distancing the agony. The alley came into focus around me again, as the illusion gave way to reality. Unsteadily, I stood up, shaking and breathing hard. I looked back across the street, seeing the woman peeking out of the market's door in fright. That was twice she had assaulted me with alien apparitions and cerebral pain, and I began to realize, though I hated to admit it, that perhaps I was out of my league with this assignment. Torn between my pride to finish the job and fear of being crippled again, I just stood there. Uncharacteristically, my fear won out and I hastily retreated toward the water.

*****

Angelina had found herself in desperate need of food in her undersized refrigerator. She had been reluctant to venture forth, both for the unwanted attention she always received and the nagging thought that the shark man might still be able to track her here. Now she was left with no choice, she either had to buy enough groceries to allow her to seclude herself again or she was going to have to go to some sort of restaurant to fill her gut. So she dressed and left for the first time in nearly a week. She moved casually down the stairs, actually looking forward to getting out of that dreary motel room. She pulled her sunglasses down over her dead eyes as she stepped into the sun, and turned to walk toward the small local market on the next block.

Angelina was about to enter the store when a feeling passed over her. She turned and searched the street, seeing no one about at this early afternoon hour. But still the feeling that she was being watched would not dissipate. Doing something she loathed, she sent forth a tendril of a probe, searching for any unseen watchers. She hoped that she was being paranoid, and almost convinced herself of it when she encountered a brain pattern that was all too familiar to her. Feeling the skin on her neck begin to crawl, she fumbled for the door behind her and slipped inside even as she searched again for the owner of those dark thoughts.

Angelina stared in horror, finding her watcher not two hundred yards from her in an alley. He was on his knees and writhing as if in extreme pain. After some time he seemed to recover, but looking one last time toward where she stood, he turned away and left. She watched the retreating form of the shark man through the store window. There had been no duress that time, no real thought of a threat, yet she had again disabled the creature with a probe. She had not even known he was there until he was crippled and unable to cause her any harm.

She looked one last time out the window before doing some hasty shopping. When she had gathered what she needed and paid for it, she stepped cautiously out onto the street, wondering if the shark man had returned to resume stalking her. Somehow she doubted it, but to be sure she aggressively probed the area, ensuring the creature would be incapacitated even if he were there. She encountered nothing except for the small thoughts that the storeowner was thinking. She moved up the street slowly, reviewing these most recent events. It had been exactly the same as it had been at the bar. From the pain the creature had seemed to experience, to the visions she kept seeing from her time in college. This had been the graduation ceremony, only instead of watching enviously from the audience as David had given his speech as Valedictorian, she had stood behind the podium. It was like a dream come true, erasing all of the envy that she had felt at the time. She shook her head. It must have been a daydream, but again that did not explain what had happened that had crippled the gemue contracted to kill her.

*****

I pounded a fist into the wall, ignoring the sharp stab of pain that radiated up my arm. "What the hell is wrong with me?" I growled, pacing the narrow outcropping in my entry pool. It seemed every time I got near that bitch my head went over the edge. "I was made for pain tolerance! Fuck! I get one little headache and all my training goes to shit! You'd think she was the one stalking me!"

My pacing stopped momentarily and I ran a shaky hand through my hair. These last two encounters had definitely shaken my confidence in my ability. She got into my head so easily as if she'd been there before, all the worse for the sights she leaves behind, dreamy portraits of a normal life, of college, and the love of a woman. Things I had always wished for all my outcast life, things I could never have because of where and how I had grown up.

Suddenly, I found myself wondering where that was. I could not recall. I tested that blank wall that had severed my early memories from me with that question, only to be met with the same rhetoric I had already memorized.

*****

Angelina ushered herself into Max's office without any warning. "Max!" she said, seeing him in.

The young man started. "Angelina," he returned, and there was a note of irritation in his voice. "What can I do for you?"

"I need a favor."

61

"A favor?" He shook his head. "I don't know. I'm out on a limb right now with The Movement because of you. They nearly ostracized me right there."

"They'd be doing you a favor, bunch of hypocrites."

Max raised his hand in a silent request to stop. "I don't want to hear it . . . just what is it that you want?"

"You know that incident I told you about?"

"The one about the shark gemue? Yeah."

"I need some information about that creature: who he is, who he works for, you know," she said as she fiddled with one of the postmodern sculptures sitting on his desk.

"That's trouble and you know it."

She turned to face him, pointing at him. "Just get it for me. What I do with it is my concern!"

"Hey, I wouldn't be a friend if I wasn't concerned about you chasing after a proven killer."

"I know. I just have to find out something."

"My circles don't run through gemue territory," he said, trying again to distract her from her line of thinking.

"You must have someone who can get connected in that said same circle," she replied, not deterred in the least.

"Well, I'll see what I can do. Don't get your hopes up."

"Thanks Max."

About two weeks after making her request of Max's resources, there was a message waiting for Angelina on her vid net. She immediately dialed his vid and waited impatiently for him to reply.

"I don't have much," Max began upon seeing her face, "but I thought you'd want what I do have. To begin with, no one will admit to knowing who he is."

"Someone's got to know."

"All the sources will say is that he hasn't been in Fresno waters long. They seem to think that he just appeared one day. The story is corroborated by the fact that there have been no sightings anywhere up or down even the open water coast until just about the time you met up with him."

"What else?"

"Since he's been here he has made very few contacts, mostly other gemues, but he is rumored to have a dryworld spy network. He doesn't seem to hang with any particular group; he goes his own way and does his own thing. There have been several other slayings in the area, though none of the hits were our members. More than a few of them were high ranking officials of several conglomerates in the area, and all had the same MO."

"Maybe we should hire this guy," Angelina stated dryly. "It would sure make our jobs much easier."

"Funny," Max replied without humor. "The guy has all the styling of a merc. A well paid one, evidently, if he is getting mixed up with conglomerate politics and espionage. We have no trace yet of who is paying his salary, nor how long he's been working."

"Any idea where he stays?"

"Nothing specific. He seems to maintain a thirty mile radius in the waters around Old Fresno, though there is an unconfirmed sighting as far south as San Angeles. I couldn't get anything more."

"Why not?"

"Well, I think my sources are truly afraid of this guy."

"And why is that?"

Max held a picture close to the vid. He continued to talk hidden by the graphic scene he was showing her. Angelina swallowed hard against the bile backing up into her throat. "This is his MO. His favorite weapons are his teeth and claws; no one has ever seen him with a true weapon. He carries a stunner at all times but never seems to employ it. His strikes are precise, hitting the leg or thigh, enough to keep his victim from running.

"I will say this for him, he's no sadist. Gives them just enough time to see who he is and then he kills them. He has three favorite ways to kill: stabbing through the sternum, slashing the throat, or tearing into the neck. Painful deaths all, but relatively quick."

"Lovely," Angelina replied, swallowing again and rubbing her throat . . . That had almost been her.

"Angelina, please, as a favor to me, don't do what I think you're about to do. I lost David on the last mission; I don't want to lose you too."

"I'm sorry Max. I have to, especially now." She turned her eyes down, her tone quieting considerably. "Y'see, he found me again."

"No! Jesus, are you all right?"

"Yeah," she replied softly.

Chapter Seven:
What's in a Dream?

This job was really starting to get to me. I haven't been myself since that incident at the Bar Topical, and our last encounter only served to ingrain my growing phobia of this woman. The image of that dryworld restaurant, the college graduation, and the raven-haired beauty just would not leave me alone. They had begun to manifest themselves as dreams and fantasies about a relationship between her and me. The dreams are always the same: It's before my process, I'm human again, and after the luncheon at the café we go back to her place. Once we get there one thing leads to another and I find myself making love to the raven-haired beauty.

In the throws of passion an incredible pain fires my brain and when it subsides I am back in my current form. She looks up at me at first with loving eyes for the pause, but when she sees my face, she begins to scream, and tries frantically to get away. In a growing wash of rage and panic

I quickly slash her throat, watching her bleed over the white satin sheets. Then in horror I start screaming, finding that she was someone very important to me. I always wake up scared and confused about the portent of that dream.

As a result, my search for this woman had been going around in circles. Not because there were no leads, just because I couldn't get it together mentally to track the mark. I found myself afraid of what she might do next. I was also well aware of how impatient Cortez was getting with my continued delays. He had given me several smaller jobs to accomplish for a bonus. They were easy, almost boring tasks and all too soon, I was right back where I started, contemplating what all of the dreams meant. Did I actually know this girl? If so, where from? Or was it all some elaborate plant that the witch had put into my head to keep me off guard? Whatever the reason, it was affecting my performance and I was going to be hard put to bring myself back to the matter at hand.

*****

As a habit, Angelina did not get into New Age reading. All that stuff about metaphysics, and astral planes and stuff just seemed too far-fetched even in this crazy decade. But her current circumstances had drastically changed her view about the world and what she believed in. After an exhausting search, she returned to her shanty of a room to go over in more detail the books she had borrowed from the nearby store of the supernatural. She was looking for anything that might relate to her particular dilemma.

In the wee hours of the morning, Angelina came across a book that paralleled her experience eerily close, close enough to send shivers across her skin. It was a book heavy with undertones of government conspiracy regarding the uses of telepathy and the causes of regressive memory. It talked of one man's experiences with what he referred to as "wipes." The man was a telepath of some talent and had been on a super secret government project when he had bowed out of the program. He evidently was of more use to them and they were unwilling to let him just quit. They would hound him with these creatures, creatures that at some point had been human. They had no real wills of their own, just programs to carry out, with just enough personality to blend into society and not be spotted outright.

"The only way of detecting a 'wipe' is by mindscan, passive or active," one passage read. "This act will reveal to the scanner some piece of the creature's artificially suppressed history. This can often cause violent unnatural reactions from the 'wipe', for a telepath in contact with a suppressed memory causes acute physical pain to the cerebellum of the host."

That one passage fit her encounters with the shark man, from the pain the creature seemed to experience to the memories she gleaned from his consciousness. The only puzzlement came from the visions, for she should not be seeing things she knew and experienced in his head. The shark man could not know what her past had been. She laid her head down, puzzling over everything she had learned and observed, and before she knew it, she was asleep.

*****

Angelina heard a voice, resounding everywhere, calling her name, a bodiless sound that was oh so familiar. She found herself standing in a fog, in what she perceived as a room. "Angelina," again the familiar voice called plaintively, "where are you?" She recognized it immediately and her search became more determined.

"David?" she asked of the misty air. Around her, flashes of light illuminated the fog at irregular intervals, alternately blinding her with light and shadow. She was unable to adjust enough to see around her.

"Help me . . ." he implored in a pained whisper. Angelina jumped as he suddenly began screaming in torment.

"I . . . I'm coming, David, hold on!" she yelled, finding herself running through the mist toward what she thought was the source. She skidded to a stop, nearly slamming into the opaque pinkish wall that loomed out of the mist to block her path. The flashes of light had ceased momentarily, allowing her to adjust to the dark. She noticed that the barrier was backlit with a fleshy pink light. Vaguely, she could make out shapes moving on the other side of the wall.

"David where are you?" she asked, searching back and forth along the wall for an entrance or opening. None was visible from where she stood.

One of the vague shadows gravitated toward the barrier, the outline becoming clearer as it approached her perch. From the build, it was a man. Her heart leapt as she thought she recognized the shape of him. Hands lay against the wall opposite her, followed by the stern features of a man's face. The surface gave slightly, forming around the face and, giving it a ghostly appearance.

"Help me . . . I need you," he said hoarsely. The mask backed away abruptly and she could see him looking to one side. She heard an odd sound like a cross between a howl and a scream. She watched in horror as another shadow rushed in low and tackled the shadow that was David, pulling him away from her; his hand dragging across the pink surface before her.

"No!" she heard herself scream, pounding on the slightly yielding shell. Then she whimpered through her tears, "Not again."

She ran along the wall's boundary in the direction they had gone, trying to find a way past the smooth unbroken surface. Frustrated and guilt stricken, she stopped and fell to her knees, sobbing in anguish. Her cries echoed back at her, severely distorted. She heard a strange sucking sound *and looked up to see a hole opening slowly before her, a great pink maw beyond which was darkness.*

"Find me . . ." she heard David's pained plea from the black beyond.

Compelled by his voice, Angelina slowly stood and stepped into the opening.

She blinked as she stepped through into the bright light of a mid-afternoon in the city. People were bustling around her in a claustrophobically thick crowd, determined to get where they needed to be by yesterday. She caught a glimpse of David, his five seven frame taller than those around it as if everything was in miniature. "David!" she called out but he didn't seem to hear her, moving away toward a building that she recognized as her uncle's. "No!" she yelled. "Not in there!" She ran faster, trying to catch him before he entered it, but the crowd hindered her. He, on the other hand, was unaffected by them, seeming to move through, rather than around them.

"You must find me . . ." she heard him whisper as he disappeared in the door. She accelerated again, her heart pounding and her head hurting, as she attempted to close the gap between them. She pushed brusquely past the bustling people around her and squeezed between two exiting the building. Inside, the lobby was as crowded as the street had been, and she looked around frantically for her beau. She caught a glimpse of him as he stepped behind one of the decorative lobby tanks and was moving to her right behind it. The four species of sharks swam through the water of the tank languidly, as if they were swimming through ice blue gelatin. She could just make out David's form moving beyond them, a water distorted white blur of motion.

Angelina veered that direction, intent on cutting him off. She slid to a halt in front of him, beginning into a litany of tearful relief in having found him. She looked up, her eager face becoming blank as she found that the person in front of her was not David. Slowly, her gaze moved up the form in front of her. It was a man, but no human; it was a gemue. Her initial reaction decayed into naked fear at the realization that she faced the shark man mercenary that had almost killed her once before. She began backpedaling, trying to change her momentum and get away from the mad creature, to no avail. He leapt forward in one exceptionally graceful movement, grabbing her by the throat.

"You're not wanted here! Get out!" he bellowed.

The thing drew a hand back and swung for her.

*****

Angelina started awake, filled with the vision of five preternaturally sharp claws ripping into her flesh. Her cheek hurt from resting on the unyielding surface of the book that she had been reading. She tried to remember at what point she had fallen asleep, but couldn't pinpoint it. She stood and stretched, moving to her bed. She lay down but was unable to sleep.

The last words David had spoken haunted her. *"You must find me."* At first, she had been sure that her guilt had formed that strange, frightening dream. But the more she thought on the dream as a whole, and the message, she discounted the idea that it was merely a nightmare. What the sequence of images suggested to her was that she was in contact . . . with someone. The presentation was just like when she got around people and received what they were thinking. This, however, was a direct two-way link, as tentative as it was. She had been actually communicating with another . . . with David!

David was still alive?

If so, where was he?

Where had he gone in her dream? Her uncle's building, of course! If there were to be any illegal operations the best place for them to be hidden would be in his building. But what would that have to do with the shark man? Was it that he was protecting her uncle's secret? Then why did he take David's place in the dream?

Angelina sat up in the dark as her thoughts turned back to the shark man and the recent encounters she had experienced. She mulled for long moments over his reactions when he got close to her, how he had been so pained that his threat to her was neutralized. The content of the book that she had read struck a chord again, particularly what it had said about regressive memories.

She had originally thought that maybe she had projected a part of her own memory into the shark man's head, and that is what she had touched on. In light of what she had just been privy to, that could not be the case; if it were, he should not be experiencing any pain. She mulled over that for a long while, playing each memory in her head, searching for clues or anomalies that would lead her to an answer.

Slowly, she came to realize that there was something amiss about the visions she had seen in each encounter. The events in both cases were accurate in every detail, but what was odd was their point of view. In the vision of the café where she and David had had their lunch, she had been sitting where David would have been and she had been looking at herself. Her voice had been David's, not her own. The graduation ceremony was the same way. She spoke in David's voice and, peering out over the audience in the gloom of the theater, she could see herself four rows back scowling at the speaker.

The correlation was long in coming, but when it did, it hit Angelina like a hammer. She felt herself go cold and begin to shake at the thought that was looming in her mind. *"You have to find me,"* echoed in her head again. The dream . . . that contact . . . she had followed David into the Cortez building only to find the shark man . . . did that mean that thing was he? Angelina shook her head in horror.

71

"Please, Lord, say it's not true," she whispered hoarsely. "Please tell me that that thing was not him!" Yet every time she reviewed those memories the notion became harder and harder to deny. "Tell me that was not David," she sobbed as the old ache came back.

Had she left him to that fate? She hoped that she was wrong, that David had died at the hands of those monsters. Death would be better than what she was beginning to believe. At least he would be at peace.

As the night wore on and she had convinced herself that she was right, she began to obsess about getting confirmation, about finding out for sure. And there was only one way to do that. It was obvious that he did not remember who he was . . . if it was David, he would never act the way this creature did. She would have to confront the killer and perform a probe strong enough to bring David's memories back to him. The rest of the night she spent pouring over her books and practicing her ability, something that she had loathed to this point. She still did, but it was her best . . . her only chance to prove to herself that Cortez had stolen David from her . . . and not killed him.

Chapter Eight:
Curiosity Killed the Cat

I woke from my restless slumber to a hunger stronger than usual and, groaning, I pushed myself up, staying at full arms' extension until the water ran out of my hair and down my face. I took a deep breath and then sat up and stretched. I was still exhausted but knew that my stomach was not going to let me rest any longer. It had been a night full of vaguely disturbing dreams, something about pain and bright lights, about shivering in the cold. Thankfully, however, I had no dreams about that albino bitch that was making my life so miserable. I didn't bother to dry off as I headed for the entry pool, stumbling and bumping into the walls of the passage as I tried very hard to wake up. I didn't even slow down as I reached the edge of the shelf, taking a giant step into the pool and allowing the cold water to wake me the rest of the way. I surfaced again, shaking my head and exhaling in shock at the brisk feel of the water. Waking up had also awakened my hunger further and the rumble in my stomach came back more insistent than ever.

"All right," I said to no one and slipped under the surface again. I swam quickly out the entrance toward my feeding area, and had little problem following the pheromone trail to where the fish had moved. The first few I went through with no pomp, taking the edge off of my hunger so the next portion would be concise and controlled. This was my gym. Every feeding I spent practicing my techniques; capture and kill scenarios that had made me one of the best mercenaries above and below the ocean surface. I practiced maneuvering in the water; speed runs, killing blows, all of it ensuring that my skill would not fail me at a critical moment. This was my day to get everything back on track. I was going to get myself pulled back together and do my job in the most efficient manner possible. There was one thing I needed to clear up in my head first, however, and that would require me to capture that white witch alive. For only she had the answers I needed. And again, for that I was going to need my skills as sharp as possible to keep from falling victim to her telepathy again.

As I worked, I felt the anxiety I had dealt with the past few weeks burn off. My thoughts came into focus and every fiber of my being was at max performance. It was the best I had felt since taking this assignment. I worked for another fifteen minutes tearing through the large school until it had scattered so badly that I lost track of most of the fish. There was one small knot that was insistent of staying together and I started off after them when a different pheromone trail caught my attention. I paused a moment, sorting out just what the scents were telling me. They were unnatural smells, neoprene, plastic, rubber. There was a diver in the area. Then the last of the scent reached me, a whiff of the person intruding on my section of the ocean, and my heart leapt. It was the mark! That woman was here.

Why?

I decided that it didn't matter; here before me was my chance. Pinpointing where the smell was coming from, I made strong strokes to catch her before she could get away.

*****

Angelina had searched for weeks trying to find where the shark creature was staying. She had been convinced that the creature could be found at the Marlin Inc building. That would coincide with her contact, and the dream that went with it. To that end, Angelina had convinced Max to do some research. The urge was there for her to go herself, but she had realized early on that she was highly conspicuous and such an act would only hand her back over to the stable of mad scientists.

Max had concurred heartily with that assessment and agreed to do the work. What he had come away with was less than discouraging. The creature, if he had ever worked for Cortez, was not currently staying there. They had found evidence that he had been there, but had also discovered that the shark man was currently absent for a reason that the executives at the company would not discuss. Max had succinctly told her that was as far as he was willing to go to provide her information on the matter. He only added that the creature had been spotted northwest of New Fresno near a series of underwater caves.

Since that report, Angelina had spent a lot of time just diving in different places in the San Joaquin Sea. She had finally caught a break when she had actually seen the creature entering the water near this point. Angelina had quickly followed him in the hopes of locating his lair. She had witnessed him entering a small opening in the rock wall. After she had located it she spent the next several days waiting for him to come out of there. There was not an ounce of will in her to go into the creature's lair when it was evident that she would never return. She checked her air again, knowing that she was getting low and figuring it was about time to stop for the day. When she looked up, her breath caught in her throat. She had to force herself to keep breathing as she hunkered down. As if by magic, he was now swimming before her.

She peered from behind a large volcanic outcropping, watching the shark man intently. From what she could tell he was fishing, swimming through a school of black rockfish, catching the fast swimmers easily, and tearing them to shreds before swallowing them. It was disgusting. Blood soon filled the water, attracting scavenger fish to suck up the remains drifting with the currents. As she watched she began to realize that not only was he feeding, he was practicing. Each strike was a precise calculated maneuver. He would cut off a fish from the school, then tease and track it through the water. When he was satisfied with his attack, he would end the chase, violently taking the fish's life. She was still questioning the wisdom of her decision to seek out this creature, especially after her last encounter with the shark man. Yet she felt that she had to be sure that this was not David Scott, not the man she used to love. But then there was the matter of how she was going to be able to perform the probe. He was not just going to sit still for her performing a scan on his mind with enough duration and strength to find out who he really was. He would kill her long before that happened.

The shark-man paused abruptly mid-stroke while chasing a large rockfish. He raised his nose almost like a dog testing the wind. She hunkered down closer to the rock as he turned to face her hiding spot. He was motionless with the exception of a flick or two from either his hand or foot, and those odd fins at his elbows moved constantly to maintain his position in the water. His lip curled slightly into a half smile, and he made deliberate strokes toward her position. "Oh shit," Angelina muttered, torn between staying put to see if he actually knew she was there, and making an attempt for the surface with the hope that she could outrun him. As he came closer and seemed headed straight for her rock, she panicked.

She kicked off with as much strength as she could muster, hoping to gain an advantage with the extra distance. She swam hard, not looking back, and not wanting to know how close the creature was to catching her. Her effort availed her nothing, for within yards of the surface a large webbed hand closed over her faceplate and dragged her back. The other arm wrapped tightly about her waist, and the creature angled his feet up, twisting them both in the water and swimming back towards the depths. She struggled, not ready to give up a fight to this killer, and that is when her hand found the hilt of her dive knife. Angelina drew it up as best she could and plunged it down and back, hoping to make contact.

When she heard its cry of pain she knew she had struck home. She raised the knife a second time, bolstered to try again, but before she could, a sharp set of serrated teeth cut through her wetsuit and sank into her arm. The pressure of the bite felt as if her arm was going to snap in two and the wail of agony that escaped her lips echoed loudly in her mask. He released her with the exception of the grip on her arm and began to twist and shake in the water, causing her to lose her grip on her only defense. She watched helplessly as it sank in to the murky depths. He spit out her arm again, but wrapped her up in a rescuer hold before she realized she had been freed. He swam faster for the depths.

Angelina could see nothing but the surface getting farther and farther away. Even that sight was cut off as they entered a narrow tube in the rock. She felt the quick ascent he took in her ears and fought to clear them before they began to hurt. They broke surface in the dark, but the shark man seemed to know exactly where he was going as he lifted her bodily out of the water, tossed her carelessly onto a hard rock shelf, jumped up beside her and dragged her stiff legged across the uneven floor. Abruptly, he let go of her and she fell ungracefully to the floor, then he left her sitting scared in the pitch. She jumped as she heard a snort and the splashing sound of water forcefully hitting the deck.

Lights abruptly came on and Angelina blinked painfully several times, trying to adjust to the brightened surroundings. He was suddenly near her again, holding a small lantern. He set it down as she looked around slowly.

He reached roughly under her chin and, easily finding her seal, ripped the helmet from her head. He glared at her. "I oughta rip you apart for that stunt!"

She flinched. "Well, you can't expect me to just let you drag me to the deepest trench and kill me! I'm not stupid you know," she yelled at him, brazen in the face of her fear.

"Oh, yeah, that's why you go around following someone who is under contract to kill you. You've either got some big cajones or no regard whatsoever for your life."

"Go to hell!" she screamed, frightened. The creature was much more intimidating up close and she felt herself cower as he towered over her.

He paused, and Angelina saw a glint of humor in those foreign eyes as a grin crossed his stretched mouth. She thought she saw her blood still lingering on those saw edged, multi-rowed teeth that grin exposed. "You've got spirit, I'll give you that," he replied, turning away from her. He raised his right arm to survey the damage Angelina had inflicted on him. A two-inch gash showed nastily about halfway down the ribcage on his side, more toward his back. Streaks of red ran from it, hastened by the water still dripping off him to stain the waistband of his pants. He touched it gingerly.

"And a hell of an aim," he added as he disappeared into the shadows. "You're lucky I got a thick hide."

Angelina took the opportunity to take a quick look around her. There was not much to his hideout, at least at first glance. It was a small shelf that sat just inches out of the water and only about three feet from the wall to the edge of the water. The landing was long though, and the light from the lantern did not illuminate the far reaches of it.

Angelina glanced over at where the shark man had thrown her dive mask. She peered again at the darkness where he had moved out of her sight. She licked her lips and, hoping he was not watching, she leaned toward it.

"I wouldn't do that were I you," she heard his disembodied voice say.

He appeared again, carrying a towel and a robe in one hand, another towel around his neck, and a square of gauze pressed to his side. "None of your damn mind grenades either, that shit hurt." He tossed down the towel and robe. "I would suggest you get out of that wetsuit and dry off. I don't even stay wet in this place; it's too damn cold. For you it's a pneumonia risk." He sat down, Indian style near her.

"I'm going to die anyway, right? Why should I?"

"Look, you would not be in here," he stabbed a nail into the rock he was sitting on, "if my intentions had been to kill you out there. That may have been what I was paid for, but . . ." He stopped, shaking his head as if he did not want her to know the details of his reasoning. "I don't let just anyone in here . . ."

She scowled and began to take her gear off. She sucked a pained breath as she tried to pull the sealing collar off over her head, aggravating the bite on her arm, which now pounded with dull fury. Without a word, the shark man reached over and pulled the sealing collar off for her, then assisted her in removing the rest of the bulky gear, and the

79

tight fitting wet suit. She watched, quietly impressed at his deft handling of the setup as she reluctantly toweled dry.

"You seem to know your way around a rebreather tank," Angelina said suspiciously. "You dive before you submitted for your change?"

"No," he replied simply as he closed off the valve and rebooted the mixer system, not elaborating.

"Then how . . ." She trailed off, pointing to his handling of her gear.

"After spending seven years in the water, I would think learning dive equipment to be a logical offshoot, don't you? I mean, not everyone I work with is a gemue," he said, and when she pursed her lips he scowled. "You think I'm not capable, just 'cause I am gemue...just 'cause I don't need equipment to breathe underwater?"

"Well . . ." she started, scratching her head, knowing she was skating on thin ice.

"Y'know," he interrupted before she could answer, "that's just the attitude I'd expect from a dryworlder gemuephobe. You people don't know shit about the situation, but are judge and jury for the lot of us. I had no fear of drowning with this soggy valley when I had my change done. I was confident in my decision to do this. You assume we're all stupid and reactive, and that puts us beneath the rest of the human race. And you're dead wrong."

"I never said that!" Angelina defended, even if it was exactly what she had been thinking.

He grunted dismissively as he stowed her tank in a cubby by one wall. There was a long silence punctuated only by water dripping into the pool somewhere.

He stared at her and after some time returned, grabbing her arms, one hand tightly compressing the wound there, which drew a squeal of pain out of her and buckled her knees. He then roughly sat her down. Angelina grimaced at the lingering pain and marveled at the strength of his grip.

She laid a hand over the newly bleeding bite. He scowled openly, moving away again before she could get a good look at his face; not that she could see much through her pain induced tears anyway.

She watched him closely as he worked, looking for some hint of resemblance. His features were so stretched it would have been difficult even with David's most recent picture handy to make any kind of determination.

"They did one hell of a number on you, you know that?"

He turned to face her, not sure how to take her comment. When he decided she was serious, he replied, "You like it? It's the best money could buy. Took just about everything I owned to pay for it...my first two years' salary as well."

"You talk as if you had a choice."

"Of course I had a choice. Why do you say that?" His brow ridge dragged down, emphasizing his irritation.

Angelina just shrugged. "Oh, no reason." She tried raising her arm, wincing at the pain. Looking down, she noticed that though smaller in width it was exactly like the bite of a true shark. The wounds were angry red and beginning to swell. He returned to her side, flipping a roll of gauze nonchalantly and catching it, and she wondered where he had hidden it. "Did you have to bite me?" she asked incredulously, her anger rising again.

"Did you have to stab me?" he quipped in return.

"We've been over this already," Angelina returned sullenly.

He shrugged as he settled next to her, oddly looking apologetic as he assessed her injury. "I wasn't about to let you stab me twice."

She grimaced at him, and as he reached over to dress her wound, she cringed.

"Don't!" he growled. "Look, I'm trying to help, okay? You move you get cut, got it?"

She nodded, wide-eyed. She wondered why he was bothering.

He held up one hand, his fingers splayed wide, giving her a good view of the two-inch claws adorning each. "After all, these nails aren't exactly graceful when you're trying to do precision work."

He very carefully wrapped her arm and she noticed the pains he took to keep those lethal claws off of her skin. A more morbid voice also chimed in, wondering how easy it would be to break those long, delicate looking fingers. That might be enough distraction to get her out of here. She did not trust his conviction about not harming her.

"There," he stated, tucking what was left of the gauze back under the fin at his elbow. He stood, seeming quite proud of his work.

He started drying his hair, which Angelina regarded as redundant, for his hair was near dry the moment he stepped out of the water.

"You'd better take that bathing suit off too." He sighed, and she looked back, glaring at him.

"That how you get your jollies? Accosting women and telling them to strip?"

"Lady, I gave up women seven years ago. Girls just don't go for gemues. The ultimate in birth control, forced abstinence," he replied lightly. "Besides, how can I 'accost' someone when they came looking for me?"

Her lips thinned and she sighed angrily, unable to argue with his logic. "Well, do you mind?"

"Yes, actually, I do. I can't have you trying to escape. My boss is expecting me to kill you, and he won't be happy when he learns I had you if I just let you walk a second time." Her eyes widened again, and she began to back away. "Calm down. Right now, I could give a shit less what he thinks. Our deal is starting to sour my stomach."

"Are you sure it wasn't all those fish you devoured?"

"Cute," he said, smiling again. He nodded her way. "I just want some answers, and I'd rather have you comfortable to do it. Don't worry. I'm the perfect gentleman, really."

"When you're not killing people for profit, that is," she retorted hotly, still not budging.

He scowled. "Oh, Jesus. These days, teens go to school topless and you're afraid to strip down to save yourself a cold?" When she still did not move, his temper snapped. "Fine!" he growled, throwing the robe against the wall. He glared at her and then moved to the far end of the landing. She noticed that he never left his back turned to her for long. It reminded her again that he was very good at his chosen profession.

He watched her, scowling, as the damp air began to steal her heat. It was not long before she was shivering uncontrollably. Angelina's pride and what little modesty she had left kept her from doing what he asked.

"Uh huh," she heard him say.

He was shaking his head as he leaned down to retrieve the robe he had discarded moments earlier. He stepped up to her, robe in hand, and Angelina thought he was going to be kind enough to give it to her. He instead dropped it at her feet, and in a motion she did not quite catch, he sliced through her shoulder straps, bellowing, "Now get the damn thing off!" He resumed his place at the opposite end of the landing. "Damn a woman's pride," he muttered. He continued on for long moments, something about not being able to stand suffering.

Angelina stood there a few moments, jaw hanging slack. It was slow to shut and she found herself swallowing a lump of fear that had not been there earlier. Realization dawned that he could have just as easily taken her life in that split second. She turned around quickly and as discretely as possible undressed. She picked up the robe with trembling hands and wrapped it around her, tying the sash tightly about her waist. That done, Angelina sat down, knees to her chest, trying to warm up fast, and sat as far from the creature as possible. Out of the corner of her eye she kept watch for any sign of him approaching her.

What had possessed her to chase this man down?

"He isn't David," she thought angrily. "Can't be. The way he talks, he's been a gemue for a very long time. And his mental feel tells me he believes it. It has depth enough to be true. Was I projecting a memory into his head? No, that's not right. Why would they be from David's point of view? Remember what you read Angelina . . . 'A telepath in contact with an artificially suppressed memory causes the subject of the probe sudden acute pain.' He had definitely been in pain at that bar and at the store. Maybe he's had a memory implant, a rewrite to suit Uncle Marlin. That would be just like him," she thought bitterly. Marlin had always possessed a twisted sense of humor.

Chapter Nine:
Truth Hurts

I observed unobtrusively as she shyly got herself out of the wet swimsuit. I averted my eyes to fulfill my promise, but I saw enough to know that her skin was pale all the way down and that she had a beautiful body. I looked back her direction as I saw the flash of white that told me that she had gotten the robe on. I watched also as she sank dejectedly down and curled up, her eyes losing focus. I was unsure whether it was to keep warm or that she thought all hope was lost.

"You have yet to answer my question," I told the girl, looking at her sidelong. In the white robe I had given her, she looked very pale indeed, almost like a snowflake that had been trapped in Hell.

I kept asking myself why exactly I had brought her in here. This was my personal sanctum as it stood, and not even Cortez knew where it was. I was curious, certainly, encountering a telepath, and one of such raw talent was unheard of. When I made my decision to submit myself for alteration I had read everything I could get a hold of about genetic anomalies. I could think of no mention of that kind of talent.

Another voice argued that it was ridiculous to think that she would be willing to just tell me her life story. Killing her and taking her back to Marlin's lab would certainly be easier. His machinery could strip the memories of a person from the brain, alive or dead.

The idea had little appeal however, especially with the treatment I had received from him lately. He had me feeling more like an errant child to be looked after, and locked away, than a trusted employee. He would almost certainly verify her death then be rid of the evidence. I would lose my shot to learn what I wanted to know.

So here I was breaking every rule I had learned about being a merc, and for what? What exactly did I want from her?

She stared uncomfortably in my direction before she spoke. "I don't know," she said softly. "I thought you were someone I used to know…a person who was separated from me forcefully about nine months ago."

My eyes widened a bit, as I was definitely not expecting that kind of answer from her. Then again, it made her being here a whole lot more sensible. "I'm sorry to disappoint you, but I never saw you before the Bar Topical incident."

"So you say."

"What do you mean 'so you say'?"

"You remember those 'mind grenades,' as you called them?"

"Yeah, it saved your life. That's one hell of a trick, planting those images in my head."

"I didn't plant them, any of them. Those images are your own memories."

"What? Oh, come on," I replied in disbelief.

"You may not want to believe that, but I didn't put them there."

That shocked me into silence for a minute. She continued, "You see, I'm very new to the telepathy game. I have neither the control, nor the experience, to plant a memory and make it come off.

"I suspect you are newer to being a gemue than you think, as well. A very ruthless man captured a man named David Scott and I while we attempted to gather information on him to expose his underworld dealings. One of his specialties has been illegal gemue experimentation. David and I were separated and in a very short amount of time they were able to do this to me." She indicated her pallid complexion. "I got away, but David wasn't so lucky. He remained behind, and who knows what they were able to accomplish with him. I suspect that you could very well be that result."

"And just what proof do you have?" I asked intrigued by this stretch of fiction she was trying to feed me.

"I was in your head, remember? I saw what you were seeing. I saw the café. It's the place that David and I went when we first started dating. That memory is yours," she started boldly. "The pain associated with its recall comes from the mental wall they put up when they rewrote your memory . . . essentially; they blocked your past from you. They don't want you to remember us. They made you into someone else. You're an experiment, nothing more."

I scoffed, pointing a finger accusingly her direction. "You put those there . . . I have no memory of ever living Uptown."

The look in her eye was dead serious, as she replied, "No, I'm not capable. I only pick up others' thoughts, and I can't project."

"So you're saying I'm this boyfriend of yours and this 'bad man' turned me into a fish against my will." I could not help but laugh. "Lady, I feel for you, I really do. But this body, the changes to it, they were my choice. I've been this way for seven years. I took up merc'ing five years ago and I am paid well for what I do. Don't think your little story is going to have me start questioning my existence."

"Then tell me something," she continued. "Where did you go to school?"

"I dropped out," I replied easily. "School was too slow for me."

"That doesn't really answer my question," she uttered.

I looked at her sternly, not giving her further details.

"What were the names of your family members?"

She stopped me dead with that one, and I felt my mouth thin as I said, "I don't remember. Procedure induced amnesia." I wondered why I was indulging her inquisition.

"No, it's because they rewrote your memory to suit their needs. There are large gaps in your memory that they try to explain away by saying that your transformation caused selective amnesia." She drew a deep breath, sensing that she had my attention, and more than just in passing. "Do you realize how unrealistic that explanation is . . . how asinine it sounds?"

My thoughts roiled for a moment, as a part of me actually wanted to believe what she was saying. I felt my features harden then, realizing she was playing with me.

I quipped, "Do you know how asinine YOU sound?" I rolled my eyes, muttering, "Boy, its no wonder Cortez wants you out of the way. You are very good at playing mind games. The way you talk you probably suckered some unsuspecting tech out of the information you stole."

Even as the words were uttered I knew at least the last part wasn't true. I had done a little digging, and found no record of a security breach. Even more perplexing was the fact that no one I had contacted knew anything about an alabaster-skinned woman working for Marlin Incorporated. Yet another reason I was having this discussion instead of swimming her body back to collect my fee. The stout executive was trying to snooker me, and I wanted to know why.

"Is Cortez who you work for?" she asked, and I nodded. "And that is what he told you?" I nodded a second time. She smiled wryly. "Oh, Uncle Marlin, you connive with the best of them."

I looked up, astonished at her words. " 'Uncle?' Marlin Cortez? Now you're reaching."

"He's the one David and I was after," she said with sincerity.

I wagged a finger; she couldn't get me on this one. His only niece, Angelina, was in New York on a very important business trip. "I know for a fact that he speaks very highly of Angelina."

I actually saw color tint those white cheeks as her temper flared. "Boy, he's really got you duped, doesn't he? He rewrote you so well you can't even access the truth. That man cares for nobody but himself, and he considers his family members nuisances. One of the first big businesses he took over belonged to my father, Paco Cortez, and without a hint of emotion he left us out in the street. He gave us one or two token visits to his estate to gloat about how rich he was getting, but that was it.

"He personally oversaw my experimentation, y'know. He laughed at the pain he inflicted on me." She was right in my face now. "I am Angelina Linda Lupe Estrada Cortez, and Marlin Cortez doesn't give a damn about me except to see me dead!" There were tears running down her angry face. "Now you either kill me and get it over with, or give me my stuff back so I can leave. I've got other idiots to avoid, besides you."

I stood there, confused; the vehemence of her word was shocking. Even the best liars couldn't pull that off. So what do I do? If I released her Marlin Cortez would have every reason to rip up our contract and let me go. He would probably ruin my reputation as a merc. Compassion was not supposed to be a strong suit in this line of work.

I felt my brows furrow as something dawned on me. Shaking my head, I decided that she was just playing another head game with me, a very good one I might add. "How about this: I take you back to Cortez and you can try using that line of bullshit on him. I don't buy it." Her eyes widened, and slowly she sank to the ground, looking dejected. "Get up. I'm tired of playing games . . . Get dressed. We're leaving."

She dragged her feet as she dressed into her suit; not that I blamed her, but the longer I waited the more I was considering looking further into her story. She seemed to be fussing with a leak on her rebreather tank and I came over to see what the matter was. The sooner I got out of here and deposited this girl with Cortez, the better I would feel. I wasn't expecting her next action. Out of sight, she had removed one of the small emergency tanks from her pack, and as I neared, she swung hard for my head. I couldn't duck the swing in time. It connected squarely just above my left eye and sent me reeling into the adjacent wall. I felt my dorsal fins twist painfully and the impact as I hit the deck, before darkness overtook me.

*****

Angelina finished dressing quickly, not sure just how badly she had injured the killer, and not wanting to stick around long enough to find out. She glanced back once before sealing the helmet over her head. He was much too still, and Angelina wondered if she had killed him. She dove into the pool and made strong strokes toward the entrance.

It wasn't him, she tried to convince herself, it just couldn't be. That arrogant, strutting, wisecracking killer just could not be the man she had loved. Angelina had just been deluding herself for thinking that it was he and for thinking she could undo whatever it was that had been done to him. There were tears running down her face inside the mask, blurring her vision as she swam to the surface.

So David was dead, but where did that leave her? She was disappointed, and emotionally spent for keeping herself so wound about that question. She slowly climbed into the dinghy, stripped out of her rebreather, and motored back to shore wondering what was left to live for. She still had all of Uncle Marlin's normal flunkies to avoid and she began to question if it was not just wiser to move away from New Fresno and start over again. Maybe she could have The Movement hide her again, somewhere away from Cortez, and away from the ocean.

*****

I woke up several hours after the girl claiming to be Angelina Cortez had assaulted me, unable to see out of my left eye. My back was on fire from the muscles and tendons torn when I had run into the wall, and my head pounded like King Kong was trying to bust out of my forehead. I pushed up, groaning in pain, and looked about for the woman, knowing already she was long gone. The only evidence that she had ever been there was the robe she had discarded in one corner.

I raised my hand to my head, feeling the warm trickle of blood still oozing from my brow. She had laid my forehead neatly open with the force of the blow. I felt as well as heard the growl building up in my throat as I straightened. "That does it, bitch," I bellowed up at the ceiling, listening as it echoed back at me. "I catch up with you, you're meat!"

I could not believe that I let her lure me into such a compromising position. What kind of a merc was I? She had almost convinced me that her mark was not worth the fee.

My thoughts crystallized. Her attack had strengthened my resolve to get her buried.

I decided it was time for me to check back in with Cortez to update him on my lack of progress. I was sure that I probably was suffering from a concussion, for I was sick and dizzy. Might as well let them patch me up while I'm there. I slid myself carefully into the chimney pool and headed for open water, cursing the pain in my back and the sting of the saltwater in my open wound as I swam.

"Well, Tigershark," Cortez gushed as I stepped in, "we were beginning to wonder if you were coming back. And by the way . . . you look like hell."

"You wish," I muttered, trying to ignore my injuries.

"Well?" he asked. "Did you find her?"

"You could say that," I replied enigmatically. "Slippery little fish, she managed to get a jump on me . . . knocked me out cold. When I came to she was long gone."

"This particular mark seems to be giving you a lot of trouble. I thought you were the best . . . are you sure you won't need some back up on this?"

"Oh no, she's mine. I have a score to settle with her now."

"If you're sure," he said, smiling darkly. I just nodded, wondering about his overly cordial tone. He sounded as if he was placating me somehow.

"You've already got someone else on this, don't you?" I asked sharply.

"If you don't start performing I will," he returned. This time there was no humor in his voice.

"You keep everyone else out of this!" I warned. "I will take her, and I will collect my fee."

"I'm glad to hear that," he replied dryly. "You may return to your quarters."

I turned away slowly, breathing, "Yes, master."

Making my way down through the hidden ways unknown to the executives who buoyed the corporation, I mulled steadily over the many things I had discovered this night. Marlin had not disclosed all I needed to know about my quarry. The "facts" that the woman had told me, the embarrassment I felt at having her outwit me in my own territory, sent another wash of anger and a want for retribution through me.

I was too spent to even get upset when they once again locked me in my quarters, barely turning my eyes to them before I hopped into the shallow pool and eased my aching body into the warm saline. I couldn't have said whether a coherent thought had run through my head before I had fallen asleep.

Later that night I jumped up, sloshing saltwater over the floor of my quarters. I was breathing heavy and my hands quaked with an uncontrolled adrenaline rush. If I were human, I'd have been drenched in sweat. Yes, the nightmare was that bad. I sat for a moment, calming my nerves and trying to recall the particulars of that intense experience. But as I did, the details blurred until the only thing I could remember was a bright light, and agony. I rubbed my eyes aching from REM, and then I slicked back my hair. looking around, I wondered what time it was. Nobody was on the deck, so it had to be sometime after two in the morning. My room was locked, as usual. I grit my teeth, wishing they would stop being so paranoid. It was like they were expecting me to just jump ship one day and never return.

*****

My quarry had gone dryworld to New Fresno. She had gone into hiding, or so my sources had told me. I fell back on my network of spies to help find her. Their information was leading me to an electronics factory plant, just on the other side of the city. The place was nowhere near the water and that made me edgy. I hadn't been out of water for more than an hour since I had taken this form. Most of my previous jobs had been underwater, or they only required me to come out of the water long enough to make the hit, then disappear. I was thirsty, something that I never worried about, because in the course of my feedings, I got more than enough directly from the ocean. Now that I was on land I was acutely aware of the dryness in my throat and how my eyes burned from lack of moisture. To add to that nuisance, my body seemed extraordinarily heavy out of the water and the longer I remained the worse it became.

I passed the dryworld shops, hardly glancing at the baubles showing so prettily under their intense lamps. People moved quickly out of my path, shocked or horrified looks showing on every one of their faces. Most of them had probably never seen a gemue in real life, much less one as intimidating as I was. They spent their entire lives in their warrens of tall buildings and dreamy pre-fab suburban housing tracts. Few, if any, ventured down near the water, a place considered too foul for their lovely countenances to behold.

The offices faded away, giving way to a more industrialized area where warehouses and factories sprawled across several dozen acres. The place I wanted, according to my source, was the second on the left. The gray warehouse was as nondescript as the rest of the buildings in the area, but the last thing The Movement was going to be was high profile.

As I moved closer, I pondered how exactly I was going to gain entrance. After all, my appearance did not bode well for just strolling through the front door. My previously bold tour through the city turned to a cautious trek as I drew near my objective. I sneaked to an adjacent alley, ensuring no one witnessed my departure from the street. I listened very carefully for the whir of surveillance cameras, but the silence of the trash-ridden corridor was only punctuated by the sound of a few voices talking further down. As I moved farther toward the back of the place, I found the source of those voices. There was a noxious cloud of cigarette smoke that clogged my nose and threatened to make me cough. About six people were huddled around a double door, polluting themselves with what most people considered cancer sticks. I avoided detection by sidling behind a pile of accumulated rubbish. All the other doors that I had tried had been securely locked. So I moved around to the back of the building.

I was beginning to think of a more drastic means of getting in when I came across a door that had been blocked open. Someone had placed a fan there to circulate the outside air through the hall and some of the nearer offices. I ducked under the fan without disturbing it and proceeded down the passage.

I paused at the first junction and took a sample of the atmosphere. Here was less congested with unfamiliar odors, though they still tainted it. There was the tang of well oiled but overworked machinery, sweating bodies and a mixture of wood, paper, and leather. It surprised me. I had expected this place to be a front, but I detected no traces of what could be considered the spy ring The Movement was purported to be. It smelled exactly like it looked: a factory, with a few office spaces for the managers.

Disappointed, I moved further away from my entrance, taking a path through the mazes of corridors that got me closest to the scent of offices. At the last moment, I detected a group of people approaching my position, and back-pedaled hard, hiding myself in a small nook where the water fountain was. The group dressed in business suits moved past me without as much as a glance, talking excitedly about some new project. I sighed quietly, relaxing and looking out from my cubby. I saw no one, but paused a bit longer, wondering why I had not sniffed that group out sooner. They had been almost on top of me. I also took advantage of the water, trying vainly to soothe my parched throat. I hoped it was my imagination, or the stark whiteness of the walls, but it seemed that my vision was getting dimmer. I shrugged, telling myself it was just nerves, and moved on.

After several more corridors and two more close encounters with the workers of the plant, I was about ready to give up and go home. I was not feeling well. My chest hurt like I'd been running too hard and my eyes were scratchy. But my pride kept me there; I had told Cortez I was going to finish the job, and damn it that was what was going to happen. That bravado failed me after several more lengths of seemingly endless hall and I turned to backtrack to the door I had entered through. I took a step and miraculously caught a whiff of the girl who claimed to be Angelina Cortez. So, she was here. Immediately, all ails were forgotten. I picked up my pace as the trail became stronger, and it stopped at a plain wood door of just one more office in this section of the building. I closed my eyes, drawing a deep breath and sorting what the pheromones had to tell me. There was someone else in the room with her. But that was okay; I was given a bonus for every Movement member I took down. I would kill her and her accomplice and show Cortez just what I was worth. Get someone else would he . . .

*****

Max and Angelina had been discussing the latest intelligence to come in regarding Cortez's operations. They were getting much closer to the information they needed to shut him down. The Movement was, that is. Angelina was no longer a member in anyone's eyes with the exception of

Max. He still relied heavily on her to gather information for him and do legwork that his position didn't allow time for.

Max's front was as curator of the local aquarium, but he came to this office, his white room, to take care of any official Movement business that arose, usually involving scrambling transmissions between the higher echelons of the organization.

Angelina and Max both jumped up in shock as the door exploded inward. Somewhere in the back of Angelina's mind she knew what was coming next. Following the momentum of the door was the creature she thought she had seen the last of. Three feet into the room the shark man paused, assessing the situation before him. He was crouched low, snarling. He lunged at her with lightning speed, grabbing her by the throat and lifting her bodily off the ground. His expression darkened at the sight of her and his growl was feral and menacing. The swelling in his eye was unsightly purple and the stitches holding his brow together showed bright blue against his pale skin. Angelina sucked in a breath, wishing suddenly that she had made sure he was dead.

He slammed her hard into the nearest wall, compressing her lungs and shocking her diaphragm until she couldn't breathe and once she was securely pinned he looked to the thin young man who also occupied the room. Angelina watched, after several terrified moments, the snarl on the creature's lips fade away as it looked at Max. She felt herself slide down the wall as he continued to stare at her friend. The shark man squinted, releasing his hold of her as he slowly moved toward Max.

Angelina stood there rubbing her throat, trying to catch her breath. Max looked horrified, backing away until the desk behind him hindered his retreat. He had heard Angelina's description, but never thought he would be privy to actually seeing the creature. The gemue stopped just two paces short of Max's frozen form, looking oddly at him.

97

Angelina thought she saw the mercenary's body shaking. Its eyes narrowed as he moved a step closer, causing Max to cringe.

Angelina was about to put herself between them, when her assailant stopped, and the shaking she had previously noticed became more pronounced as he stood there. "M . . . Max?" she heard him say in a querulous tone. "You . . . I . . ." The statement ended in a sigh as it slumped to the floor at Max's feet. Holding his heart, as if he was having a heart attack, Max lurched into the desk behind him. By the time that the creature stopped quivering, Max was practically on top of the furniture. He hopped down after the gemue stilled, saying, "Jesus Christ! I thought you said this thing wasn't going to follow you! I thought for sure I was a dead man!"

Angelina ignored him for the moment, kneeling beside the downed individual and assessing his condition. His yellow-gray slitted eyes were half opened, covered by a second opaque set of lids she had never noticed before. Mr. Merc's breathing was shallow and fast, and moving his mane away from his neck she noticed how his gills were convulsing. His skin looked dry and puckered. When she pinched it and it stayed that way, she knew he was dehydrated.

Max overcame his anxiety and moved up next to her and the being. "Did . . . that thing say my name or was I just imagining things?"

"No," she said quietly, her mouth a thin line. "He called you Max."

"But, I mean, how did it know?"

"I don't know," she replied. She had not informed him of her reservations about this man. In fact, she had all but forgotten about it, until now. Her suspicions seemed to be reconfirmed. David had introduced her to Max when she had first joined their group. They had been like brothers, only with less of the fighting. It was too much of a coincidence, with all of the other evidence she had already compiled. "If we want to find out for sure then we had better do something."

"Huh? What do you mean?"

"He's dying, Max. He's got all the symptoms of someone who's suffocating."

"Let the thing die then! I'm not that interested in keeping it alive, and I'm not that curious about how he knows me!"

"MAX! He's a living being, remember?"

"He's a gemue, and he works for Marlin Cortez. If he lives and gets loose, our whole operation is sunk!"

She had forgotten how gemuephobic Max was. "Look, nothing says he's going to escape us. Besides, I want to find out why Cortez wants me dead." She already knew that and such a boldface lie hurt her head.

"He's your responsibility. I'll have no part of this."

"Fine, Max. Call Doctor Thomas. We're going to need him in on this one." Doctor Thomas was one of the few professionals that had allied with their cause. He was the closest thing they had to an expert on gemue biology, and he would kill her if he didn't get the chance to study this creature. "Meanwhile, we're going to need to get him down to the aquarium."

"The aquarium?" asked Max, pausing in his conversation with Thomas.

"Do I have to explain everything to you? He's got gills, y'know, like a fish. He certainly breathes better in the water than from the air." She had a feeling that somehow they had tampered with his ability to get a proper air exchange through his lungs.

The building was about ten minutes by car from their district headquarters. They recruited a few people to help them pack the shark man into their van, and he now lay across Max's lap. Max was very pale next to her, pulling up on one of the man's lips and getting a good look at the teeth that mouth contained. He grimaced, and quickly removed his hands lest the gemue come alive and relieve him of some of his digits.

"Why in the world would anyone want to do this to themselves?" he said, his tone heavy with disgust.

"Why do people do drugs, why do people drink, and why do people commit suicide? Why are you asking me?" Angelina retorted from behind the steering wheel. Several minutes later, they had pulled into the consignment area and several workers greeted them grimly. They had the equipment all ready for them, loading the man onto a gurney specially designed for dolphin transfers. The gurney slid along tracks in the roof of the hall, coming to a stop over a shallow tank usually used for spawning salmon. It was past spawning season now and the tank was perfect for what they needed.

Walking into the holding area from the public section of the aquarium was Doctor Thomas, looking excited at the prospect of seeing the gemue they had. Two workers were now lowering it into the tank.

"Up the temperature, saline, and oxygen content," Angelina was saying as he stepped up next to her.

"Oh, my God!" he said, astonished. He moved over to the tank, taking every detail of the creature in. "Whew is he a piece of work!"

"That's what I said," she replied, getting his attention back. "He seemed quite proud of himself for it."

"Hello, Angelina." He smiled, and then turned back to his examination. "I would be too if I was into this sort of thing," he said with his back to them.

"I hope we're not too late," Angelina said.

"Not that I really care, but why?" asked Max in irritation.

Angelina frowned. "He's been without oxygen for fifteen minutes. That's enough time to render a human a vegetable, or worse, it could kill him."

"Good, then we'll not have to worry about him snitching to Cortez about my cover."

"You're a real humanitarian, Max. If you weren't my friend, I'd smack you."

"Why's that?" Max asked angrily.

"For being so callous."

"Callous? For heaven's sake, he tried to rip out your bowels! For that, I say he deserves to die a slow painful death!"

Angelina smiled wryly, admiring Max's loyalty, even if it was misplaced.

The doctor stepped up a ladder that had been provided, and pulled out his instruments. The man had both the conventional and the state of the art in his medicine bag. Angelina and Max made themselves comfortable as he continued his work.

Chapter Ten:
Behind Enemy Lines

After about an hour Doctor Thomas rejoined them. Angelina saw a light in his eyes that she rarely saw: he was excited about this guy.

"Magnificent transformation process-The lines between what he was and what he is now are so fine as to be almost nonexistent. He was changed rapidly." He turned on his holoprojector, lighting up the space between them with three-dimensional pictures of the gemue's skeletal structure. He pointed to different spots as he spoke to further illustrate his supposition. "The areas with the most change, here in the jawbone, face, and between the knuckles on the fingers, show signs of stress, of being stretched too quickly. They re-grew this guy's bones literally to fit the new DNA pattern, and faster than any growth of bone with the exception of that of a fetus. In order to accomplish such a feat, it is my guess that they exposed him to large doses of radiation.

"Additionally, there are signs of extensive surgery, mostly removal of what his creator considered unnecessary organs. The gills look to be surgically implanted and then rapidly grown to support this man's size, though I can't make that determination for sure.

"His mass has been increased from what I can tell, indicated by faint stretch marks on his skin, appearing as slightly darker stripes." He shook his head. "He was much smaller when he was human, probably only five seven, weighing about 155 lbs."

"But have you been able to determine what's wrong? Why'd he collapse?" Angelina queried, missing Max's look of disapproval in her interest.

The doctor nodded, changing the hologram between them. It showed a close up scan of the gemue's chest cavity. "Remember I mentioned they removed some organs?"

They nodded; before them was a picture of what was left of a normal pair of healthy lungs. They had been reduced to one-third normal size and the remaining tissue looked shriveled from disuse. It was not near enough to support the air exchange needed by a humanoid the size this creature was. What had taken up the remainder of the space in his chest cavity was a bladder much like fish used to change depth.

"Dear Lord! They butchered him!" Angelina exclaimed.

The doctor nodded mutely, and then said, "The bladder seems to be supplemental to the natural buoyancy of his lungs. I would have to say it was an afterthought, as if they stripped him of his lung tissue and then discovered that he couldn't really swim easily without it."

"Or that they wanted to restrict the amount of time he could remain on land," Angelina interjected, giving voice to her thought when he had collapsed.

Doc looked reluctant to agree with that. "It is possible, but I could not confirm that from the information we have. It has certainly affected him. He was meant to be a primary water dweller, and from the look of his lungs, that has been the case. He collapsed because his lungs cannot provide enough surface area for the blood to get adequate oxygen to his cells, and not nearly enough to carry waste gasses out of his body. Therefore, the CO_2 gets recycled through his system, accumulating in his tissues. And if he is out of water for any length of time he will pass out."

"How long would you say it takes?" This time it was Max who asked, actually sounding interested in the discussion, even if he looked appalled by what he was seeing.

"A rough guesstimate?" He shrugged. "Probably about three hours by his rate of out gassing since being in the tank. It seems that his gills are ridding him of the by products that get stored in his muscles when he is on land."

"Is there any way to tell how long he has been this way?" Angelina asked next.

"Medically, no, but the advanced technique used and the quality of the work suggest that he was not created more than a year and a half ago."

"But he insists he's been a gemue for seven years. I got the impression that this has been his only alteration," She argued.

"Where did you get that information?" Max asked in astonishment.

"He had me as his prisoner for a while, and he was long winded. Look, I don't have time to go over it in detail with you."

*****

"It is not likely he has been in this form for that long," the doctor replied to her statement. He narrowed his eyes a bit as he continued to look at Angelina, noticing her

105

uncharacteristic interest in this subject. He wondered silently, why? He knew her too well to think that she had changed her attitude about gemues, yet she was saving this one. While he was grateful that she had given him the singular opportunity to work on such an advanced specimen in gemue biology, he wondered what had brought her around. Could it be that her current altered state had affected her way of thinking about what gemues were worth? He shook his head slightly, discarding that thought, as an inkling of suspicion dawned on him.

*****

Several days later Angelina returned to the aquarium to check on The Movement's new charge. She stepped into the eternal twilight of the warehouse and moved to where Doctor Thomas sat. He had his feet kicked up on the desk and was reading a newspaper.

"How's he doing, Doc?" Angelina asked as she approached.

He looked at her, smiling as his legs slipped from the desk. The expression faded quickly. "He's slipped into a coma, I'm afraid." He moved over to the converted tank that held the shark man. "Oxygen deprivation has injured his brain, and I'm uncertain how much that may affect him. All my assumptions are based on humans and those gemues that are more commonplace. If they hold true, he could be a vegetable by now, or at least should be. Because his procedure was a radical and a different template was used for his genetic supplementation, I could be greatly in error." He looked thoughtfully at the tank, rubbing his five o'clock shadow. "You know, I've broken four needles trying to get an IV started on him. I ended up having to cut through the skin with a serrated blade, and I made an amazing discovery in the process. This man's skin has two distinct layers of epidermal tissue. The top layer, which is very tough and pliant, is just like the shark's he was patterned after. Under it is a distinctly human layer of tissue, like the new just grew over the old instead of replacing it as a DNA sequence change is purported to do."

"He's got to belong to Marlin Cortez. That would fit perfectly with his obsession," Angelina mused, not really hearing what the doctor had said.

"No doubt, and he was very recently reintroduced as a member of society." The doctor turned to face her, laying his cards on the table regarding his suspicion about her motive. "You think he's David, don't you?"

Doc Thomas knew a lot about her and David, though he had never actually met him. Thomas was an old friend of the family and had been her personal physician for years. When David and Angelina had started dating, she, of course, felt very comfortable talking about it with the old doctor.

Angelina took an involuntary step backward, trying to hide her shock. "What makes you say that?" she asked in a bad try at nonchalance.

"Oh, come on Angelina. I know your distrust of gemues well enough to know that you would not have tried to save this creature without some ulterior motive."

"I want to know why he's after me," she insisted.

"He was after you because you're a threat to the Cortez Empire, that's simple. Now tell me the truth."

Angelina went silent for long moments, and then she nodded at him, looking up momentarily into the doctor's eyes and then away again. She laughed shortly. "You know, I thought that I had convinced myself it wasn't him. But after he barged in on us, I began to have doubts again. I mean this thing called Max by name, even though the creature had never seen Max before.

"Max and David were good friends long before David and I became an item. That compounds on the evidence I got right out of his head. Cortez had us both less than nine months ago. Six months ago, this critter shows up and starts hunting me. It's got to be more than coincidence. I mean, that would fit Uncle Marlin. What better way to get revenge than to sic my boyfriend on me to eliminate me?"

Doc Thomas stepped up and laid a hand on her shoulder knowingly. "I hope you're right. I hate to see you in such pain."

Angelina went silent, not even able to look at him. She listened as his footsteps faded into the distance and allowed her gaze to move back to the tank, her eyes automatically studying the features of the shark man's face, barely visible behind the canvas sling supporting his weight in the water. She thought vaguely that she should know them well enough by now, but she was still noticing things about him that she hadn't before; the details in his countenance, how peaceful he looked lying there. There had always been strain to his expression at each of their encounters, something that went beyond concentration or anger. It was like there was something that he was trying to hide.

Angelina looked to the dorsal fin peeking just over the thick wooden poles that gave the sling rigidity. She had noticed that there were three of them spaced about four vertebrae apart, the one between his shoulders being the largest, the one near the small of his back merely a nub of cartilage, and the one in the middle was somewhere between the extremes.

Her eyes moved to his shoulder and slid down his arm dangling lax in the water, as it moved forward and back with the artificial current. She looked his arms over closely, noticing that not even the fins on his lower arms were moving to counteract the motion of the current, they just plied back and forth as the water played with them.

Again she wondered if she was right in her assumptions about this killer. A pang of anxiety went through her; if she was wrong he could be the death of them all.

"What the hell is she doing? Why doesn't she just let it die?" Angelina heard whispered behind her, bringing her out of her depressing thoughts.

"Why do you have to be so damn callous, Max?" Angelina growled. "I told you, he has information we need."

She expected a hot rebuttal from her friend, who had somehow come in without her hearing him. However, the room fell deathly silent behind her. Angelina slowly turned, seeing Max standing there with an inscrutable expression on his face, his green eyes large and his white face paler than normal.

"What?" Angelina said grumpily.

Max shook his head minutely, his eyes not leaving her face, looking as if she had turned into a monster herself. "I . . . I didn't say anything," he said in a shrill, almost frightened voice.

"Sure you did . . ." But then she stopped, and a wave of heat flushed over her as she realized just what had happened. "What do you mean?" she said instead, trying to cover her slip. She had picked up his thought, and being preoccupied had assumed she had heard it aloud.

"I didn't speak," Max repeated. "But you knew . . . you knew what I was thinking."

"No," Angelina tried to deny it.

"How did you know what I was thinking?" Max said and again his voice gained pitch. He took a reluctant step closer to her, his head cocked to one side and his expression one of concern. "Does this have something to do with . . . with . . . the experiments?"

Angelina remained mute, her own eyes now wide and fearful of what he would think of her.

"Angelina," Max said in a much softer voice, "please, tell me . . ."

She continued to stare at him and had to force herself to breathe when she started to feel faint. "Yes," she finally blurted at him. "I've been able to . . ." she couldn't bring herself to say what she was able to do, "since I escaped."

"Why didn't you tell me?" Max said softly, sounding hurt that she had kept it from him.

"Because," Angelina whined, feeling and sounding very undignified, "because of how you are. I thought you would excommunicate me for something like that." she refrained from naming her skill. "Look at how you regard him." She threw an arm in the general direction of their ward. "I just knew that you would look on me like a freak, like some sort of monster that you couldn't bear to lay eyes on me."

"I wouldn't," Max denied.

"You would!" Angelina insisted loudly. "Only gemues have abilities like those . . . And I'm a gemue!" She paused at that admonition, realizing that she had been denying that to this point. "And we both know you hate gemues!"

"I don't hate you," Max said, blinking.

"Why does the fact that it's me make it different?" Angelina flung at him. "What if it were David standing here instead? Would you act the same? Or is it because you love me that it's suddenly okay?"

Max looked taken aback at those words as his body stiffened. And Angelina was suddenly standing there with her hands over her mouth, realizing that she had pulled that reason out of his head, and then spouted it to him to help her argument. She was also bothered by the fact that she had never realized before that he had felt that way for her. She watched as his body slowly relaxed with a heavy sigh. He blinked replying softly with, "It shouldn't make a difference. You're right, but it does. I never said I was perfect." He looked away, adding disjointedly, "You know that David was like a brother to me. You don't know how much I miss him."

Angelina nodded emphatically. "Yes, I do know."

Max stepped forward, merely a step of space between them, but he didn't touch her, as if to prove that what she had pulled out of his head was a falsity. "You having this ability does not stop you from being my friend," Max said, still softly, and Angelina thought she heard pain in his voice.

"I'm sorry," Angelina said with a shake of her head. She hoped that he knew it was both for her angry words, and an apology for not being able to reciprocate the love he felt for her. She liked Max, considered him a close friend, but she had never felt that way for him. David was the only one she had ever had eyes for. She couldn't bring herself to say it, however. So they stood staring at each other for long moments before Max sighed.

"I've gotta get back to work," Max said.

"Okay," Angelina said, nodding and not able to meet his eyes.

*****

Angelina rushed into the dusky storage room, and tried vainly to catch her breath. She had gotten an excited call from the doctor, but he wouldn't explain over the phone what was going on. She found the doctor monitoring the equipment to one side of the creature in their charge. She stood recuperating a moment more before straightening and stepping over to him.

"So," she said finally, "what's so thrilling?"

"He's come out of the coma," the doctor responded excitedly.

"What!" she said incredulously. They had kept the shark man in high saline, high oxygen, warm water bath for over a month with no progress toward recovery. But a glance at the monitors told her this was not a joke.

"His brain functions are off the scale and his respiration and heartbeat are up. He should be waking up any time now."

For over two hours they kept watch for some sign of consciousness. They were both bored, Angelina especially. Looking at a monitor that was telling one, "Yes, this guy's brain works," lost its thrill after the first ten minutes. Angelina was now seated at the desk reading yet another newspaper that the doctor had neglected to finish, while the doctor anxiously observed the monitor, licking his chapped lips. When she had read it three times she decided that it was time to put it down. She stood up and stretched, moving back to the tank for nothing better to do. "Any change?"

He shook his head mutely, and they both turned away and headed back for the desk. As the doctor settled behind it, Angelina sighed again. "Well, shit, this has been a hell of a waste of time. You know, I'm real tempted to just pull the plug and forget the whole thing!"

*****

I was led to a raised disk in the floor, made to stand there as they closed containment over me. The electric humming was omnipresent around me. I looked up, seeing a similar disk to the one at my feet above me vents, and lights alternating around its circumference. The outermost edge glowed slightly, the field keeping contaminants, and me, in. The floodlights became brighter around me; an effect that allowed a subject to know that it was time. I couldn't smell it, and I couldn't see it, but its effects on me were very physical. Radiation flooded the small cylinder, and immediately I began to itch. The itching was quick to turn to burning sensations centered in my hands and my face. I did all in my power to keep from screaming as the intensity continued to rise.

My hands felt as if I had set them in hot coals, and I raised them up even as my eyes moved down to look at them. I had been expecting to see flesh falling from the bones in those extremities, surprised and even more shocked when that turned out not to be the case.

There was a pulling sensation now, adding to the excruciating burning in my hands. Through the tears in my eyes, I watched, horrified, as they began to stretch as if someone was pulling putty to the limit of its elasticity. The pain became more than I could bear and finally the scream that I had been holding back ripped from my throat.

My body jerked with the sound of the scream in my mind and I felt water stirring about me violently in reaction to my movement. I panicked again, trying to gain purchase and get out of the water, but something held me; I found that it was something pliable and form fitted around my prone body. My fingers found a tenuous grip only to slip off again and send my face back into the water. For some reason I couldn't open my eyes to see just where I was, as the scenes from my dream looped through my mind over and over again.

I flung my arms out, bumping my fingers painfully into something cold and hard, and desperately I scrambled closer to it and freed myself from the material. My feet drifted slowly down through the water even as I pulled myself up on the corner of whatever container I had been housed in.

I overbalanced, reaching out blindly for something to break my momentum on, only to find empty air and instead I tumbled down. A second later, I impacted on a cold and wet floor, curling into a ball as the visions still haunted my conscious thought.

"Get up," my mind said. "Open your eyes and get up!"

And I tried, making it to hands and knees, but I crawled forward, toward the tank I had been in, and still unable to see though my eyelids were now open. I worked my hands up the base of it and then the glass until they found the lip, where I was able to pull my body upright.

A wave of mental anguish washed over me, coinciding with the vision of stretching hands. As it peaked I reacted, sending my elbow crashing into the glass of the tank, and listening to it crack under the blow. I could no longer hold my feet, the grip I had found loosened as my fingers lost feeling. I sank back to my knees, incapable of doing anything but lay there panting, still overcome by the visions in my head and powerless to see just where I was.

*****

Angelina and Doctor Thomas whirled as the sound of struggling began in the tank where the shark man was being held. He seemed to be trapped in the canvas sling, trying to work his way free. Angelina could see that his eyes were open, but the inner lids were solidly shut, and he was flailing sightlessly. Finally, the shark man was able to pull his body clear of the tank. There was a look of incredible pain painted across his features. She watched in shock as the beast hit the deck with a thud, curled into a fetal ball, and began shivering violently. She started toward him, intent on helping him, but the doctor restrained her. "I don't think it's wise to get close to him right now."

"I'll be okay," she insisted.

"Don't let your hopes of it being David blind you. That creature is no longer who or what he was, and now, my dear, he is a killer."

Reluctantly, Angelina relented.

After a few moments, the creature pushed himself up on all fours and crawled to the tank, clumsily reaching out for something to hold onto. When his hand encountered the tank, he snatched it in one hand, using it as a support, and he pulled himself upright. Both eyelids were now open but remained unfocused and unseeing. He was gripping the lip of the tank, forehead resting on the glass. His features twisted into a grimace of pain and he punched the tank, creating a spider web of cracks along the surface. He then sank back to his knees, hands wrapped tightly about his head.

Angelina, unable to wait any longer, pulled free of the doctor's hold and cautiously approached the gemue. She knelt near him, studying his pain-wracked face. Slowly, she lowered the novice built mind shields she used to screen what she received, and sent forth a tentative probe into his mind. She reeled momentarily as the images hit her. There was a blinding light, heat, and excruciating pain only dulled by her observing from the outside. She saw normal human hands as they began to stretch before her mind's eye. That was all she received before she sensed awareness in the man. She brought herself back to the real world to find the gemue standing above her and staring down at her hatefully. The fading bruise on his temple was testament of her own act to free herself from his murderous clutches.

"I told you before," he growled, "stay outta my head!" His fist hit her square in the jaw, knocking her to the floor. He grabbed her lapel and started to lift her off the tile, claws poised for a finishing blow. "And this is for the concussion, bitch!"

"That's enough!" Doc warned, pointing an old-fashioned forty-five at the shark man's temple. The gemue looked out of the corner of his eye at the older man. He allowed his grip to slacken and Angelina's limp, unconscious form thudded to the floor. He straightened, arms hanging slack at his sides, warily watching the wielder of the gun. Angelina lay for long moments unmoving in an awkward looking position. The physician kept one eye on the perpetrator and the other eye out for any signs of consciousness.

Finally, she twitched and then groaned, but she was slow to push herself off the ground. "Angel, dear, are you alright?" he asked in concern, but his eyes never left the shark man. The creature was glaring at him, surely thinking of a way to turn the tables. Dr. Thomas backed out of arm's reach of the creature.

She was in a half-seated position, her legs folded up on the right side of her body. She spit blood. "Yeah, I guess so," she said in a small, cracked voice; her eyes were glazed with anger. "...that's gratitude for you."

"Where am I?" the creature demanded, moving aggressively toward the threat of the gun.

"Unless you want me to undo all that we've accomplished in bringing you back, I suggest you stand still," Doc warned the creature, but he kept coming. Angelina's friend reversed motion, stepping away from the shark man's advance, as he cocked the hammer. The creature blinked, pulling himself unhappily short. "You are at the New Fresno Aquarium," he replied when the creature had stopped his advance.

"And what, pray tell, am I doing here?" the gemue grumbled, slowly crossing his arms, trying not to look woozy, and he almost but didn't quite succeed at it.

"We brought you here after your collapse," Angelina replied through her swelling mouth. "I'm beginning to think that was a mistake," she muttered, finally pushing to her feet.

"Collapse?" he asked in confusion. His small eyes darted back and forth as if trying to recall what they were telling him, and his brow heavily furrowed.

"They didn't design you to travel dryworld very long, did they?"

"Huh? What do you mean?"

She moved around behind her collaborator in this. "They didn't tell him," Angelina whispered in Doc Thomas' ear. She said it with such confidence that the shark man knew she had violated his mind again. He must have been developing some kind of mind shield because she wasn't crippling him as she had before.

"I mean, they designed you so well to be a fish that they forgot to leave you enough lungs to survive as a human."

"Oh, really?" the creature said, sounding skeptical. He turned away from the two of them and the gun, pacing. The shark man looked at the tank, the gurney, and the general condition of the area. "You actually did all this to keep me alive?" he asked incredulously, as if it surprised him that humanity would do anything to help a gemue. They both nodded in unison.

"But, why? Her, I have been trying to kill for the last seven months . . . and you . . . I don't even know you. Why would you help me?"

Angelina remained stoically silent, but Doc replied, "I am just doing Angelina a favor."

The creature glanced from the doctor to Angelina, around the room again, then back to the two of them before turning his eyes to the floor. He seemed to consider all of this for a very long time. It was obvious that he had come to a decision but that it was one he was not comfortable with. His mouth set in a thin line as he approached the two of them. This time there was no aggression showing in his frame. "Then I guess . . . I owe you my life." He reluctantly extended a clawed hand, which the doctor looked at warily. Slowly, the gun drifted down, and the older man took the proffered appendage.

"They call me Tiger."

*****

My life just gets more and more complicated. I've been living as a gemue for seven years now and never realized that I had limitations on my time dryworld. Doctor Thomas had said that I was lucky in that I wasn't a vegetable after my ordeal. He had informed me that there had been severe damage to my brain, but he had been surprised to find that the cells somehow had either regenerated, or their function had been taken up by another section of my mind in the month that I had been comatose. There had been no trace of scarring noted and all of my abilities were intact.

After Doctor Thomas filled me in on the extent of my previously unknown medical changes, I wondered why the team who did my transformation never informed me of it. I was glad for the fact that I had not found out the hard way sometime previous to this, and also that he and Angelina were more gemutarian than I had given them credit for.

I keep replaying the same events in my head since waking up. Visions of pain, of watching my hands grow before my eyes. These were much more detailed versions of the dreams I had been having for months now. Now I knew I was starting to recover some of the memories of the processing I had undertaken to become what I am. I'm beginning to think it is something the doctors had suppressed when they altered me. The only reason I can come up with is that they were trying to lessen the trauma, and as bad as the memory is I'm glad they did. I know that woman . . . that Angelina, was there as I came around, in my head, as I was reliving the pain. That made me leery. I did not trust her, for she had intruded on my thoughts many times without my knowledge or permission, and I am uncomfortable with someone who cannot or will not allow someone else their privacy. I had been avoiding her since waking, unsure of my reaction if I did see her.

I had caught a few glimpses of her, however, and in the past few hours the swelling on her face had become unsightly purple against her unnaturally white skin. I felt little remorse for my action; I was still angry for the fool she had made of me when she had tried to split my skull open. That one act had marred my previously spotless record as a merc and ruined my boss's trust in my ability. As far as I was concerned, she deserved it. Now, however, I was bound by my word not to try to harm her further, in order to repay her the debt of saving my life.

I was preparing to go back to Cortez's headquarters. A month and a half was way too long to be out of his sight. Corporate powers are a suspicious and paranoid lot and I have no wish to be on Cortez's bad side. Of course, preparing meant recovery, and that was exactly the reason I was back in the tank they had put me in for a month. The doctor hypothesized that twelve-hour recuperation was required for me after long periods in the air. And I was not about to doubt him, for he had managed to keep me going after a serious bout of oxygen deprivation. So here I sit at the bottom of the tank, Indian style, watching the darkness of the warehouse beyond.

I caught a glimpse of someone moving outside the tank and I pushed myself closer to the cracked glass to take a look. Angelina was standing there with a blank expression on her face. My heart started beating faster with anxiety, but I broke surface anyway.

"Something I can do for you, Angelfish?" I said blithely, resting my chin on my folded arms.

"Angelina," she snapped, paused, and then went on. "So you're going back to that mad man, huh?" she said, with was an edge of hostility.

"He is paying my fee . . . and it would ruin my rep if he found out I was consorting with the enemy, even if I'm not." I shrugged. "Besides, I get the impression you people don't like me. Even the doctor is more interested in me as a specimen than as a being. I can't say I'd like to remain in this company."

"I don't mind you being here." There was something in her tone.

My head came up in shock, and then I scowled. "Oh, now wait. You're not still hooked on the notion that I'm . . ."

119

She looked away with watery eyes. I slipped out of the tank, landing lightly in front of her, feeling like an ass for my reaction. This was obviously something very important to her, this belief that I might be this boyfriend that she had lost. "Angelina, I'm not him. I'm sorry about whatever happened, but you've got to stop it with this."

"The evidence is there, Tigershark, you're just ignoring it. You even recognized your best friend . . . called him by name . . . I know David's in there somewhere."

I couldn't recall the event of which she spoke, something that was supposed to have happened just before my collapse. I searched her face, her sad eyes. She really did believe what she was saying. I changed the subject. "I've really got to get back in the tank. I've got to leave soon." I turned back to her, raising her chin gently to make her look at me. "I owe you both my life, and I won't forget that. So what if I don't get my money?" I shrugged.

"Small comfort," she replied. "I just have the other 99 gunners to worry about."

I grimaced at her sarcasm. "I can't help you," I said in a softer tone yet, meaning both with her other pursuers and her quest to find her lost boyfriend. I turned back toward the tank and climbed slowly in. I pivoted in the water as I sank to face her, and watched, as she stood there several more moments before walking dejectedly away.

Chapter Eleven:
What Am I?

I left just two hours after the conversation with Angelina, making quick time back to the water, intent on not setting myself up for another collapse. I was going to have to research how long was too long to be away from the ocean. Once in the water it took me only forty-five minutes to get to Marlin Cortez's water entrance. I broke the surface and strode onto shore, acting as if nothing was wrong. I really expected to be cut down before I got very far, but was surprised when no one even appeared to escort me. I made for the stairwell leading to the lower floors of the high-rise that stood over this spot. There was no use in my delaying the inevitable. Eventually I would have to face the man.

The halls were unusually deserted. There had always been a few executives or rookie guards to stare at me as I visited the boss before, but today there was no one and that immediately raised alarms. I felt my hackles rise, realizing that I could very well be walking into a trap. He obviously knew I was here, so I stepped into his office without the preemptory check-in. I didn't really care if I disturbed anything. As the door silently swung in, my senses told me that he was alone. Correction: Tony was there just behind him. The room was dark, and so I could not actually see him, but his reek hit my nostrils shortly after I picked up Cortez's aftershave.

I stepped up to the desk and seated myself in the plush chair he had for visitors. I realized that it probably cost him a small fortune to keep this chair clean after my visits, as it got wet every time.

"Where have you been?" he asked immediately.

"I fell ill. I decided to hole up until I felt better," I embellished.

"For a month and a half?" he replied with raised eyebrows.

"No. For two weeks or better I was tracking my mark. I was almost on her when I got sick," I said. It was the truth, so why did I feel like I was guilty of something?

"Why didn't you return here? We could have taken care of you. We have excellent facilities. After all, we did take care of that concussion the girl gave you."

"I didn't think it was necessary. Look, it was just enough to dull my edge, it's not like I came down with pneumonia." I might as well have.

He picked up a piece of paper on his desk and began to summarize it for me. "You were tracked dryworld, to the industrial section of town. You entered a building suspected of being a front for The Movement, and for all intents and purposes disappeared until this very moment."

"You were tracking me?" I asked incredulously. There was a sinking feeling in my gut that told me I was had.

"I always track new employees. I can't afford not to!" he growled. "Now, what were you doing for them?"

"Look, I wasn't lying. I got sick, collapsed. The next thing I know, I'm waking up in a strange place, strung up like a damn corpse," I said, again padding the truth. "I disconnected myself and high-tailed it."

Marlin seemed to consider that seriously for a moment. "Tony?"

"Yes, sir?"

"See that Tigershark is safely incarcerated in his quarters until I can verify his story." I saw a smug smile pass over Tony's scarred face.

I stood up. "Now, wait a minute. That's against my contract!"

"Contract? What contract?" he said innocently.

"The one detailing my services. We both agreed to the provisions. There is nothing in it about staying behind bars, especially for questions of loyalty. If you don't trust me, fire me. I'm tired of this shit."

He laughed heartily. "Oh dear, they did do a good job on you." He looked up at Tony with mirth and Tony returned it with a wan smile of his own. When he looked back at me I knew I was in trouble. "I'm sorry, there is no contract."

"What are you talking about?" I stammered, as I felt the situation quickly spiraling out of control. More guards had appeared near Cortez.

"Tigershark, you're bought and paid for, my creation . . . I made you from scratch. So, contrary to what you believe, I can do whatever I want with you. My will is your will whether you know it or not."

"What?" I asked in confusion. Creation? He began to chuckle at my annoyance. "WHAT are you talking about?"

I started for him, intent on wringing the answers from that smiling mouth. He ignored me and nodded instead. Upon seeing that, several of his goons wrapped themselves around my arms, wrestling me to remove me from the room.

"I want a rewrite. Tell Marcus to reset the previous memory set . . . erasure of all memories to this point. And this time tell him not to give him so much free will. Maybe with a bit less intelligence as well. I don't need him rooting through my files again, trying to find the truth."

"You can't do this!" I growled, struggling lightly, trying to get a feel for my opponents.

He was saying, "I can and I am. When we next meet you will be as loyal as you were supposed to be the first time."

"No!" I uttered in panic. I wrenched around, throwing the guard on my right across the room into the opposite wall. I followed through, snarling as my nails sank deep into the other soldier's throat. I turned to the other man on that arm, grabbing him around the forehead and thigh, and lifted him bodily. He stiffened as I expected, and I brought him down forcefully onto my knee. His back broke easily.

That done, I headed for the large desk again. All I could see was Cortez, haloed in red; I wanted answers or I wanted blood! Two feet from the rosewood piece of furniture Cortez raised a large caliber pistol, smiled, and pulled the trigger. I reeled back as the slug tore through the meat on my left shoulder. I stumbled and barely realized that I had fallen to one knee. My vision faded out as the pain tried to overtake my world. As my sight grayed, my thoughts turned inward... Cortez's words resounded in my head . . . his creation, I was a figment . . . my whole history was faked. The mental tail chasing began to spiral out of control and I forcefully centered on one thing . . . there was only one option now . . . escape. There would be time to think of the implications later; an answer would do me no good if I were dead.

That shot had knocked me back to the reality of my situation. I was trying to kill this man in his own office, and that was about as smart as trying to kill a queen bee in the middle of her hive. I'm good but not stupid enough to throw away my life . . . whoever I was.

I looked around, quickly assessing my choices. The soldiers were beginning to close the circle they set up to detain me. Without giving away my intentions I prepared myself to make a hasty retreat. I jumped up, slashed the two guards blocking my exit, and made a run for it. I bolted down the stairs leading to the cavern, as my chest began to throb from so much demand for air. I hoped I could make it to the water before my system shut down. Bullets whizzed by me on both sides as I sprinted across the rock toward the pool of water that would provide me my escape. A second slug found its mark not far from the first bullet wound on my arm and buried itself into my bone, causing me to stumble. Knowing if I went down there was no getting back up, I twisted convulsively. I recovered and leapt the last three feet to the water and immediately swam for the depths. The salt water stung miserably in my wounds, and my left arm was nothing but agony every time I tried to use it. I swam on though, intent on losing my pursuit in the depths of the sea.

*****

Cortez slowly sat again in his oversized chair, surveying the aftermath of Tigershark's escape. One man twitched spasmodically as the severed nerves in his back tried vainly to help him move. Against the wall to his left was a broken heap that had been another man in his employ. And just in front of him was a man who had died just shortly after Tigershark had left. The man's blood drained from his ruined throat and pooled on his Persian rug, staining it beyond hope of recovery.

Two other of his soldiers sat in one corner, nursing deep gashes, one to the face and the other on his upper chest. Cortez slowly shook his head, feeling his anger rise. "Tony?"

"Yes, sir?" The older man said quietly

"Send everyone we have. I want that destructive bastard found and I want him returned to me. Equip every squad master with a tracking device. Bring him to me . . . Alive".

"Yes, sir," Tony said aloud, then turned smartly and started away, muttering, "Too bad."

*****

I was still on the run two days later. Cortez's minions were hot on my tail, having an uncanny knack for knowing where I was even after I had lost sight of them for hours. Usually, I would rid myself of the tail on land. That was great, but sooner or later I had to go back in the water, and that was where they would find me. I was almost certain that they had some kind of water activated tracking device on my person. When I had originally come up with that correlation, I had gone totally stiff, as if the signal would stop if I didn't move. Silly, I know, but desperation does things to the mind.

By now, every crony and junkie on the streets of Old Fresno was looking for me. I'm sure Cortez would have made it worth their while. That left me little option as far as whom I could go to for help. I clacked my tongue on the roof of my mouth in consternation. But would Angelina, Max, and the doctor be willing to help me? I had made a pretty hasty exit, and they may have moved operations somewhere else on the offhand chance I had spilled the beans about their location.

Cortez made me? That thought kept coming back to me now. I would have given it little more credibility than a ruse to throw me off, if it had not been for Angelina's persistence in telling me that I was not who I thought I was. But if I'm not Tigershark, who am I, and who was I? I had tried several times to recall my life before transformation, to remember my name or where I used to live. All those queries to the gray matter between my ears went unanswered. The same old rhetoric about being a teen looking for a kick and finding it in being turned into a gemue was all that answered those inquiries. There was no memory to find other than that. That now made me as suspicious as any of the rest of the evidence.

*****

I crashed through the doors of the New Fresno Aquarium with little concern for who saw me. One arm dangled limply at my side from the damage of the two bullets I had taken in my escape. They were also infected from my exposure to the less than pristine waters of the Sea of San Joaquin. With the pursuit close behind me I was given no time to pause in my flight and care for them. I strode up to the receptionist, who backed away from the desk. Checking my watch, I realized that I was close to my three-hour dryworld limit. "Get me Angelina Cortez, this is urgent." I whispered, and then pointed toward the warehouse. "I'll be in the back when she gets here." And I headed for the double doors without waiting for her answer or her protest.

Half an hour later, the alabaster skinned woman burst through the door. Seeming more than a little mad about the situation, she pulled to a stop just shy of the tank, and Max was half a step behind her. I pulled myself awkwardly from the tank and hopped down in front of her. She looked at me cockeyed, and then at the tank. I could see her lips move as she counted the fish. I leaned into her view. "I didn't eat any of them. I just needed some 'air.' "

"You've got some nerve threatening our exposure like this!" she started angrily. "What is it you want? You were in an awful hurry to go back and save your reputation."

"I need some help."

Her eyes went blank a moment and I saw her wince as she replayed the events of the last few days; it was the one time I did not mind the intrusion, not if it was going to save my hide. Funny thing was that there was no pain associated with the invasion as had been true of all the other times. Vaguely, I wondered why.

"He finally showed you his other face, huh?" she asked, and I nodded. She looked me over. "Jeez, you're hurt!"

"Nice of you to notice. Look, they have a bug on me somewhere. I need to know where the transmitter is and have either removed or disabled."

"Okay, look, I'll talk to Doc Thomas, but I can't guarantee you anything."

"Fair enough. Now, do you have some fish I can eat?"

She actually smiled at that.

*****

Within the hour, Angelina provided Tigershark with a tank full of live fish. She had to walk away as he began to feed, wondering if the filters would be able to handle the amount of blood and bits of flesh that would be left behind.

After an hour she returned to find him sound asleep on his stomach at the bottom of the tank. There were about ten or twelve fish left swimming cautiously around him, picking pieces of their brethren from between the rocks. Well, that was one tank full of fish they would not have to feed. Occasionally, one would get bold enough to nip at the glaring bullet wounds on Tigershark's shoulder. He would twitch, sending the fish scurrying as far from his prone body as possible.

Angelina noticed that Tigershark was dreaming. She began to wonder just what he might be dreaming about. Was it a nightmare, maybe? Was it a dream about his transformation? About his life before, or was it something more insidious? Perhaps he was reliving all of his hunts, and the pleasure he took in killing his victims. She was

128

curious to find out, and the thought crossed her mind to peek at what a mercenary might hide in his subconscious. She dared not, however, for fear of waking him. Somehow, he was preternaturally sensitive to telepathic contact, even though he claimed no talent of his own. Was she that clumsy or was it something else?

Angelina stared at his sleeping form intently, and the longer she looked at him the more he began to resemble what she remembered of David's appearance. Yes, his features were out of proportion, but it did look like him. She shook her head, smiling ruefully. "Doc's right," she muttered, "I'm hoping too hard that it's him."

David had been about as gemuephobic as Max. He grew up dryworld, and out of a rich family. He had been sheltered most of his life from what existed at the water's edge. He had never even heard of a gemue until he had begun attending college. He had been disgusted with the notion of haphazardly splicing genes together to make a new life form. He did not mind it if it was used to strengthen crops to grow in this age, but his tolerance stopped at living beings. If he *was* David, and regained the memory of who he actually was, he would go crazy

Angelina still had doubts about Tigershark, even with all of the evidence she had gathered as to his identity. His return was just a touch too convenient. Her probe of his thoughts revealed no deception, but that meant nothing considering her limited training on the use of her new ability. She wondered if she could determine the difference between true memory and a carefully constructed ruse. She sincerely doubted it. And that came down to what was worrying her, for she had allowed Tigershark back into their fold. She had gotten the impression that he was concerned about his reputation above all else. If it turned out that he was a plant to get to the higher echelons of The Movement, it would be her fault. Her eyes fixed on his arm; the wounds there were real enough, and his plea had seemed genuine. She decided to let it be for now, to watch him very closely and just see what happened.

*****

Doctor Thomas came by the aquarium late the next afternoon. He had explained that it had been a very busy week.

"Don't apologize, Doc. I know your primary purpose is as a human doctor," Angelina said gruffly still perturbed by the situation she had been forced into.

Tigershark was waiting patiently in the back when they stepped in, but looked a bit embarrassed by the situation. "Doctor," he said shortly.

"It's good to see you again, Tiger," Doc said warmly. Angelina wished she could be so enthusiastic. "I understand they've got you bugged."

"Yes. Do you think you can remove it? I'm tired of an electronic leash."

"It depends on where they installed it. If they put it into a vital organ, there's nothing I can do, not here anyway." He laughed. "I could just see escorting you into my surgery theater."

Tigershark just smiled, looking down. "Do what you can. If it comes to an office visit, we'll see what can be arranged."

After about twenty minutes, the doctor revealed his findings to the shark man. "Well, I'm afraid the tracer is going to have to wait. It's butted up right against the jugular and it's going to be a bitch to get out. Your gills cover that entire area."

"Great," Tigershark grunted, sounding disappointed.

"But, I can get these wounds dressed while I'm here. Putting yourself in harm's way again, I see."

"Always," Tigershark laughed, watching as the doctor scanned his shoulder with a pocket hologram, and then began work on extraction of the bullet lodged in the bone in his upper arm. The procedure should have made him howl in pain, but the only sign he felt it at all was a slightly strained look on his face. "Maybe I should have just let them lock me up. My story would have panned out, but stupid me, I had to argue it was against my contract."

"Oh?" Angelina queried, pricking up with interest. She exchanged a glance with the doctor.

Tigershark nodded. "Then, not only did he tell me there was no contract, but that I was his property; his creation. That parallels just a little too closely to what you said to me, Angelfish . . ." he added, shaking his head emphatically. "But he can't be my creator." His eyes ridges furrowed as he repeated in a whisper, "He *can't* be . . ."

"I believe he just may be," Doctor Thomas chimed in.

"No, you don't understand. I have been gemue for seven years. I've only worked for Cortez six months, and that was the first time I had ever met him."

"Let me show you something," Doc said, pulling out one of his holographic projectors. "These are slides of tissue samples from gemues I've worked with over the years. The first is from one whom would have been a test tube buddy if what you are telling us is true. As you can see, there is a distinct division between the human and the template cells. This particular mutation was a dolphin gemue, and not a very effective splicing of genes." He changed slides. "This is a sample I took the first time you were here. Here you can see, the structures from the human and template creature, in this case a shark, are well melded. There is little or no distinction between the two. Which is why you turned out to be more . . . graceful a creature. This kind of accuracy was not possible until a year and a half ago, and even then, it was used only on fetal tissue. That they made it work for a fully-grown man is amazing to me. As amazing as the thought that they mind wiped your whole existence to that point, and is the fact that they wrote you a new history."

"I can't believe that!" Tigershark was starting to get scared. Angelina felt the part of him that beginning to believe what they were saying. It was becoming as loud as that portion that was denying it, and it was driving him toward panic.

Angelina was unable to stop herself as she added another thorn, despite his obvious discomfort. "Remember I told you of Marlin Cortez's illegal dealings?" He nodded slightly, his thin lips tightly pressed together. "The man has the money and the less than scrupulous doctors to pull this kind of trick off."

That did it, he had heard enough; she felt his mind snap shut even as she heard his words boom through the room. "You're trying to tell me I'm him, aren't you?" He stood abruptly, knocking over the chair, tearing the stitch that the doctor had been tying, and backing away from the both of them. "Well, I'm not, Goddamn it. I don't know what you people are trying to pull," he turned to Angelina, "but you can't make me into your dead boyfriend just to save yourself some heartache!" Hands pressed to his temples suddenly; he practically doubled over in pain. "God!" he swore. "Just leave me alone!"

Tigershark ran from them, back toward the tank in the warehouse. Angelina moved to follow him.

"Angelina, don't," implored Doc.

"He was remembering something," Angelina whispered to him.

"Don't force him to face this, Angel. He needs to ask for help. Don't push it on him, or we'll lose him."

"I'll keep my distance," she said and trailed the gemue. She watched as he vaulted over the lip of the tank and splashed down into the water. He sat with his back to her, shoulders slouched and head pressed into one corner of the fractured tank. His large hands were wrapped around the back of his head.

She felt his misery even without touching his mind. "Tigershark?" There was no response. "Are you okay?" He shook his head slightly. "Is there something I can do?"

He stood up slowly, turning in the water as he broke surface and glared at her. "You've done enough. Just leave me alone." He looked into the darkness a moment. "Coming here was a mistake," she heard him whisper.

She started to reach out with her mind but he seemed to anticipate her move.

"Keep your Goddamn probes to yourself," he growled menacingly, pushing halfway out of the tank as if to physically stop her.

She retreated from him.

"If I wanted the world to know how I feel or what I'm thinking, I'd tell them. Every time I get near you another piece of my world shatters irrevocably," his hand made a slicing motion through the air, "And if it's one thing irritates me the most, it's people who don't respect another's privacy." He started to settle back into the water. "Go play voyeur somewhere else," echoed through the room.

Angelina took another step back, because the words were perfectly understandable even through the distortion of the water and the thickness of the tank glass.

Chapter Twelve: Insurrection

The young executive burst through the doors of the company president's office without bothering to be announced. "Sir, I think we may have something." Marlin looked up from his stock reports with a raised eyebrow. "One of our contacts has forwarded a copy of a shipping invoice. It is a large shipment of live fish headed for the New Fresno Aquarium."

"Why is that news? They get shipments of endangered species all year round."

"This shipment consisted of black rockfish, mackerel, lingcod and several other species of common game fish." Marlin was leaning across his desk now, intrigued. "It is the first such shipment ever for that particular aquarium. And an aquarium that displays no predatory fish or mammals needing the size shipment they received."

"Really?" Cortez purred. "Good work. It sounds as if Tigershark found himself a roost."

"He's definitely defected, sir."

"No shit?" he said lightly, and then hollered, "I thought that was clear when he disemboweled three of my best soldiers!" He smoothed back his hair and sat down, his demeanor restored. "Get a squad ready, I'm about to reacquire my prize creation. Tony, I want you to lead this one. He comes back with you alive or he stays there dead, and anyone aiding him is to be killed either way, got it?"

"Oh, yes, sir!" Tony said with relish.

*****

Tigershark appeared in the doorway of Max's office, his face drawn up in consternation. His eyes locked on Angelina without even seeing Max. He took three determined strides toward her. "Do it," he stated in a low growl.

"Do what?" Angelina asked in confusion.

Tigershark sighed impatiently. "What you've wanted to do since the Bar Topical. You want to know, and now I've *got* to know. Your trick worked, Angelfish, I hope you're happy." He paused a moment. "I had another 'dream' . . . about you and I," he finished in a whisper, looking away.

Angelina's heart skipped a beat. "Y . . . You're sure?" He nodded grimly. "This may be very painful for you, in more ways than one. Unlocking suppressed memories is an excruciating experience, from what I've read."

"I don't care."

"And . . . David was a gemuephobe." She could not believe she was trying to talk him out of this. Here he was providing her with a golden opportunity to answer her own questions and she found herself trying to convince him not to.

"I'll deal with it if it's true."

Max became tired quickly of not knowing what was transpiring, so he stepped between them, facing Angelina. "What are you two talking about?"

Tigershark pushed Max roughly out of the way, pointing a finger at him. "Stay out of this . . . If it turns out to be true, you'll know soon enough." He then turned back to Angelina. "Meet me at the tank in half an hour."

"Half an hour," Angelina repeated, as she watched him disappear as quickly as he had appeared.

"Angelina?"

"Hm?"

"What was that all about?"

"It's a very long story. I'll fill you in as I get ready for this."

After her explanation, Max was dumbfounded. "There is no way in the world that that creature is David. Huh uh, I'd know if it was."

"Would you?" she sighed. "Hell, Max, I wouldn't even recognize him anymore. That's why I want to do this. I need to know if it really is him or not."

"This is major dangerous. I'm not letting you do it. That thing is a serious killer."

"I'm doing it with or without your permission," she stated, stalking toward the door.

"At least let me come with you, in case something goes wrong."

Angelina rolled her eyes. "Sure."

*****

Angelina was relaxing in preparation for this mind probe, or at least she was trying to. She blinked seeing Tigershark stare warily through the glass of the tank at her. She was nervous about this and was beginning to wonder if she had chosen the best course. Tigershark looked no less anxious.

Angelina tried to shut out his almost palpable anxiety about this situation, as well as Max's discomfort and mistrust of Tigershark. She could not let herself get distracted. She was just about ready to begin when a commotion began in the public area of the aquarium. Angelina started and Tigershark was already out of the tank and heading for the adjoining room.

"Wait!" Angelina whispered emphatically, grabbing his shoulder to restrain his advance. She shook her head when he looked at her, and he seemed to catch her meaning. He approached more cautiously, and opened the door just enough to see what was happening. Fifteen soldiers were setting up a tight formation in the lobby.

"Can you see the emblems on their sleeves?" Tigershark breathed in Angelina's ear as she slid in next to him to get a look.

"They're Cortez's men," She said with conviction, anger evident in her voice. "You son of a bitch!" she uttered hotly. "You brought them to us!"

"What!" Tigershark said, shaking his head ardently in the negative. "No! I swear to you, Angelina, I didn't." She continued to stare at him angrily, unconvinced. "You read my mind when I arrived . . . did you detect any deceit then?"

"No, but . . ."

"Search my mind again if you must. You have to believe that I didn't expect them to be able to find me here!"

Angelina nodded once and then did what he suggested, aggressively probing for the deceit she was sure was there, uncaring of the amount of pain she put the gemue through in her search. Yet she found no evidence that he was lying; in fact, he was genuinely surprised and a bit scared at the predicament they were in now.

When she had finished, it took a moment for Tigershark to straighten, nearly crippled by her mind search. "You couldn't have been a little gentler? That felt like my head was going to explode," he grumbled, rubbing his temples.

She did not respond immediately.

"Well?" he prodded.

"It proves nothing!" she refuted, though she realized deep down he was right. "It may have been planted there!"

"Angelina!" he growled impatiently, taking her by both shoulders. "You have to believe me! We don't have time right now to discuss my supposed guilt. If they find me here, everyone dies. You don't understand how ruthless your uncle has gotten."

Angelina relented, looking back out through the slit in the door as most of the soldiers completed their rounds. The majority of the visitors were now being held in a small corner of the lobby. Tony motioned six more toward where the two fugitives now hid.

"I'll go out and see what they want," Angelina stated gruffly, not wanting to stay in her current company.

Tigershark grabbed her arm, forcefully dragging her back and spinning her to face him. "Are you crazy? You're pretty high on their hit list too, remember? You're the reason all this got started and you're not exactly easy to miss! They'll cut you down before you get two steps through the door."

"We can't just wait here for them to find us!" she whispered vehemently, ripping her arm from his grip, barely missing laying her arm open on his claws.

"We can retreat," he answered her simply.

Reluctantly, Angelina nodded. "Max, can you get the . . . ?" Max was no longer behind them. "Shit, where'd he go?"

Tigershark shrugged. "A good sense of self preservation?"

"That's not funny!"

Just then a muffled, "Can I help you gentleman?" was heard. Max had stepped through one of the office doors into the aquarium. The ensuing conversation fell below an audible level for the two of them.

"Jesus! What's he doing?" Tigershark growled.

"Possibly saving our asses," Angelina commented.

*****

The younger of the two soldiers spun toward Max as he stepped forward.

They looked at him sternly before the young man responded, "We are looking for a renegade gemue and a female accomplice he has with him . . . We have reason to believe that they may be taking refuge in this building. With your permission, we would like to conduct a search of the premises, Mr. -?"

"Just call me Max," He stated evenly, shaking his head he added, "I'm sorry but I don't know what you are talking about."

"I'm sure you don't, sir. If you would just give permission for the search?" the younger soldier asked.

"I can't let you do that, gentlemen. We have some very sensitive projects in work right now, ones I would rather not disturb," Max responded.

"Do you recognize this?" the older soldier interrupted, producing a document. Max glanced over the bill of shipment dangling in front of him.

"Of course, I approve all shipments in and out of this facility."

"Can you give me a reason a facility such as this would need a large shipment of the more common game fish?"

"As I said, there is some research going on. It has to do with toxicity, I believe."

"You don't know?" the older man inquired, leaning in suspiciously.

"I get over twenty requisitions a day; I don't have time to know the intimate details of every study going on in this facility," Max replied, aloof.

"Uh huh," the old man said, leaning even closer to the redheaded man. "Look, you hippie freak," Tony whispered, "I know that gemue is here and I know you're helping him. And we are going to search this place with or without your permission."

"Unless you have a warrant, sir," Max said coldly, "you had better take your men out of here before I call someone with some real jurisdiction."

Tony's face clouded over with rage, and what happened next went down altogether too fast.

*****

"No," Tigershark whispered suddenly, becoming very agitated as he watched the scene unfold.

"What's the matter?" Angelina queried.

"He's going to . . ." He leapt to his feet and was through the door before he finished the sentence.

Angelina jumped up and followed his lead. Tiger ignored the six that had been dispatched their way, pushing past their startled forms as he headed for his objective. Halfway to the trio a shot was heard, and time slowed down as Max began to fall. The younger soldier fired at them and Tiger ducked each of the shots deftly as he closed the gap between them. Knocking the gun away, Tigershark punched the younger soldier in the face and still managed to catch Max before he thudded to the deck. Angelina stood there watching as Tigershark gently set Max on the ground. When his gaze moved from Max, to her, to the two soldiers Angelina could see that there were tears in those slitted eyes of his.

"Get him out of here," Tiger growled. Angelina nodded and struggled to get Max into the storehouse in the back.

Tony stared at Tigershark reproachfully. "Just like a gemue to change alliances as it is convenient," he sneered.

"Well, well, well, Tony . . . What an unpleasant surprise," Tigershark grumbled, straightening.

"Y'know, I tried to convince Mr. Cortez that hiring you was a mistake. Gemues are nothing but trouble. It's really too bad he didn't listen. If he had, I wouldn't have to deal with you now. But, hey, on the other hand, this could be fun."

"You can let the hostages go, Tony, it's me you want. I can't promise you you'll get me, but I'll give you a hell of a fight."

"This is business, Tigershark," he replied. "I've got orders: either you come back, or you die, and all who helped you."

"If that's the way you want to play it," Tigershark shrugged. He lashed out without uttering another word, catching the man Tony across the already scarred face, and raking long furrows into his cheeks. He followed through with a punch to the gut. Tony doubled over as Tiger grabbed him by the scruff and waist band and threw him bodily into the six soldiers who were now headed back for them, intent on carrying out their orders.

Angelina had thought she understood Tigershark's nature. She realized now that she had sold him seriously short of his potential for destruction. It didn't take him more than a minute to kill the guards surrounding the visitors and release them before moving on to the stragglers left searching the building. Angelina watched protectively over Max as the carnage mounted.

*****

Sirens became audible in the distance just as I was finishing with the last of Cortez's henchmen. I pushed through the dividing doors, grabbing Angelina by the arm and pulling her up. "We've got to get out of here."

"But, Max . . ." she muttered, staring at the bloody prints I had left on her sleeves.

Seeing that she was worried and anxious, I knelt down, sampling the air about him. Trying to assure her I said, "He'll make it, even if we leave him behind." I stood again adding, "They can't tie him to this. They'll write it off as being in the wrong place at the wrong time."

"You're sure he'll live?"

I nodded tugging on her gently. "He doesn't smell of death, but if you and I don't leave now . . . Well, let's just say the day gets much less pleasant."

She yielded and we headed for the loading dock. "How did you know that man was going to shoot Max?"

"I smelled it." I answered, to which she shot me a confused expression. I added, "See, when humans have an adrenaline rush their scent changes. It was just a jump of intuition to determine what Tony's next action was going to be."

"Do you think you killed him?"

"Nah, doubt it. I only hurt him bad enough to get him out of my way."

"You enjoy your work, don't you?" she asked me.

I looked at my hands and down my front, seeing the blood spattered on and staining both. "Let's just say I'm good at my job, and leave it at that."

"So, now what are you going to do?"

"Doc Thomas- I need that tracer removed, and I don't have very much dryworld time left to do it in."

"Can we drive, then? I mean it will get us there that much faster."

I looked at her, bemused, not previously considering *that* option. I guess I have been in the water too long. I nodded silently, not willing to give voice to my oversight. Angelina had gone on musing, "We are never getting into the hospital looking like we do. I have to wash and change."

*****

We made our way through the streets, ending up back in front of the drab motel I had been casing a little over two months ago. Without pausing, she jumped out of the van and headed for the lobby door. I was slower to get out, unsure whether she wanted me to follow her or not. Halfway to the door, she turned back and motioned to me impatiently to come along. As I caught up with her she said, reminding me of the blood on my clothes and hands, "You need the shower more than I do."

As we entered, she headed straight for the stairs. Out of habit, I took in the surroundings. There was not much to the lobby; it was not well lit and the walls were stained with a combination cigarette smoke, urine and about four other unmentionable substances. There was what had once been a very nice Persian rug in the center of the lobby. It was tattered, frayed, and stained with thousands of footprints that had been across it. The check-in desk was an old piece of pressboard that looked as if it was about to collapse, leaning precariously to the left.

Behind the desk stood a man whom I can only say fit neatly into the picture of neglect this place presented to the eyes. He was overweight with a once white shirt that was now more the color of urine. His face was flabby and loose, and as he moved, the folds jiggled and shook like a tent in the wind. A scraggly beard grew haphazardly on his face, and through it he grinned, showing a mouthful of rotting teeth. He looked from me to Angelina, returned to me, and then finally settled on Angelina's retreating form. "Hey, babe," he called after her. "We don't rent rooms by the hour, y'know!" He had not even seemed to notice the condition of my clothes. Shit, he had probably witnessed murders in

144

the lobby and "not seen a thing." Angelina shot an acid look his way before continuing up the stairs. "Sweetie, you can do better than the gemue. Hey, I know, give me a try . . . I'll rock your world!"

I glared at the manager, growling, and the man stepped back; this, despite the distance between us. I turned away, smiling thinly before heading up the stairs. The hallways were drab as we gravitated toward her dwelling these past several months. She stopped in front of a dark door, on which the wood was peeling away, and Angelina fought with the lock for several moments before it relinquished its fight and allowed us entry. Once inside, she wasted no time; she began rooting through several drawers and came up with a fresh set of clothes. She turned to me and said, "I won't be long." Before I could say a thing, she disappeared into the lavatory.

I stared at the bathroom door for several moments before, feeling uncomfortable, I turned away to take in the surroundings, a habit after so long in this profession. I noted immediately how immaculate the place was, and I was sure it was by no effort of the management. The sheets on the bed were so tight that a coin would bounce if dropped on its surface, and a small holey blanket was folded neatly at the one end. At the other end, the pillow was fluffed and neatly tucked up under the sheets. There was a pressboard dresser to one side of it and I noticed that there was not a speck of dust on its surface. Curiosity got the better of me and, with a quick glance over my shoulder, I opened the drawer I was nearest. It was one that she had not disturbed and, looking down, I took in an obsessively neat arrangement of garments. I shook my head; what kind of nutcase was this girl? I slid the drawer shut but just before it closed I noticed something tucked into the front of it by the mirror's reflection. I pulled it quickly back out and gingerly plucked the picture from hiding. I looked in the mirror to be sure that Angelina was not standing behind me while I violated her privacy, but what I saw froze me where I stood.

I didn't see my reflection, instead I saw a stranger. He was shorter than I, relatively thin with a strong build and a stalwart face. His hair was blond and cut into a style I thought was odd looking. It was short over the whole of his head with the exception of a few wispy strands hanging loose at the back of his neck. His eyes were bright sea blue and something pricked at the back of my mind with familiarity.

I could hear my own breath coming in short gasps, but I found myself unable to move as I stared at this odd face in the mirror. He was adjusting a tie for the dark suit he was wearing and he was talking, or so it seemed because I couldn't hear what he was saying. I gazed to whom he was speaking, and my heart leapt again, this time in panic. I whirled around, ready for an attack, and froze when he was not standing over my left shoulder as had been reported by the reflective surface at my back. I slowly turned toward the mirror, confirming what I had seen, thinking suddenly that I was slipping into insanity.

The vision still held, there in the mirror stood Tony, though his appearance was askew of how I remembered the man. He, like the blond who had taken my reflections place, was well dressed and appeared to be talking paternally. My gaze drifted back to the stranger before me, wondering who he was that he was a friend of Tony's.

"Tiger, are you okay?" I heard cutting through the vision that held me. I blinked several times as the vision of the strange man and Tony bled away until I was seeing Angelina's concerned face staring over my left shoulder, and my own reflection. I shook my head, clearing the last of that disturbing image out of my brain. With a start, I realized that I still held the picture I had purloined from the wide-open drawer. Trying not to appear obvious, I dropped it back in the drawer and leaned on it slowly until it was closed. As I turned to face her, it dawned on me that I had never gotten the opportunity to see what the picture contained.

"I'm fine," I finally replied, hoping I sounded more sincere to her than I did to myself. I also hoped she was not going to use her talent to find out one-way or the other.

"Uh huh," she replied slowly, as if she didn't believe me. "Well, I'm finished. Your turn."

"Thanks," I said quietly and slid past her before she felt a need to inquire further. I did catch her suspicious sideways glance at me as I moved toward the shower.

I moved into the bathroom and, adjusting the water temperature slightly lower, I stepped into the stall. I stripped down, using the available water and soap to clean the dried blood out of my dive pants. I then turned attention to myself, scrubbing hard to get the stain off my textured skin. When I was satisfied with my cleanliness I stood under the steady stream of warm water, opening my mouth and letting the water wash over my gills in an attempt to delay my drytime limit.

As I stood there, I thought over this latest in a line of strange visions that had been assailing me over the past few months. This one was vastly different from any that I had previously encountered most of which consisted of the raven-haired female and me in one way or another. This man, I didn't even recognize and was friends with Tony, my sworn enemy. I was hard put to even correlate why this vision was presented to me. My head had been playing games with me for too long now, and I was severely taxed to keep my sanity intact. So deeply entrenched was I in my soul searching that I started when Angelina pounded on the door. "C'mon! We don't have all freakin' day!"

"All right!" I barked at the door. I stood there a moment more, trying one last time to extend drytime. I then shut the water off. I wrung out my pants, then dried off and donned the still wet garment. That was a struggle in itself, wet neoprene and sandpaper skin it was like trying to pull up velcro.

As I stepped out, she already had her few possessions packed and slung onto her shoulder. She looked very impatient, keys in hand, "Well? Let's go," I growled. "It's not like *I* have to pack."

We retraced our steps and I hung back as she headed for the desk to pay up her bill. The man at the counter didn't miss a beat as he said, "Wow that was fast!" He looked past Angelina to me and said, "It been a while for you buddy?" I scowled at him, but his attention was already back on Angelina. "Babe, you couldn't have been satisfied with that . . . Let me show you how a real man treats a woman." He ran a thick hand suggestively up her arm.

She jerked it away, looking disgusted. "Please, you wouldn't know a real man if he hit you," Angelina retorted.

"Well, at least I'm human, unlike fish lips over there. Gotta give me some points in that respect."

By then, I was up to my gills with this guy and, my temper flaring, I bolted toward the raised desk. Five feet from him, I made a flying leap, timing it perfect, and, just missing Angelina. Sliding across the slick surface, I kicked the clerk square in the chest. The momentum of it drove the man into the wall and as I landed lightly on the other side of the desk, he slumped to the floor unconscious. As a counterpoint, the desk decided to collapse behind me.

"Perverted bastard," I growled as I stepped around the other side of the now dilapidated counter.

"Was that necessary?" she scowled as I passed by her.

"I feel better," I replied. "The guy was an ass."

"That's a given, but your reaction was a bit extreme."

I looked at her with a shocked expression. "Angelina, pause a moment and consider this . . . Three months ago I would not have thought twice about cleaning that stain from the gene pool. Really, do you think that was an extreme reaction for me?" I shook my head. "Hanging out with you is making me soft."

Angelina shrugged. "Point taken," she said, and simply walked toward the door.

Chapter Thirteen:
Nail in the Coffin

Thirty minutes later, we were standing in a storage room on the first floor of the hospital. "He's on the fourth floor."

I sucked air through my teeth. "Dicey situation I must say," I remarked, looking down the crowded hallways.

She pointed over my shoulder at a point across the hall. "That's the main freight elevator for the building, and we could use it to get to the fourth floor, but it's well used and we'd have to traverse the hall to the other end of the building once we got up there."

That was not what I had wanted to hear. This was a strictly human hospital, as the posted signs in hall stated. I would stick out here like a man wearing neon green in a gospel choir.

"There!" Angelina exclaimed, pointing to a pile of laundry, next to which was a folded wheel chair.

"You don't mean . . ."

She nodded. "We could dress you up as if you were a patient, and no one would bother us."

"Except maybe a doctor. Look, I'm not built to sit in any normal chair."

"Well then, slump forward, it would add to the illusion and would be good enough to hide your face."

I shook my head. This was going to be so embarrassing. "Okay, I'm not happy about it, but I see no other way to do it."

Yep, I was truly mortified. Within minutes, Angelina had dressed me in a patient's gown. It felt inadequate; my largest dorsal protruded from between the ties. Moments later, she returned with a robe that she draped over my shoulders. She had put a shower cap over my hair and ears and had stuffed my long feet in booties at least two sizes too small. Not only did I look ill, I looked as if I had gotten ill in the shower.

"Now you're going to have to keep your hands and elbows hidden under the robe and your head down. Anybody gets a good look at you this is all going to be over."

"What about you?" I asked. "Surely you don't think your looks are going to pass for human."

"Give me about ten minutes and you'll never recognize me." And with that, she disappeared. When she returned, her face hands and arms were covered in make-up that gave her skin some color. It looked odd to me, probably just because I was used to her being pale, but it struck me how much she looked like the woman from my visions.

"What about your eyes?" I pointed out. She raised a finger, turned away, and a moment later was wearing contacts shaded brown. "Hope they think your pupils are just white because of the lighting." I sat down in the wheelchair and hunkered over as if I was ill. It did not take long for the position to get uncomfortable. "Let's get this over with, okay? I'm not going to last long like this."

"All right," she replied and I heard her open the door. She pushed the chair casually across the hall and hailed the elevator. Shortly, it chimed and the doors opened. I heard no one come out of the elevator and I caught no odor, but I remained silent in case my senses were deceiving me. Angelina sighed, which I took to mean that the coast was clear.

"I feel ridiculous," I hissed

"You got a better idea? Let's hear it."

I shook my head slightly. "No, none."

"Well then, keep quiet."

The door announced their arrival on the fourth floor before I was ready, and I doubled over quickly, trying to get all my abnormal features hidden before the door parted. As they opened, I could hear dozens of sets of footsteps all around us, as well as sounds of a busy ICU. Angelina was pushing the chair slowly toward the far end of the hall, and it was making me nervous. Suddenly it occurred to me that she could easily betray me in here. She surely held some doubts about my motives, and she could leave me and make her escape while hospital security dealt with me.

But I felt no change in the motion of the chair, no indication that she might just stop and leave me sitting in the hall.

She startled me as she leaned over and whispered, "We're here."

*****

"What happened?" Cortez growled. Tony stood in front of the screen. Several bloody, long furrows were raked down one side of his already mangled face. One section of his lip was neatly split and he was having a hard time relaying his report.

"He killed then, sir. All of ny group is dead."

"How did you get off so easy, soldier?"

"I have no explanation for that, sir. I underestinated his avility. I understand if you're utset with ne, sir."

"You should have realized that he was not one of the gemue cows you're used to hunting. He's as much a killer as you are. I expect you'll not make that mistake again," the executive snapped.

"Yes, sir." He nodded, one of the flaps of his lip emphasizing the motion. "What do you suggest?"

"His dryworld time is running out. He's going to try and avoid confrontation. Exertion cuts down on what he has available," he mused, then addressing Tony he added, "He'll try to make it back to water quickly. Cut him off. I want him stuck on land until he is incapacitated. I want him back in a position where I can keep tabs on him."

"Consider it done," Tony agreed.

"And Tony," he sighed, "get those wounds tended. They are, to say the least, unsightly."

Tony's hand went to his face. "Yes, sir."

******

Tigershark sat on the table, staring at Doctor Thomas. They had expected a confrontation from the receptionist but were surprised when she just let them by, reminding Angelina to remember the report when they were finished.

"You took a real chance coming here," he admonished them. "What if I had been with a patient already?"

Tigershark just shrugged. "Wing it? It's what we've been doing to this point."

The doctor just shook his head. "I think I have figured out how to do this without risking oxygen deprivation."

"And?"

"Well, we still have a few tanks we used to use for burn victims. Y'know to keep them from sticking to their wrappings. If we put a saline solution in it and oxygenated it, we've got a fool proof surgery bed."

"Interesting solution," Tigershark replied approvingly. "So how do you propose to take the tracer out?"

He held up a fine tube. "With this."

"A borescope."

"Yes, it will do the least amount of damage and is delicate enough to get the device without disturbing the jugular. But this kind of surgery will require a general anesthesia," he insisted.

"No, that requires recovery time. Tony is not going to give up on me that easily and he is very good at anticipating an opponent's move. He may be on my trail right now. No, I need to be able to leave on a moment's notice."

"But it's a delicate procedure. One flinch and I could kill you."

"I won't flinch."

"But I can't even use local, the pain . . ."

"I can handle it. Just perform the procedure." His teeth were grit as if he was losing control of his temper.

It took about a half-hour to get everything prepared for the surgery. With a sigh, Tigershark lowered himself into the water and lay on his side. Half of his body was exposed to the air, but because his head was under water it served its purpose. Water ran out of his gills at intervals and Doc Thomas shrugged. "Guess I won't have to worry about blood getting in the way."

Angelina felt a shiver run through her as she noticed that Tigershark's chest did not move when he used his gills. Suddenly, it felt to her as if they were working on a cadaver.

Doc Thomas turned on the monitor for the CAT machine, examining the area and the best angle from which to get around the backside of those gills and at the tracer. He pointed out his objective to Angelina. "Are you ready, Tiger?"

"Do it," he growled impatiently. The doctor took a step back. It was an exact duplicate of the reaction Angelina had to clarity of his speech through water.

The doctor brought out a scalpel and made a small incision at the division between two muscles in Tigershark's neck. He inserted the borescope slowly and Angelina saw Tigershark's eyes roll back as he fought the pain. His whole body began to tense, and she saw the clutch on his arm tighten.

The procedure took almost two hours to complete. Angelina was in awe over Tigershark's self control. He had managed to keep entirely still, even as obvious as his pain was. It appeared that Tigershark was sleeping, but as soon as the scope was withdrawn, his eyes opened. He looked at he doctor expectantly from the corner of this close eye. "Can I get up now?"

"Just a minute," the doctor told him. "All right. Slowly, though."

There were claw marks evident on Tigershark's arm where he had been gripping it tightly. "I hope to God I don't have to go through that again," he said, and winced at the pain talking caused him. He raised one long hand toward his neck, which the doctor immediately grabbed, shaking his head.

"You're not done yet. Go sit on the table, I need to stitch that up."

*****

Tony made his way through the hospital in a dour mood. He did not like it that the gemue bastard had gotten the upper hand with him. He hadn't expected him to react that quickly. He paid no attention to those around him, nor did he care if they thought his face hideous or were afraid of him because he had a gun. It had been worse when he had taken the grenade in the face because of that chicken shit private of his who had saved his own skin. He had believed in teamwork back then, believed he was a part of some great army machine. It had taken losing half his face and sight in one eye to realize the real golden rule: you can only count on yourself.

He entered the elevator and selected the fourth floor. There were several people that had been in the elevator already and he noticed their poorly hidden stares. That brought a slight smile to his face. He was always happier when people feared him.

He was the last one in the car by the time it reached the fourth floor and he barged into the reception area, heading for the operating theater. The receptionist barred his way. "I'm sorry, sir, the doctor is with a patient at the moment. If you would care to wait, I will tell him you're here." Her disgust was barely disguised by her manners.

"Lady, I need to see the doctor now. As you can see I'n in fetty desferate need."

"I'm sorry, but he's in surgery right now. Please have a seat and I will call a nurse to help you."

"You don't get it, do you? I don't wait for anyone." He pushed her down and leveled his gun at her temple. "Now stay fut."

He stepped over her and moved down the hall.

*****

Tigershark was much more relaxed now. In fact, he was asleep, sitting up, while getting stitches in his neck. The doctor was shaking his head. "I have never seen so high a tolerance for pain."

"Maybe he had to. You said yourself he was grown in this form very quickly. That must have been excruciating . . . maybe he just learned to shut pain out. You saw the way his eyes just kind of rolled away."

"You may be right."

Tigershark's eyes popped open suddenly, causing Angelina and the doctor to startle, and he drew in a breath. Reaching up and cutting the floss, he uttered, "Shit. Time to go!"

"What? Why?" Angelina asked.

"Tony's here. In fact, he's coming down the hall."

"Shit."

"That's what I said," Tigershark replied, deadpan, jumping off the table. "You got another way out of here?" he said, this time to the doctor.

"The landing out the window. There are ladders down to the first floor."

"Good, that'll work."

"Let's get this 'bed' out of sight first. No use raising his suspicions"

Tigershark slid the table into an adjoining room and jogged back in. "Thanks, Doc. I owe you two."

As they disappeared down the fire escape, Tony flung the door in and stepped inside. "Hello. I'n in need of your services." His brows furrowed. "Your recettionist said you were with a patient."

"She says that when I'm trying to take a break. Please have a seat."

He seated himself, never relinquishing his gun. "What happened to the floor?"

"Oh, I spilled my decanter. I was just about to clean it when you came in."

Tony nodded, seeming to accept that story.

*****

Angelina stood in the half-light coming in through the broken windows of their new hideout, waiting anxiously for Tigershark's return. She peered around her yet again, trying to familiarize herself with it, knowing that they could stay here quite a while. Tigershark had mentioned something about it having been the Sunmaid Raisin Plant before the meltdown.

The immediate area that she was sitting in was part of a very large boardroom in the management section of the factory. The furniture was long gone, looted probably just after the flooding. Out the door was a long balcony that had once looked out over the factory floor. Now, however, the view was a placid indoor lake. Towards the north end of the room were several offices attached directly to the boardroom. Down the length of the boardroom were huge bay windows that had at one point watched over the lush valley. Most were cracked or completely broken. The few that weren't were so thick with dust that plants had actually found purchase.

Tigershark had been making forays to and from his former "sanctum" for the last several hours. It amazed Angelina just how much crap he seemed to have. A lot of it was things she thought he would have no need of. So far he had brought over towels, robes, sleeping bags, several first aid kits, packets of MREs, and cans of fruit, vegetables, and soups. Angelina jumped as she heard the splash that announced Tigershark's return. She glanced from the can of food in her hand to Tigershark as he pulled himself up onto the shelf. "And here I was thinking you only ate sushi, freshly killed," Angelina said, tossing the can into the air with a flourish, as he stepped up to her.

He leaned over her and caught the can midair, and then stared down at her fleetingly. When comprehension dawned, Tigershark smiled wanly, watching the can as he turned it in his hands, seeming to read the label. His nails were making clicking noises on its surface, and he appeared to be exhausted. "I crave human things occasionally: foods, pastimes." His eyes traveled over her over momentarily. "Longings."

"Oh?" Angelina said, backing away quickly, not liking the inference.

"Contrary to popular belief, gemues are made anatomically correct," he said, smirking at her. Then he leaned over to retrieve something from the water. "We were all full blooded humans once," he grunted as he fought the water resistance to remove his objective. Angelina's eyes widened in silent appreciation, as his muscles stood out in sharp relief. He moved past her with a dripping pallet, and she shied from him as he stacked it in one corner. He turned toward her, shaking his head. "Don't worry, I'm not one to take what is not offered me. If I was, you would have been in trouble on our first meeting," his gaze moved up her body and back down it again before he returned his attention to his work, "as pretty as you are."

She stared at his back. "You think I'm pretty?"

"Well, yes," he said twisting around to face her, with an unidentifiable expression on his face. "Especially the way I see you in my head. The way you were before, when we were in school."

"What did you say?" Angelina asked, squinting at him. His voice had lost the gruff quality when he had said that, and the feeling she received behind the words was not Tigershark's. That had sounded too much like David.

"What?" he said, his brows furrowing.

"You said, 'When we were in school.'"

"I did?" he asked incredulously, but he waved it away. "It must have been a slip of the tongue."

He stood up and resumed stacking old crates to create a dry spot. He then grabbed several of the waterproof bags and started emptying the contents onto the crates. He spread out a down sleeping bag over which he laid a blanket. The second bag contained a pillow, which he set out at the head of the pallet. He came back over to her. "That should be adequate, don't you think?"

She nodded. "So, where are you going to sleep?"

"Downstairs."

She peered at him quizzically, and he pulled out a length of nylon braid with clips at either end, comprising a tether. "Just below the floor I'll tie myself off. If anything happens, just stomp. I'll hear you." He began rubbing his neck as he stood.

"Is something wrong?"

"My neck hurts, no big deal."

"The stitches?"

Tigershark nodded.

"Let me see," Angelina said. She stood and pulled away his coarse mane to look at his incision, brushing fingertips against the skin on his neck. It was soft, nearly human textured skin, and just slightly cooler than hers was. She swallowed as a feeling rose up in her unbidden. She centered her concentration, detaching herself from her suddenly raging hormones, noticing the white and puckered appearance around the blue stitching. As she was examining them she discovered another scar. This one was barely visible just behind his elfish ear, and was jagged and old. The scar reminded her of another that she knew too well, and she suddenly found herself remembering David and how he had gotten a scar just like that.

*****

Angelina's gaze was drawn to the loud conversation coming from the bar, heard even over the din of music and the myriad of loud speaking that was going on around her and her friends. She leaned back to see the source of the argument and she rolled her eyes, seeing that David had found himself in another of his many fights. It was clear that he had been drinking, heavily, by the way his expression was glazed and the sway of his body as he confronted the day's nemesis.

161

He'd chosen a real winner too. It seemed that a biker club had decided this was the place to be tonight, and David had picked the largest of them to confront in his inebriated state. She watched a moment longer, quickly becoming bored with the loudly audible taunts he was throwing at the 250-pound man. She had seen it too many times in the past few years; instead, she turned back to her drink, making rude comments on the man's stupidity with her friends.

"Look out!" someone yelled suddenly. It had sounded like one of David's closer friends, and Angelina turned back toward the bar just in time to see the biker lunge forward with a broken beer bottle aimed at David's throat. She drew in a gasp of fright as David reacted, just a bit slowly, to his friend's warning. He ducked down and slightly to one side, which only served to get him cut in a different place. She watched, horrified, as the broken shard laid the back of his ear clean open, the point sticking out the cartilage just forward of his ear canal.

"Oh, my God!" she heard her friend screech next to her.

Several of David's friends as well as some of the other bikers restrained the man with the bottle, who was still struggling to get at David and finish the job. David was half leaning on one of the barstools, his hand to the back of his ear, and Angelina blanched to see blood streaming from between his fingertips. She expected him to try for revenge; it would fit with his acerbic personality, but he surprised her when all he did was push himself to his feet with help from his friends. Once standing he moved some ways away from the other man and sat down. He was shaking his head as if regretful of his choice this day.

*****

Angelina was frozen next to Tigershark as that remembrance ended and she glanced into his pointed ear, seeing the exit scar just where David's had been. She continued to stare into his face, finally noticing that he was looking sidelong at her with a look that was halfway between concern and anger.

"Well?" he asked, having finally caught her eye.

She glanced away from his gaze quickly and cleared her throat as she said, "Just as I thought, you've got to let them dry or they are going to pull out."

He glared at her in an irritated manner, his eyes bleary despite his alien face. "How do you propose I do that? I need at least eight hours of sleep; I've been run ragged. I've only got three, maybe four hours of drytime before I suffocate and die. Do you see a solution I don't?"

The feeling that had possessed her dissipated under his harsh tone and her defenses came back into place. "Yes, actually, I see two. You can either seal up the stitches with a waterproof dressing, or sleep half out of the water like you did during surgery. No, on second thought that won't work either. Your exhalation will wet them anyway. Can you get enough oxygen through only one set of gills?"

He glowered at her momentarily, angry, then away. "I don't know. I've never tried it."

So, Angelina set about taping down the gills on the left side and then placing a watertight bandage over the stitches before he returned to the water to catch up on his sleep. After he left she gawked a long time at the tinted window, watching the colors play across the surface as the sun went down. She ate a meal of cold soup before settling down on the pallet that comprised the only dry spot in the room.

She lay down, staring up at the ceiling as her mind continued to work. "What had that been?" she asked herself. When she had touched his skin it had dredged up something she couldn't believe that she felt. Longing . . . her body had suddenly ached for something more intimate and primal. She felt her face screw up in disgust, thinking, *Am I that hard up that I want a gemue? Ewww, oh, jeez, say it isn't so!*

But that was what it had been. No matter how desperately she wanted to deny it she knew it was true. She wondered a long time why . . . then her thoughts turned perversely to what it might be like. A shiver ran through her and she shook her head, trying to clear that vision from her mind.

Then she thought about the scar on his head, and she was more than ever convinced that he was David. How many people have scars like that one? She reviewed the memory. A pang went through Angelina as she remembered the rest of that chapter in her life.

David had received fifteen stitches for his stupidity that night. The bottle had nearly scalped his ear straight off of his head. As it was it had never healed properly, and rewarded him with one of the ugliest scars she had ever seen.

When David had returned from the hospital after the bar fight, Angelina had ribbed him for two weeks running about being too slow to get out of the way. One day he had stopped dead in his tracks and turned to face her with a look she had never seen before on his face; she remembered suddenly being chilled. He had stepped over before she could retreat and grabbed her by both shoulders, shook her once, hard, and in a tone of controlled fury said, "Stop."

Then he had simply let her go and walked away, though she could see his whole frame shaking with his anger as he receded into the morning crowd. What had her scared about it was that there was murder in his eyes. She had never seen the look before but she recognized it immediately when it was there. She had avoided him for a very long time after that.

It was hours before Angelina could get to sleep, in part because she wondered how she could convince Tigershark that he needed his old personality back. It was nearly sunrise when she finally was able to stop thinking of it and go to sleep.

Chapter Fourteen: Changed State of Mind

As much as I professed to be tired, I found myself unable to sleep. I suppose I could blame it on the "congestion" I felt, having only one gill to breath through, but I knew that was not the reason. So much had happened in just the past two days, and it was all trying to recap its highlights behind my eyes. I had been happy with my life before Angelina came into the picture. I had a good paying job, and I was content knowing who I was and what I stood for. That contentment no longer existed. Angelina had introduced the doubts that raced circles through my brain, and each circuit found pockets of evidence I had never noticed before to support them.

There was my "anxiety attacks" at being submerged. I had truly thought I was about to drown that day I was released to pursue this, to point, unpleasant task. I was beginning to think that the familiarity both before each incident and that had asserted itself afterwards had been something artificial.

Angelina thought I was David Scott, her former boyfriend. Doc Thomas insisted my transformation was no more than two years old. Cortez had said it himself: I was his creation, a pet project for a madman with an agenda that made no sense. It all made for a very strong case that I was indeed a construct for Cortez's machinations, and possibly David, just as Angelina insisted. My stomach convulsed in anxiety.

All of this built up in support of Angelina's theory…and the dreams.

They were something that I had only hinted to Angelina about. The visions, what I had thought were dreams, were becoming something much more ominous to me. They were constant and insistent, coming unbidden when I slept. And each night they returned longer and more detailed than the night before. Each one seemed to be an account of a life I had lived with . . . with Angelina. Alternately, I had the nightmares of pain, bright light, and feelings of nausea.

Looking back they were too vivid, the surreal quality was missing, and when they started happening in the middle of the day it had raised a huge red flag behind my eyes.

But I was comfortable with my life now. Did I really want to upset things by accessing memories that may or may not be there or mine? If all of her hopes turned out to be true, then what? "David was a gemuephobe," that's what Angelina had said. As David, would I refuse to function, hating what they had made of me?

I sighed heavily, shaking out those thoughts, trying to slide into oblivion. I would worry about it once I had time, once the probe was complete, and if it was true.

*****

Angelina woke late the next morning and for a moment was disoriented. It took her a bit to realize where she was. She stretched, feeling stiff and sore. "I'm a piss poor outlaw," she muttered as she stepped into the cold water that submerged the fourth floor. "Well, that's a hell of a wake up call. If we stay here much longer I'm definitely going to make more of the floor dry." She found herself hoping that it wouldn't come to that.

She looked around the room, figuring Tigershark would have beaten her in waking up, but he was not to be seen. Angelina shrugged and moved to a corner where the bags of foodstuffs floated. She opened a bag and began rummaging through it, finding something that looked appetizing for lunch. She was startled by the loud splashing behind her and whirled around, unsure of what she would find.

Angelina relaxed visibly when she saw that it was Tigershark. She watched him a moment as he shook the water out of his hair and approached. She returned to what she was doing. She thought of how ironic that was; only months ago he had been her waking nightmare, making her check every corner and wonder how soon he would catch her. She found herself surprised how quickly she had become comfortable around him, and she could only guess that it was the current circumstances.

"Are you hungry?" she asked him without turning her eyes.

"No thanks, I've had my breakfast." He responded strongly

She grimaced at the sack, realizing just what that breakfast had been. " 'K."

She straightened, selecting the least disgusting of the choices available, moved back to the dry spot on her pallet and worked to open the can. "In all that stuff you brought over you'd think you'd have had a heating unit."

He shrugged. "It wouldn't fit into a bag," he replied simply, "I had to leave it, or else it would do no one any good."

She shrugged in turn and fell reluctantly to her meal. She glanced up at him. He was lounging on one elbow on a half-submerged pallet, watching her strangely.

"You look like you've got something on your mind."

"What? You didn't try to pull it right out of the old gray matter?" he replied in a tone of sarcasm.

"I think I learned my lesson after almost having my jaw broken."

"No, only upon threat of death," he corrected quietly, a slight smile turning up the corners of his stretched mouth. He momentarily gazed up again, a strange light in his eyes. "Tell me about this guy David."

The chunk of cold stew she was chewing stuck in her throat. She swallowed hard, trying to get it to go down. "David?" she asked. He nodded ascent, and she set the can aside, her eyes for her hands rather than that curious face. She was noticeably uncomfortable.

"How long did you know him?" he asked to jump-start the conversation.

"Five years. We met in school, college. We were studying for the same major, political science. He was from one of the rich families, 'old' money, if you know what I mean. In fact his family lives up in the mountains, far from the corruption of Old Town. That's what David told me his parents called it." She shrugged. "His dad died just after David graduated college. His mom still maintains the property in the hills above the city."

"Oh," he said, his brows furrowing, saying, "Were you dating?"

"Oh no." She smiled. "We hated each other. It's hard to be in any kind of relationship when both are shooting for top honors. We were very competitive. I mean, we rarely spoke, and if we did it was only for the sake of polite hatred. You know, more to stick a thorn in each other's sides." She sighed. "He ended up being valedictorian, much to my chagrin, and I swore I would never talk to him. It seemed an easy enough promise to keep. He was going into the family business, and I was getting a job in San Angeles. But the job fell through, and I ended up stuck here working for a small firm at the edge of New Fresno." She turned her gaze up to find Tigershark laying belly down in the inches of water. It swirled around his neck as he breathed, with only his eyes, ears, and fins visible. "If I'm boring you, I can stop."

"No, please continue," he said without lifting his head free of the water.

"Well, we ran into each other again about a year later outside the Comtec complex, a place he was doing 'research' on. It was so good to see someone from the good old days that I forgot our rivalry. He bought me lunch, and we seemed to talk forever. We started dating shortly thereafter."

"That is the memory that I saw on our first meeting," he stated matter-of-factly.

"Yes," she answered simply.

"W . . . what did David look like?"

"I have a picture, if you'd like to see it."

He nodded, sitting up, water running quickly off his features as he did. Angelina handed a slightly water stained photograph to him.

*****

I shook the excess moisture off of my hands, took the picture gingerly, and stared at the man. He was tall, just inches shorter than I. He was also thinner, though he was muscular and in very good shape, and his skin was almost brown from exposure to the sun. He was blond haired and blue eyed and blessed with what I judged to be an easygoing personality.

"He's very good looking," I said, looking up at Angelina.

Her expression was unreadable, though she acknowledged my comment. I tried not to let it show, but I realized that this was the man I had seen as my reflection in Angelina's motel room. The thought made a hard knot in my stomach; it was another clue, and one that pointed to Angelina's theory about me. What did that say about Tony? Did that mean that I was once friends with him? I shook that from my head.

I then moved my gaze to her past image, shocked at the sharp contrast between her then and now. Her skin was almost the color of milk chocolate, her hair was raven black, tinted a dark red at the ends, by the sun. Her eyes had been dark brown and peered out with playfulness that I never saw in Angelina's dead white eyes.

I swallowed hard as something came unbidden to my mind. I felt my hand raise up to shade my eyes at the mental pain of the recall. I vaguely heard Angelina asking me if I was all right. I raised my other hand to stop her from speaking as I concentrated on the images forming in my head. I found myself suddenly on a white sand beach where a hot wind blew across my skin, and the sky above was as blue as the water. I watched as the dark skinned woman ran past me to dive into the incoming surf, felt myself laughing wholeheartedly, as her swim top came floating to the surface and I saw her humiliated face as she tried to retrieve it.

"Yes!" a stranger said in my mind. He whispered urgently, "Free me!"

I came back to my surroundings more than a little shaken. There were tears running down my coarse cheeks to drip into the water at our feet.

"Are you okay?" Angelina asked, and I found myself wanting to accuse her of playing with me again. That would be simpler than the truth insinuating itself through my carefully constructed alibis.

"I," I started, beginning to tremble, "I remembered that day. I was there . . . It was at Playa Nueva in Mexico."

"Yes," she stated in surprise.

I felt my brow furrow. "It was . . . our vacation." I gawked at her shocked face. "You . . . didn't put it in my head . . . did you?"

"I . . . swear," she breathed, she seemed as surprised as I was, "I didn't lay one tendril of thought in your mind."

"Then it is true, isn't it?" I muttered; she looked hopeful. "It means you've been right all along?"

I couldn't continue looking at her, considering carefully what I was about to say to her; what I was about to ask her to do despite my thoughts about the consequences. It would be a dangerous situation if I could not function afterwards, especially with Cortez hot on our tails. But my mind didn't want to wait; the stranger had no patience for it, creating a steadily more painful headache. My concentration was gone.

"I need to know for sure, Angelfish." It was hardly audible. I was surprised she had heard it. "Please?" It sounded pathetic to another part of my mind, one that suddenly seemed very foreign.

"Are you sure?" she asked.

"Angelina, these lapses are beginning to taunt me," I replied softly. "I want to know for sure one way or the other."

*****

Angelina felt the involuntary shudder from Tigershark as she laid a tentative tendril into his thoughts. She felt the whispers as he forced himself to relax, to give over to the probe. When he was no longer fighting her she moved forward through tangles of thought and memory. She avoided prolonged contact with those bundles for two reasons: they were not what she was here to find and, having been a part of some of them, she did not want to be witness to any more. Before long, there rose before her mind's eye an opaque barrier, beyond which shifted shadows of hidden thoughts. She had no doubt that this was the suppression placed over who Tigershark really was.

Angelina realized with some trepidation that she had been here before. She had seen this perception prior to this. It took her a few moments to realize where. It had been the dream, or what she had thought had been a dream. It was just as she had envisioned it, the vague impression of being in a mist enshrouded room, and the pinkish hue that she "saw," the opaque barrier that she had contacted David through.

She felt herself shiver with anticipation, hoping she was right about what she assumed lay behind this milky curtain. She quelled it lest she lost concentration and broke the link. She searched back and forth along the wall, looking for the scar that would mark the breakdown in the overlay of memories. There had to be one or more, because without a defect no memories of his past life would have surfaced. If no clue had been presented then they would not be in this situation. Then again, if he still believed in the ruse then she would have been long dead, she thought grimly.

She centered again and continued her search. The barrier was smooth and featureless, and the shadows on the other side moved languidly across the inner surface. Angelina pushed her probe against the barrier, testing its strength, only to be stricken away. She grimaced inwardly; the scientists who had wiped him had put safeguards in place to counter what she was trying. If forced, the barrier would implode and "blind" the telepath's talent. She had read that some telepaths died when their minds were trapped in the collapse. And more often than not the wipe died as well as the shock overloaded their brain. She put the doubt out of her mind as she moved on.

As she searched, she became aware of a presence and, looking up, she found one of the shadows standing just opposite her. His hands and face were pressed against the opaque barrier, creating a ghostly image. Angelina stared at the shadowy face and she watched anxiously as it shifted slightly as if to bring her into better view. She was drawn back to her "dream" as the wide sockets turned away from her and down as if looking at something else. Her gaze followed it down to find the scar that she had been searching for directly below where he stood.

"Free me!" she heard echo through the space around her. She looked back up to find the shadow face gone. She was alone, surrounded by mist and shadow, faced with the barrier. The scar was low on the division in her perception and looked as if it was in the process of deterioration. And she estimated that it would not be long before he retrieved all of the memories locked away here with no external help from her. She knew, however, that Tigershark had little patience for waiting. Angelina's shadow-self pushed against the scar, feeling it give, but it held against her persistence. Needles stung her incessantly as the failsafe beat her away. She backed from the barrier for a moment, regarding it with a critical eye. Yes, the opening did look wider. She rushed in, hitting the scar forcefully, ignoring the white-hot pain that she experienced, intent on getting through this time. Angelina thought that she was prepared to retreat before the safeguards shorted her brain, but she was one moment pressed against the barrier and the next she was floundering in a sea of memories both familiar and foreign. Angelina felt her contact start to fizzle, felt her brain want to die at the pain of the breached security, and then everything went black.

Angelina slowly became aware that she had returned to the real world and she tried to take a breath, gagging as the flood of water she lay in cascaded down her throat. Floundering with panic, she managed to sit up; coughing to clear her airway of the water she had tried to inhale. She gasped deeply, coughing and spluttering, before she realized that she was still alive, despite her encounter with Tigershark's booby-trapped mind.

Angelina looked around, suddenly aware that Tigershark was no longer in front of her. She finally found him about twenty feet away, where he had evidentially retreated. In the process, he had pushed her over, still trapped within his memories, unable to prevent her falling prone into the water.

Tigershark's body shuddered and writhed as if from a hidden pain. He arched back several times, screaming at the ghosts of pain he had suffered. He emitted a low moan as events severed from him were forcibly introduced all at the same time. Tigershark brought his hands clear of his face, looking them over as if they had just appeared.

"You bastards," he whispered as they slowly formed tight fists in front of his eyes, "what have you done to me? You fucking bastards!" Both extremities splashed into the water to punctuate his anger and loss as his body folded in on itself, his head resting heavily on his balled hands. Sobs soon echoed off the warehouse walls.

Angelina stood, head pounding from psychic backlash, and then moving closer, she knelt before his cradled form. She did not know how to go about comforting him. His moaning had ceased and he had straightened to a semi kneeled position, but he was shivering. He glanced up, only a flickering eye contact, averting his eyes and turning his head down after seeing her there. She reached out to touch him, and he shied from her. Slowly, he uncurled his body, looking again at his hands.

"Tiger?" she finally managed to say. "Are you okay?" She laid a hand on his shoulder.

He swatted it away, glaring at her. "Leave me the fuck alone!" he moaned angrily. Jumping abruptly to his feet, he retreated to a small office space at the end of the boardroom, slamming the door. Angelina heard a loud splash she could only think was Tigershark throwing himself into the water.

Angelina was left kneeling in the liquid seeping in through the cracks in the building, more confused than ever, unsure even if the process had been a success. She wanted to think it had, but the things he had said could have been his angry response to the torturous process he must certainly have gone through. He had already admitted not knowing what had happened during his procedure.

*****

I lay in the ankle deep water, consumed by a numbness that had penetrated even my brain. I had no will, no desire to move, to eat, or to think. I just wished the room would collapse and end my misery. What had that woman done to me? What had I allowed her to do?

Thousands of images washed up behind my eyes, vying for recognition. Very little seemed familiar to me now, where it had when she had first freed my mind. Now it was a confusing jumble begging to be processed, and I had no facilities or training to handle the volume I was seeing. So many of the images conflicted with each other, taking place at what would have been the same point in time, and figuring out what was real and what was fabrication was hard. At the moment I didn't even try; I could only lie there and let the images wash over me, hoping that sooner or later they would make sense.

How long had I been laying here? My mind tried to grapple that problem, but with all the other information it soon slipped away, lost in the blur. I had seen the girl, what was her name? Angelina, yes…that was it. She had peered in several times, her face wrinkled with worry, and again my mind went to futile effort to figure out why. Slowly, the answer filtered through the whirling images. I had been contracted to kill her, and had been repeatedly thwarted by her.

And how had she done that?

Ah, yes, she was telepathic. She had mentally crippled my attack. But…if I had been contracted to eliminate her, then it begged the question, why was I now in her company? The question echoed between my ears for several minutes before an answer presented itself.

She had . . . rescued me . . . I had nearly died from exposure to the atmosphere. She and a portly doctor had saved me from oblivion, and in return I had vowed to cease my persecution of her. And yet there was something else, some other reason I had sided with this woman rather than fulfilling my contract. There was also that the man who had hired me had lied about the girl's identity and the real reason he wanted her dead. He had said that he was my creator. And yet even that was not the whole reason. What exactly had caused my defection? Again the question floated freely in my mind, threatening to be obliterated by the flood, but pieces began to adhere to the question, and began to make a picture. What it told me shocked me more than the liberation of my mind.

*****

Two days went tensely by with no sign of Tigershark recovering from the cascade of memories he had inherited in a matter of minutes. Angelina had checked on him numerous times, only to find him in the same spot, belly down in the water, staring at some unknown point on the office wall.

She hoped the he would kick his funk; they were going to have to move locations if they were going to avoid Cortez's search parties, and soon.

Angelina had just begun a cold meal when he finally stirred. He had entered so quietly that she had not even known he was there until she turned to retrieve her fork. He leaned against the wall on one elbow with his fingers run part way through his thick mane, staring oddly at her. She started at the sight of him. "Hi," she said, sighing with relief.

He just nodded, uncertainty twitching the corners of his mouth. He looked gaunt, though Angelina was sure that it was just an illusion. His swaggering self-confidence had evaporated, and he somehow seemed more diminutive for it. "Are you going fishing?" Angelina asked, knowing he had to be hungry at this point.

"I . . . don't feel up to chasing my dinner," he answered quietly. She nodded and turned to rummage through the gunnysack for another can of food. He had seated himself near her, but distant enough that she knew he was uncomfortable with any proximity to her. Angelina opened the can, stuck a spoon in it and handed it to Tigershark; then she seated herself watching him closely.

"Thanks," he said simply.

They ate in complete silence, and Angelina tried to ignore both Tigershark's nervous glances, and his lack of eating grace. He had discarded the spoon, opting instead to pour it directly from the can into his large mouth. He was done quickly, and the can slipped from his hands into the water. He was staring at her openly now, and she couldn't help but wonder what was going through his mind. "Feel better?" she finally got the nerve to say, unsure even what to expect of him at this point.

"A little. My head hurts," Tigershark replied without feeling.

"Mine too. I guess it's from the psychic backlash. It wiped the floor with my brain," she returned. He chuckled, but did not actually sound amused by it. She cleared her throat. "So, did you find what you were looking for?"

He did not answer her but continued to stare at her. A smile began to form on his lips and Angelina smiled also, though uncertain about what was so funny. It was as if he was smiling to spite his mood, a somewhat insecure humor.

"What?" she finally said.

"Nothing," he replied quietly.

"No, really. What's so funny?"

Tigershark glanced down for a moment, that odd smile still on his features. "I was just thinking. White has never been your color." And again he gazed into her eyes with meaning.

Angelina gawked at her fellow runaway in confusion. She was hesitant, not certain either what had brought him to say that or what exactly he meant by it. Slowly, and after several more times of running the comment through her head, it began to dawn on her.

Angelina's eyes went wide with realization, and her spoon clanked noisily into the can she had been eating out of, then the can splashed into the water. "David?" she said, squinting as if that would reveal his true appearance.

His eyes wouldn't meet hers for long moments, flicking between her and the water. Finally, he nodded.

"Oh my God!" she gasped as she dove across the space between them, knocking them both into the cold water. Tigershark used one free hand to push them both upright, not returning her warm embrace, and after a moment he grabbed her gently and pushed her away.

Angelina watched his slit yellow gray eyes as they moved over her features. He raised one hand and ran his knuckles down her cheek, asking, "What did they do to you?" He glanced again at his hand, bothered by its appearance, and he curled it into a ball, allowing it to settle slowly into his lap.

"Me? Mine is nothing compared to what they did to you, David."

"Please don't call me that . . . not yet." He looked down at his lax hands. "I'm not deserving of that name . . . the things I've done . . ." He sounded anguished.

"It wasn't your fault. Cortez programmed you to do it. You weren't in control," she argued. He stood abruptly, seeming agitated. "What?" she said in confusion.

"How can you stand to look at me? Look what they made me into! A Goddamn gemue freak, a fucking killing machine, that's what I am!" He twirled around to face, her agony painting his features and regret filling his voice. "I tried to kill you! God, I didn't want to hurt you, ever," he said guiltily. "Turned out to kill my own true love." He covered his teary eyes with one large hand.

Angelina stood and moved to his side. She took his free elongated hand, and wrapped it in her own. Bringing it to her lips, she said, "It's okay. I forgave you a while ago... ever since I began to suspect. I still trust you."

His hand came away from his face and he stared at her blankly. Glancing from her eyes to her grip on his, he pulled his fingers slowly from her grasp, backing away, shaking his head, and acting hurt. "I don't trust myself," he trailed off, turning from her and secluding himself in the office area again.

*****

Waking from the suppression of my mind had been a painful, confusing thing. I did not recognize this body, so radically changed by that madman Angelina was unfortunate enough to be related to. I remembered nearly every agonizing moment that I had spent in Cortez's house of horrors. Then there were the visions . . . I had memories

181

I did not recognize as my own, bloody violent memories. Yet I knew with certainty that I had performed every act stored in my head. Being introduced to them so suddenly had disgusted and frightened me, as did the capabilities of this form.

They were certainly not unfamiliar traits in me, and that's what scared me. In my youth, I was troubled and uncomfortable with my family status. In rebellion I had joined a gang of kids with similar problems to my own. In a ruthless fashion I moved through the ranks to become their leader, and we did things that people seem to think only inner city kids are capable of. It was unheard of or neatly covered up so as not to tarnish the neighborhoods we came from.

The only problem with reaching the top, especially in a gang, is there is only one way to go, and always someone willing to push you off the edge. It was not a very long to wait for me, so cocky in my "invulnerability" that I never saw the gunman. I nearly paid for my pride and vanity with my life. Sitting in the hospital for four months had given me a lot of time to reflect on where I was headed if I stayed to the road I was on. I had been vengeful when I had first awoken, intent on getting my attacker put in the dirt, but that bullet had knocked some sense into my thick skull, and time wore away my reason for retaliation.

Instead, I had come to grips with the fact that I had to make changes in my life, or I would be dead within a year. It took a lot of soul searching and even harder work but I did it, changing from last in the class in my junior year to a top honor's winner as a senior. They voted me most improved and I had even earned a scholarship for college. That was a past that Angelina wasn't even aware of. She was only cognizant of my hair trigger temper and a vague mean streak that had showed on occasion when I was in college.

Now I found myself at the crossroad again, only this time it was harder to ignore the red-hot impulses stemming from the stimulation of that aggressive side of me. I had seen Angelina's worried face peering in the door from time to time, and she was probably wondering if I would recover from this. It was something I was wondering myself. I knew I would have to. I was not the type of person prone to giving up, but it was so hard to just get up and face her, knowing what I had done, what I was now. And just how do I tell her, and what exactly do I reveal? Would she run away and think on me only as a monster?

Again the images ran through my head, images of violence. I remembered vividly the things I had done by choice as a youth; things that I had thought I had left behind me over five years ago. Then my more recent memories came back; of the terror I had unleashed on countless people, most of whom I had no clue as to their crimes. I only had my orders and Cortez's word that they were guilty, of something. I knew now that most of them had been business rivals, and their death warrants were only to gain Cortez more shares of the market.

Slowly I shut my eyes, trying to block out the sight of terrified faces, trying to forget the screams that still sang in my ears, to rid myself of the blood I still tasted on my tongue. My attack on Angelina surfaced again, and my body shivered as I realized how close I had come to spilling her blood as well, and a breath escaped me. It did nothing to fade those memories, nor the satisfaction that I had felt at the conclusion of each successful hunt. What had I become? I tucked my head under folded arms and sobbed quietly.

Chapter Fifteen: Explanations

It was early when I awoke, the sun just beginning to stain the sky with color. I easily slipped past the still sleeping form of Angelina and stood staring out at the placid San Joaquin water.

I was hungry, and not for any cold cans of prepackaged vegetables or stew. My new body craved raw fish, freshly killed, and it did not like my hesitation at going to find it. My duplicity, however anchored me here, merely staring at the glassy surface of the water.

I knew from first hand experience how well this body performed its function. My older identity was frightened though, never having been involved with living underwater for indefinite periods of time. I found myself afraid of drowning, which I knew was absurd. I had spent two days laying face first in the water of the office, but it was easy to delude myself into thinking I had been breathing through my nose.

That was the problem with having two similar yet distinct personalities. One denied what the other knew for fact. So I stood staring out at the water, feeling the hunger gnawing at me and growing more insistent as I lingered. I closed my eyes, and made an effort to slide back into Tigershark's familiarity with this. I fell into it much too easily, and in a panic I withdrew, afraid that I would lose my identity to him again.

I took a deep breath trying to calm my racing heart. I knew now the only way to get over my anxiety was to, quite literally, dive in. Hopefully, that would begin to heal my divergent memories. I jumped into the cold water before my nerve gave out and I swam deeper so that surfacing when I ran out of the breath was not an option. Knowing this body's ability did not stop me from holding that breath. I panicked just as I had the day of my introduction to my new life, thrashing about wildly unwilling to drag in that mouthful of saltwater. Finally, I had no choice. I drew it in, grateful when my gills seined the needed gas from the water, and oxygen returned to my system. Even with my small victory, I was still breathing fast and had to will my respiration to slow. I was very conscious of the water passing out the gills on my neck, such a familiar, yet foreign sensation for me. That was the whole experience so far, given a certain familiarity with this body but still feeling as if I didn't truly own it. I can't even say that David had witnessed the atrocities Tigershark was capable of; they had buried that personality so deep that it had no recollection of my period as a mercenary. My indignation only came once my previous personality had been restored to equal footing with the new. Now they both vied for control of this body.

Once I had calmed, I set to work tracking down my breakfast. The anxious feeling was slowly passing and I began to relish again in the grace of this body. The ease at which I was able to move through the water was amazing. It was faster than I had ever swum on a dive and changing direction came without effort or awkwardness.

*****

Angelina expected another long silence from Tigershark, but upon checking his perch she found him absent. She checked in earnest the rest of the facility, only to come up with no clues as to his whereabouts. "Well shit," she muttered, unsure how to interpret his disappearance. Did he panic and run away, or did he just snap out of his mood and go for some breakfast?

He splashed up minutes later, answering her unspoken question, and pulled himself easily onto the platform. Water dripped from all of his features and he sighed grandly, running a hand through his thick mane. Tigershark looked much more solid mentally. In fact, his eyes were alight with pleasure and a relaxed smile graced his elongated face.

"Good morning," Angelina offered in astonishment, "Feeling better?"

"Yes," he replied lightly. "That was invigorating."

He stretched, reminding Angelina of a cat, and then shrugged his arms back like a swimmer preparing for a race. He then moved across the room and began looking over their supplies.

Angelina smiled warmly at his back surprised and happy that Tigershark had begun dealing with the course his life had taken. That joy was relatively short lived, however. As the day wore on, Angelina began to notice how little difference there was in his behavior now, as compared to his mannerisms before she had released the shackle on his mind. There were moments of deep introspection on his part, during which times he was irritable and moody. They were short however and his swagger, humor, and manners spoke

187

all of Tigershark and none of David. That worried her, the thought of David possibly preferring Tigershark...or that the mental block ran deeper than what she had defeated in his mind. She could not confirm or discount either suspicion, for her telepathy had been crippled in her attempt to help him.

Her whole purpose in pursuing Tigershark had been to verify David still existed in him and to bring David back into her life. She realized immediately how selfish that was, but was unable to help herself. Either way she could not recall David being so cavalier or temperamental when they had been dating.

By the next morning it was irritating, and she decided it was time to find out if she had really purged Tigershark's influence. She strode up to him confidently, but faltered as she neared him. She looked down for a moment, and then cleared her throat.

Tigershark turned to look at her. "Is everything okay?" she asked quietly.

"I'm just stowing some of these things," he said matter-of-factly, turning back to his work, "We're going to have to leave soon."

She laid a hand on his arm, turning him back to face her. "No, I meant, are you all right?"

"Yeah," he replied, his brows knit in mild amusement, "why do you ask?"

"You..." she stammered, suddenly unsure how to phrase her concerns, "With everything you've been through in the last few days... You're taking all this rather well," she finally blurted out.

A look akin to anger crossed his face as he slowly sat down. Angelina sat down across from him, and he asked her, "What were you expecting?"

Angelina's face flushed, "I ... I'm not sure... Not this, certainly."

"Not what?" Tigershark pressed in a darker tone.

"Not such nonchalance," she blurted. "The David I knew despised everything about gemue's. He thought their very existence was blasphemous."

"Don't you think I know that?" he said, blinking slowly.

"I can't tell," she answered him. "My ability was blinded." His lips thinned, but Angelina went on, "I just thought that, realizing what they had done to you, you would be on the edge of insanity. But you sit before me calm and happy, as if nothing terrible has happened."

"Happy?" He smiled wryly and shook his head. "No. I'm not happy. But circumstances have a way of changing one's perspective," he replied simply, not looking at her.

"How can you be so calm?" Angelina screeched in frustration. "They turn your... our lives upside down, and you give me anecdotes!"

He stood abruptly, glaring down at her. "What do you want me to do? Bemoan my fate to an uncaring God?" He raised his hands and eyes toward the ceiling and then slowly lowered his eyes to look at her again. "Kill myself to end the misery and confusion that comes from having lived two completely different lives, having two personalities warring constantly for control?" Angelina shook her head negatively, scared at where he might be going with the line of conversation. Had she pushed him so hard that he was considering ending his life? Tigershark's arms drifted slowly down to his sides. "It wouldn't do any good. It will not change what has happened to us, no matter how much I want it to. I won't let them break me like that. It's what they want," Tigershark finished resolutely.

"But all those people," Angelina said softly.

"I know the lives I've ruined for Cortez's greed, and it is just something I am going to be burdened with. I can't do anything to change that past. And right now there is no atonement suitable for my sins."

Angelina had nothing to counter with and the room fell silent. The silence seemed to drag into hours, before curiosity caused her to break it, "What really bothers me is that you're not the way I remember you."

He barked out a short laugh, "I would think that's obvious."

"I mean your attitude... I might as well never have restored your memory. You're not David, not the one I remember."

That seemed to hit Tigershark rather hard, for he first looked shocked and then his features hardened. "What makes you say that?"

"You act nothing like David did when we were dating. Everything you do speaks volumes for Tigershark's personality."

"Tigershark is a part of me now, Angel," he replied softly. "I am as much him as I am David. I only regained what had been stolen of my life. I can't just erase what's happened since like an obsolete file. I just want to call myself me again, not Tigershark or David anytime my moods swing," He sighed heavily, "In order to do that, I have to let them heal themselves. They need to be used equally and at the same time. I have a long way to go before that happens, but I have to start somewhere.

"You think that Tigershark is my dominant personality?"

She nodded.

"You're wrong," he said, shaking his head in emphasis. "I know time softens edges, but Christ, it's only been nine months. I was always hot blooded, strong willed, opinionated, and quick to argue even when I was wrong, and proven so. I used to take over the class discussions and route them to come out in my favor."

Angelina watched as remembrance crossed his face. A smile pulling at the corners of his mouth, he ran his fingers thoughtfully over his lips, "You were my top adversary in those debates."

He shook himself free from the past, returning his attention to at her, "I haven't changed that much!" He looked down at his hands, and then pointed to his temple, "Well, up here anyway."

Her gaze fell away for long moments, "You're right, I guess I was so used to associating it with Tigershark that I never considered it was based on the David I knew."

Another pregnant silence fell over the room, neither knowing where to take the conversation next. Curiosity overwhelmed Angelina, "So... do you remember everything then?"

He gazed over at her with a small pained expression. "My memories are still reconciling themselves, but they are whole again, yes."

"Everything? Including..." Angelina trailed off, afraid to finish.

He closed his eyes against a painful memory, "Yes," he whispered, "Even the procedure."

*****

I remembered it all now, and part of me wished that I had never asked Angelina to lift the curtain. Fully detailed memories swirled through my head, wanting to be released. But first I had to break my little secret to Angelina.

"I was perfect for Cortez's experiments, even if he didn't know it when we were captured."

"What do you mean?"

"Angelina, there are things I haven't told you about me... about my past." I took a deep breath upon seeing Angelina's concerned face, "You know that I have always had a temper, right?"

She nodded as her expression clouded a bit more.

"What you don't know, what I hadn't told you for fear of losing you was that...." I stumbled again, unsure how to break the news to her.

"What?"

"Before you and I met, when I was still in high school I was a member of a gang. No. It wasn't just that...I led it. We were a group of unhappy rich kids rebelling against the system we lived in. We did things...that would have made ghetto gangs look tame. It's not a past that I am proud of." I bulled through the explanation.

"And you didn't tell me?" Angelina asked sounding at once angry and shocked.

"I... didn't think it was going to be necessary. That was wrong too, but I had long since reformed when we started dating. I managed a year of high school and all of college without letting myself slide back into that life. I never thought it would affect me again."

"Did... Did you ever... kill anyone? I mean back then?"

I stared blankly at her a long time feeling my stomach hit bottom as she asked that question. I couldn't meet her eyes when I whispered, "Yes..."

"Oh my God," Angelina breathed, looking horrified, "Then that day... after the bar fight..."

"Don't ask it, Angelina..." I warned her quietly, "You already know the answer."

It took everything in her to keep herself from backing away from me. She paused, considering the implications. "Then what made you get out of that life?"

"Well," I smiled ruefully, pointing to the small nearly unnoticeable scar just above my left pec, "I was...shot by one of my own 'friends.' I was so cocky, so sure of my leadership..." I shook my head. "My pride landed me in the hospital, on the brink of death for nearly a month. I was in recovery for the next three. That's a lot of time to think, and I began to realize that I had wasted most of the past few years on senseless violence, and that if I didn't or couldn't change I would be dead by the end of that year.

"It was a tough battle for me to break the destructive habits I had formed, and to get back to doing my schoolwork. After some time I realized not only was I good in school, but that I liked it. In a year I managed to turn it all around, even earning my scholarship.

"It was still a constant battle with that part of my personality, because the more stressed I became the easier those emotions came out. It showed on occasion in college; the fights I used to get involved with, the way I lost my temper in class. But I did so well...until Cortez got a hold of me."

I paused a moment to let that sink in, then I changed gears.

"After our capture, after the interrogation, and after they split us up, they sedated me. I awoke in a sterile white walled room, securely strapped to a gurney. A terrible pain in my neck and chest made me dizzy and ill. It was hard to breathe even with the oxygen being fed to me. I was still... human and ignorant of the process I was being subjected to against my will. When I had recovered from that enough, they moved me to a lab where I was shackled naked to the wall, shivering from the subterranean cold and the faded pain I was in. They allowed me to watch as they designed their product with the look they wanted, using a mock up of the DNA mixture. I remember being defiant then, shouting insults at the butchers for what they were about to try." I laughed shortly. "It did little good.

"When the right ratio was achieved they passed their notes to the lab where the formula was actually made and introduced to my system. After that, they brought me to another section of the lab filled with equipment most of which I could not name the function of... I'm not sure I want to. They forced me onto a raised metallic disc in the floor. There was a hum of electricity, and a containment field hindered my escape. I watched them laugh as I threw myself against the unseen wall, because I had an idea of what they had in store.

"You see, they wanted their product quickly and letting nature take its course was out of the question. They fell back to an old standard of radiation treatments. Blinding light bathed my bare form and an inescapable heat seared my eyes and skin as an inner fire was begun that would accelerate the changes they had wrought in my body. I remember screaming under that torture.

"After an indeterminable amount of time, they released me from that invisible prison. I was too weak to resist as they transferred me to a dank little cell to lose what was left of the contents of my stomach. I knew then exactly what a leukemia patient must feel like.

"They left me alone for several weeks, I figure now so that they could use it as a standard for the rate of change. It wasn't much after the first session. A slight change in bulk, thickening in the chest, and the paling of my skin were all I could recall.

"The treatments came in quick succession after that, and in turn the change accelerated. I remember almost nothing of that time, being too sick and dehydrated to take notice of how grotesque I was becoming. You saw the memory of the change in my hands. I remember tearing at my face because it burned and itched from the treatments, and finding out painfully that sleeping on my back was no longer an option, but very little else, until the treatments stopped. But I was no longer David at that point; I was already programmed, Cortez taking advantage of the weakness of my mind and body. That was when I started this whole mess, sitting in a cage waiting to be loosed to find you.

"He had sent me on several test runs before you," I averted my eyes, "I was sent after several businessmen in powerful positions. Those assignments were to not only test the body out, the killing prowess, but also to be sure that I would not die in the ocean because the gills failed to work.

"Cortez had insisted on the cage, from the beginning, it served to force me to take to my new lifestyle, the gills being untried. They were willing to kill me to be sure they got a good test out of my introduction to water. Turner had me convinced that it was just to show me off that first time.

"The first couple times there weren't any issues, the programming held, and Tigershark's confidence overrode what was truly natural. Occasionally there would be small hiccups, slight anxiety transferring from water to land or vice versa. I was prone to panic, even though my implanted memory was certain of the gills function; muscle memory was a bit more powerful. Those were easily explained as psychosomatic responses.

"Really, they were signs that the memory set wasn't as solid as they had predicted. There was an inherent flaw or else you would never have gotten the clues as to my true identity," I smiled thankfully as I lifted her chin so she would look at me.

Angelina looked pale and sick, and I just noticed a tear on her cheek. "I'm sorry... I should have tried harder to find you," she moaned, reaching out and embracing me suddenly.

I found myself actually returning the gesture and not feeling awkward, and I hugged her hard as I closed my eyes and fought back the pain of what had become of us.

"It's okay, Angel. Don't blame yourself."

I pushed her gently away, grinning lopsidedly and trying to appear steady, even if all I wanted to do was crawl into a corner and cry like a little kid.

"Let's get some sleep." I finished, standing up and offering assistance.

She took my hand and rose to her feet, heading slowly over to her pallet, glancing back occasionally to see if my mask had cracked yet.

I hoped it hadn't.

Chapter Sixteen: Complications

In the morning, Angelina found Tigershark staring out one of the cracked bay windows. What she could see of his face, held a blank expression. She leaned on a close by pillar and began to greet him. He looked at her sharply, stopping her words in her throat. He raised an index finger and made his meaning even more clearly. He motioned to her gear in the corner, and when she returned her gaze to him, he pulled an imaginary helmet over his head. She nodded slowly in understanding.

Angelina moved over to her gear, preparing it and hooking up her tanks. She turned to see Tigershark slide away from the window as if to avoid detection. Clearing the area, he quickly joined her stuffing necessities into waterproof sacks. He spared a few words to say, "They don't actually know we're here yet," as he grabbed another sack to put more supplies in.

Angelina dressed as quickly as her tight neoprene suit would allow. Once she had that on, she shrugged on her rebreather, and began to gather her smaller items. Tigershark was finished with his task quickly, and proceeded to help her with the remainder of her gear. He took another glance out the window before motioning her to the stairwell that had gone to the next level down when this had been land. Tigershark provided his support while she donned her fins and adjusted her faceplate. She then stepped down a few more steps before pushing off, creating little sound as she did.

Waiting several feet below the surface of the pool, Angelina paused to allow Tigershark to catch up. The wait was not long, for he joined her very shortly. As he swam up, Angelina heard his voice reverberate through the water, "Can you hear me?"

"Yes," she replied vociferously. "How's reception?"

He adjusted the volume on the receiver in his left ear, before answering her. "It's a little loud. Let's go."

Tigershark wove a path through the submerged machinery with an ease that made Angelina envious, and several times he nearly lost her. They descended through the building to the first floor, pausing as they reached the exit. Tigershark glanced cautiously out into the murky water, checking for any sign of an ambush. He tested the water for any pheromones that might give away their pursuers. Angelina mirrored the motion. They turned toward one another and nodded when they were satisfied that no one lay in wait.

They pushed off simultaneously, swimming just far enough off the bottom so that there was less chance of kicking up a trail of silt as they passed. Angelina glanced back, observing divers entering the building. She heard her heart pounding in her ears as she realized just how close they had been to capture. When she lingered too long, Tigershark grabbed her shoulder, causing her to start. He motioned toward deeper water, wanting to put as much distance as humanly possible between themselves and their pursuers.

They had been traveling for nearly an hour when Tigershark finally slowed to a halt. Angelina took the opportunity to consult her dive monitor, happy to find that she had just over an hour left at her present rate of consumption. Tigershark looked at her expectantly. "Everything okay?"

"Yeah," she said simply, and allowed him to check her meter for himself.

He nodded after confirming her air reserves. "Stay here, I'm going to find us another place to stay."

*****

I found myself unable to sit still, and therefore I decided to scout ahead. Angelina had seemed glad for the rest, but I knew that the break would have to be short. Once they found the remains of our camp at the factory, they would hound us until we were run to ground.

I was searching for a cave, building, or anything that showed promise of it holding a measure of air. Angelina's rebreather, while good, was not going to last forever. We were too far from the ranges to find a naturally occurring submarine cave. And the buildings in this section of the underwater town appeared none too promising. I was thinking of moving toward the shoreline, but I was unsure her air would hold out that long. Surfacing, while it would solve the problem of air, would only serve to make us easy targets.

I began to recognize my surroundings. Near here was a place that I could take Angelina. I didn't really relish the idea. Getting Scud involved in this mess was a risky proposition. She was less than trustworthy, but my choices were very limited.

I felt a twinge of annoyance about performing this search at all. I was unaccustomed to having to worry about another person. I knew that Angelina and I had been an item at one time, but that cozy past seemed so distant, so unreal in lieu of what has happened since. I felt disconnected from that past, and I knew it every time Angelina took it to call me David. It didn't feel like my name any longer, that part of me sullied by recent events. I found myself falling into a depression, not knowing just how to handle it, and doing a poor job of hiding it from Angelina. I began to wonder if that schism between personalities would ever repair itself.

I was interrupted mid-thought by a loud thump carried through my receiver and heard Angelina next, thinking it had been me, telling me to stop playing games. Her annoyed tone turned to a scream that hurt my sensitive ears. In a panic I swam back to the spot I had left Angelina. She was gone, and I searched quickly trying to locate her.

The water above me darkened and, glancing up, I saw Angelina swimming for the surface. A larger shadow then passed overhead, proving to be a true shark. It was in hot pursuit of Angelina, intent on a late afternoon meal. The creature's forty-foot body was misshapen with tumors from a lifetime of polluted food, and scarred from many mysterious battles with other denizens of the sea. I dashed after the two, assuring Angelina, "Hold on, I'm coming." It took me very little time to catch up to the ugly brown behemoth. Instinctively, I punched a straight fingered, clawed hand into the creature's right gill, watching blood stain the water. A shudder went through the gargantuan as the pain penetrated its tiny brain. It swung its head to the right, trying to catch me with its teeth, and I easily avoided the jaws. I slipped down underneath it, one hand still lodged in its gills. Drawing my feet up, I allowed my toe claws to grab purchase in the creature's underbelly. I pushed out feeling my sharp toenails slide easily through the armored hide.

The monster thrashed about, frenzied by pain and the blood clouding the water. I peered through the cloudy water, hoping that there were no other predators nearby to pick up the scent. Now the great shark was beginning to sink into the depths, and I had yet to liberate my fingers. My hand was wedged tight between the monster's inner gills, and the tugging I was doing was only causing raw spots on my wrist. I placed my right hand against the creature for added leverage and again attempted to pull my hand loose. I had paid no attention to the placement of my opposite hand. The shark reminded me quickly as it bit down on my ring and little fingers. I heard my own shriek of pain, as my left hand came free. Without pausing, I drew back and punched the creature in the eye. It released my hand, sending a new shock-wave of pain up my arm. I drew my right hand to my body, ensuring that I would not use it.

The fight with the shark had dragged me almost to the bottom again and I shot my gaze up to find Angelina nearing the surface, totally unaware that her pursuer was gone. There was an inherent danger in her blind flight, and I swam quickly to catch up with her before she was stricken, hindered as I was by my injury. My added effort afforded me nothing, for about twenty feet from the atmosphere above decompression sickness hit her like a fist. She doubled over, rising with the expanding air of her tanks toward the sun-dappled waves above us.

When I caught up to her I grabbed both her shoulders, trying to calm her writhing. I pulled her down from the surface and released the remaining air in her BCD. I checked her computer to find that she had only ten minutes remaining in her tanks. "Angelina?" I said as her head flung back with another spasm, "Angel!" I repeated. She rolled her head back around, peering at me as best she could. "I've got to take you back down."

"Not enough . . . air," she stuttered.

"I can get you more air, but if I don't get you recompressed, it will be the least of our worries, okay?"

She nodded jerkily. I swam down in the general direction of Scud's house, knowing now she was my only choice. As we descended, Angelina's convulsions slowed, until they were nearly unnoticeable. I set her on an outcropping of rock just outside Scud's dwelling, knowing that I wasn't going to bring her in with her gear on. I was going to have enough problems handling Scud on my own.

The place was just like one of those pup tents they sell for camping, only about four times the size. The dome was constructed of curved stainless steel beams supporting stretched and formed sheets of heavy plastic. I approached the underwater dwelling from below, where access to her pool would be, and entered without hesitation. I splashed up through the pool and jumped to my feet, even as Scud jumped to hers, pointing a speargun at my heart.

"Put that thing away, Scud," I growled, turning my back to her. The last thing I wanted to deal with was a paranoid mech-splice. I found a regulator and snatched it up, checking a few of the nearby tanks. "I need to borrow these," I said without pretense.

Scud inserted herself between her hoard and me. "No way, Tiger, no Goddamn way, those there are mine!" She hooked a thumb towards the tanks behind her.

I grabbed her lapel, lifting her bodily off the ground with my good hand. "I have got no time to argue with you! I am taking them, capiche?"

She nodded reluctantly, and I set her back on her feet.

"Okay, don't go anywhere; I'm going to need your help in just a minute." She folded her arms across her chest and frowned. I took it as a yes and dove into the pool, tanks in tow.

Angelina was exactly where I had left her. Her convulsions had ceased, but she was beginning to turn blue with cold and lack of oxygen. She barely managed to raise her lids to look at me as I came up.

"I'm back, Angel," I said quietly, shocked by the worry in my own voice. "Flood your mask. I'm going to give you a standard regulator."

She nodded affirmation and reached shakily up to unseal her helmet. I watched impatiently as it flooded, knowing her air was critically low. When the mask was filled to her eyes I removed it, ignoring her wide-eyed expression at the temperature of the water, and then handed her the regulator. She instinctively cleared the second stage and took a deep breath. "Better?" I asked. She gave me the okay signal. "We've got to get this stuff off," I added, beginning to unlatch the BCD and her depleted rebreather. I tethered the gear to a nearby outcropping of twisted steel and plaster. That done, I gathered Angelina in my arms, trying to ignore the pain from my shattered hand, and swam into Scud's entry pool

I gently pulled the regulator out of Angelina's mouth, handing it and the tank up to Scud. When she returned to the pool, I lifted Angelina as high as I could, grimacing in pain, until Scud relieved me of her burden. I went back out again, retrieving Angelina's gear, determined to keep our whereabouts from our pursuers. That done, I jumped out of the water as well and asked, "You got a towel or three?"

Scud obliged, handing me a towel, and I dried myself quickly. I helped Angelina dry herself, and then wrapped her in another to conserve her heat. She looked weary, pale and sick, and I hoped she would recover. At the moment, however, it seemed as if we were here for a while.

"She needs some sleep," I said, peering at Scud. "You got a place she can lay down?"

Scud thumbed toward her own bedroll. "I ain't going to be sleeping anytime soon."

"What's the matter, Scud?" I smirked, as I helped Angelina to the bed. "Don't you trust me?"

"Hell no. You tried to kill me."

"Consider yourself one of the lucky ones. I usually succeed when I try," I remarked as I sat protectively near Angelina's soundly sleeping form. "Besides, you were trying to strip mine my home," I finished in what I hoped was a lighter note.

Scud glared at me warily from the far side of the dome. "So . . . You going to do something about that hand?" she asked. "Or are you just going to keep bleeding on my floor?"

I raised my right hand up, examining intently the twisted digits and torn membranes. The damage was unsightly. "I suppose," I replied lightly. "You got a first aid kit?"

She threw it at me, and I caught it with my bad hand, swearing under my breath at the pain. I took a deep breath, then, with an audible crack, I reset my ring finger, taking perverse pleasure in watching Scud wince. I had gotten lucky with that finger; it was only dislocated and I quickly splinted it. The shark's teeth had caught the little finger, however, so the first knuckle was nearly severed and the membrane between the two fingers was shredded. "I'm going to need some help putting this puzzle back together," I said absently.

Scud reluctantly moved over to my side and surveyed the damage. She quickly pulled out a surgical needle and some cord, deftly sewing the knuckle to the rest of my finger. She then spread the two fingers apart, causing me a great deal of pain which I somehow managed to keep distant. Scud laid a piece of gauze against the tattered skin of the webbing and taped it to each of the affected fingers. That done, she turned my hand over, carefully replacing the shreds of skin in their respective places, then sewing them in place through the gauze. She then braced the fingers apart. When she was finished I had to consciously shut my mouth. Her skill overwhelmed me.

"Where did you learn to do that?"

She just shrugged. "You're going to have to lay off swimming for a while. Chances are you'll never use that finger again," she commented matter-of-factly and returned to her side of the dwelling.

"Watch me."

"So, just how did you do that?"

"Got into an argument with a shark."

Her eye ridges lifted above the green lenses over her eyes.

"It was trying to eat my friend for lunch. He didn't go down quietly."

"Is that how she got the bends?"

"Would you worry about your rate of ascent if you had a forty footer on your ass?"

"Nope, can't say that I would."

*****

A throbbing pain brought me out of the doze I had not realized I was in. I opened my eyes and glanced across the room at Scud. She appeared to be sleeping, though it was hard to tell with her implanted lenses. I then turned to Angelina's sleeping form, sighing anxiously. I remembered just yesterday wishing she were out of my hair so that I would have no one to worry about but me. The old saying, "Be careful what you wish for," drifted through my conscious thought for a few moments, reminding me how well it applied. That was Tigershark's loner attitude bleeding through again. Today? Well, David was in dominance, the good old emotional side of me and all his love for her was tearing me up.

I wondered silently, annoyed by the habit of it, when I would stop referring to my attitude swings as either David or Tigershark and simply refer to them as mine. They were two sides of the same coin, after all. The ones I was currently referring to as David's were the emotional side, the side that felt love, loss, and dismay, a side that needed companionship and interaction with others. All of those things that the scientists felt were detrimental to a weapon of destruction and therefore repressed when Tigershark was created. Those that were Tigershark, were those meaner traits, anger, frustration, viciousness, and aggression, all enhanced to make me better able to mindlessly go about the job they had set before me, killing anyone with an agenda contrary to Marlin Inc.

Angelina shivered slightly and my vision refocused on her. It took my mind off my own troubles for the moment, and I laid a hand on her temple. She was running a slight fever, but I was convinced it was nothing serious. I ran that same hand, my good hand, lightly across her features until it nestled almost of its own accord in the crook of her waist. It remained there as a reassurance that she was still with the living. My brows furrowed in worry as I continued to stare at her, trying to will her to consciousness. I needed reassurance right now, not only that she was going to be okay; it seemed that she was well enough that eventually she would pull through this. I needed reassurance that I was going to be okay. It was something that I was not sure about anymore.

I would never dream of giving back the gift she had given me, restoring me to myself, but the cost was a high one it seemed. My sanity right now was questionable, ever in flux, and I was unsure whether that was going to be temporary or permanent to my new life.

"So, I see they did leave you some humanity," I heard from behind me. I started, darting a glance Scud's direction. She was smirking at me.

I wanted to be mad, to deny my feelings, but instead I stared at the floor, saying softly, "Yeah, I guess they did."

"What is she to you?" Scud asked boldly.

"Would you believe a former girlfriend?" I asked glancing with raised eyebrows, already knowing the answer.

She turned a critical eye to Angelina, then back at me. "Nah! She's not your type."

"She was when I was human," I said regretfully.

"In what dream was this?" Scud scoffed, turning away.

"Never mind, Scud," I said in annoyance. The last thing I felt like doing was trying to convince someone I didn't really like of something I knew as truth. I grimaced slightly as the pain in my hand made itself known again. I sat up straighter, rubbing between my mangled fingers, which were the worst shade of purple I had ever seen, trying to make the pain go away. The gauze sewn to the webbing of my hand was green and smelled of the infection that was starting there.

"Let's take a peek at that," Scud said, reaching toward the sore appendage.

"It's fine," I muttered, drawing away.

"Sure, and I'm Mother Teresa," she replied sharply, grabbing it roughly, pinching the flesh between my fingers and drawing it toward her.

"Augh!" I yelped in pain and anger. "You fucking bitch!"

"And you feel pain too. Oh my, this is a day for finding secrets," she said sarcastically, her attention now on the hand.

"Of course I feel pain! I am not superman, you know," I growled, then lowered my voice again. "I have an extremely high tolerance for pain, Scud, it's how they made me. But even I have my limits, and believe me I've reached it. I've suffered way too much abuse the past few months."

She nodded, not saying another word. I wanted to take it to mean that she bought my reason, but you could never be sure with Scud. Her mind was often like quicksilver. She remained silent as she quickly cleaned the wounds, dousing the whole of my hand in peroxide to wash away the infection. I grit my teeth as the liquid worked its way into the tears and stitching, bubbling against raw nerves. She expertly daubed it dry, causing little more pain than was already there and again inspected the hand.

Shaking her head, not satisfied with what she saw, Scud then cut away the larger sections of gauze to get a better look. She examined my injured hand with a professional eye, gawking back at me a moment later. "These are healing at a rate I've never seen before. At this speed, the stitches can be removed tomorrow." She then put pressure onto the tip of my smallest finger. "Any feeling . . . pain?"

I shook my head in the negative, frowning. " 'Fraid not."

She shook her head slowly. "You probably won't recover full use of that hand, Tiger, and this time I'm not joking."

I just shrugged. "I'll make do. I always have. At least it's the pinkie and not my index finger or thumb. I kinda need those."

"Hmph, that's for sure," she laughed. "So, you trying to start a new fad? The stitch fad?" she added as she reached over to pick at one of the stitches on my arm.

My hand traced over each of the different set of stitches on my body. Some of them were near the point of falling out on their own because they had been in my skin so long. I smiled. "I told you that I had been abused recently."

"Well, most of these look as if they are way overdue for removal." And without prompting, Scud set about pulling those stitches that were no longer necessary. "Doesn't anyone believe in soluble stitches anymore?"

"For a water dweller?" I asked, trying to remain still as she trimmed floss away and pulled the tags from my skin.

"Good point," she replied.

When Scud had finished, I focused again on Angelina. Drawing out some more of Scud's unexpected medical knowledge, I asked, "Do you think she'll be okay?"

It was her turn to shrug. "Hard to say . . . The bends are funny that way. You did the best thing you could have, bringin' her back down. Not many decompression tanks available to us these days."

"Well, I hope it's enough. Access to a doctor is kind of out of the question at the moment, too."

The room went silent momentarily and I watched as her face formed a question. "Just why are you in these waters? I thought you were in good with the dryworlders."

"Cortez," I started. "Angelina has a mark on her head."

"Whoa, heavy hitter," she said. "But . . . isn't he the one you were working for? If so, why are you running with his mark?"

"Yes, he was my boss, and I was assigned Angelina's death warrant." I paused and Scud raised her eyebrows for me to continue. I scratched my temple, unsure how to tell her what happened next. "I showed her compassion; I spared her from the mark on her head."

"Why? That doesn't sound at all like you."

"She saved my life. I . . . collapsed while tracking her, and instead of letting me die knowing what I represented, she helped to nurse me back to health."

"That's it? Sounds pretty thin."

"No, I began to remember things. Things never a part of Tigershark's life. I'm not who I thought I was when you and I first met. I wasn't kidding when I said Angelina and I was once a couple, because not ten months ago I was human. My real name is David Theodore Scott II."

I caught her incredulous expression.

"No shit. I was walking around just like any other suit uptown, carrying on. Cortez made me into his prize experiment and tested me by sending me after Angelina with a false set of memories and a new identity. Angelina helped me regain what Cortez had stolen, and as you can guess, I didn't really want to work for him anymore."

She then shook her head. "You're weirding me out, Tiger," Scud said . "Though I have to say, I never really bought into that story you gave me about being around for seven years," she replied nonchalantly. "I've seen all the forms for that time and you're much too perfect for that era in gemue tech."

"Thanks, I think," I said with a crooked grin.

"Theodore?" she said with a smirk, and my face flushed hot in embarrassment.

"I never liked it either," I replied to her distaste.

"So what are you going to do now?"

I just shrugged, not looking at her.

"Well, you can't keep running, Tiger. Sooner or later they'll catch up to you."

"Just what do you suggest I do?" I growled.

It wasn't Scud who answered me. "We take the fight to him," Angelina breathed.

"Angelina!" I said, startled, spinning to see her pushed up on one elbow. I swiveled the rest of the way around to aid her in sitting up. I peered into her eyes, which were swollen with exhaustion. "Are you okay?"

"Other than feeling like a Mack truck hit me, I'm fine," she said, not seeming as if she matched her own meager assessment. "We need to hit Marlin where he lives, David: his pocketbook. That means we're going to need hard evidence against him."

"What do you mean?" I said suspiciously.

"We're going to talk to him," she said seriously.

"What?" Scud and I both said in outrage.

"He likes to gloat, David, he's sure to incriminate himself if we confront him with this."

"No, absolutely not!" I bellowed. "That's a suicide mission and you know it. I didn't spend the last month dodging his flunkies only to allow myself to walk into his lair!"

"How do you propose we get him off our backs? I'm tired of running, David . . . tired of playing the game by his rules. Sooner or later he will find us, and then your free will, my humanity, and probably Scud's life are forfeit."

I dug holes in the floor with my eyes, my jaw working. The truth hurt, but I nodded slowly. "Okay, but I want this to be carefully planned. He's not going to just let us stroll into his office."

"We'll figure something out."

It took two weeks for Angelina to recover enough to be a part of the party. We had been hashing out possible plans the whole time and now had settled on one that had the best chance of getting us in and out without being captured or killed.

In that time my hand had healed beautifully, to even my amazement. I had regained most of the use of it with the exception of the tip of my pinkie finger, which was stiff, immobile and numb to the touch. But that did not surprise me with the nature of the injury.

Chapter Seventeen: Battles

Angelina and I surfaced about fifty feet from the landing in Cortez's basement, in a small, shadowy alcove just out of range of his cameras.

I twisted around to face Angelina, whispering, "We'd better leave the equipment here."

She nodded, slipping out of her rebreather and then her wetsuit. She shivered in the cool water, but said nothing as she hung everything on the nearby outcroppings of rock. I turned away, peering around the wall of rock concealing us. There were three guards that I could see, one standing very near the stairs to the upper floors, and the other two moving parallel to the water away from each other.

"C'mon," I breathed, ducking low into the water before pushing off. Angelina followed closely in my wake. The easiest of the three marks was now very near the water with his back toward the shoreline. I motioned Angelina to hang back as I shot out of the water, lashed a hand around his throat, and yanked him into the cold sea. I silenced him quickly, motioning Angelina forward, only to find her gone.

"Shit," I muttered, searching the massive cavern for a sign of her.

After several moments I caught a glimpse of her sneaking up on the third guard. But her position was precarious, for there was no concealment in that area and it would only take him looking that direction to spot her. As she came closer, I decided to give her some advantage.

Stepping out of the alcove, I yelled, "Hey, dryworlder!"

"Son of a bitch," I heard his surprised mutter, as he raised his gun. "You don't know how much trouble you're in, gemue." He started toward me.

"I think I should be saying that to you," I replied smugly.

"Hu . . . Aulk!" he finished, as his eyes rolled back.

"That was stupid, Tiger," Angelina said gruffly, pulling the knife out of the guard's back and watching the man slump to the floor.

"I might say the same. What did you think you were doing?"

"I'm a big girl, I can take care of myself."

"I see that," I said in amazement. "What deep dark secret have you been hiding from me, now?" I jibed her, watching her face flush bright red against her pale skin. Turning serious, I asked, "Where's the other one?"

She hooked a thumb towards the shadows on our left, not saying anything.

I nodded in understanding. "C'mon, we ain't out of the woods yet."

We headed for the stairs, Angelina admonishing me, "Remember, we're not going to kill him."

"Right," I said unhappily. "You know we're just wasting our time. If the roles were reversed he'd give us no such consideration."

"I know," she stated. "But I have to know why."

"Because he's a sadistic bastard," I said under my breath, hoping that Angelina had not heard me, and glad she could not pick it out of my mind, I voiced nothing more.

Halfway to the first floor, we were met by three more of Cortez's goons, probably the relief for those no longer standing guard. Both of our parties were surprised, but we recovered quicker and did not waste time being nice. Shortly, we were in the sub-basement, looking down the long hallway lined with executive offices. We walked past dozens of executives without as much as a glance our direction. They were so caught up in their own little worlds that the building could collapse without being acknowledged.

That didn't mean I wasn't edgy. I was feeling that any moment there would be a swarm of jump suited goons to hem us in. That cavern had been covered with surveillance cameras. The only thing left to get past, however, was the personal receptionist for Marlin Cortez. I sighed heavily, unsure how to get over this last hurdle. Angelina tapped my shoulder, suddenly dressed in a sundress that left little to the imagination. "Let me handle this part," she said, sliding on a pair of dark sunglasses to hide her eyes.

"Where did you get that?" I asked incredulously.

"Never mind, just get over there by the door without being seen, and I'll get us in."

I nodded as I watched her walk off with such and air of authority I was baffled. I shook my head, moving quickly to a place near the office doors.

The elderly lady did not turn her attention to Angelina as she approached. "I'm here to see Uncle Marlin," she said firmly.

The receptionist started. "Oh . . . I'm sorry, Miss Cortez, I didn't recognize you. Is that a new look?"

"Well, you know, something different," Angelina answered enigmatically. The lady smiled and reached for the buzzer. "Uh, please, don't announce me . . . I'd like to surprise him."

"Dressing like that, you certainly will," she answered warmly. "Please go in."

"Thank you," Angelina said as she stepped away from the desk. Before she had taken two strides, the receptionist had returned to her computer dictation.

I slid through the doors as Angelina opened them, bolting toward Cortez's desk. I covered the space in the span of a breath and Cortez raised his eyes as I launched myself to the top of the desk. If I had a paycheck, I would have given it to have a picture of Cortez's face then. He leapt to his feet even as he grabbed for the phone at the same point as when I landed in the middle of the horizontal view-screen, scattering his neat piles of papers. I gathered any cord I could draw into my hands, yanking hard and disabling everything there.

I stood straight, cords still in hand, smiling grimly at him. He slowly put the phone receiver back on the desk, where the telephone had been, scowling up at me. I let the cords slip from my fingers, jumping to the floor in front of him, daring him to piss me off. He stood statue still, anger and a hint of fear burning in his eyes. I moved back around the side of the desk, positioning myself near a side door, ready for any interruption of this impromptu meeting. Angelina was just arriving at this end of the room, her face blank of any readable emotion. I watched as she stopped three feet from his expensive desk.

He glared at her momentarily and then returned his attention to me. "Well, Tigershark. Fancy you having enough balls to sneak back here," he started maliciously. "Even more so to join up with Angel's cause."

I smiled at him vaguely and returned my attention to the floor.

"Did you expect less after the way I was treated?" I said evenly, peering sideways at him.

"I treated you no differently from any other of my employees," he defended.

"Oh, yeah. You cage everyone, or just the freaks?" I said then, shifting my weight to the other foot.

"Just the fre . . ." he started, stopping himself just in time.

"It's a wonder anyone still works for you. I don't like being toyed with, Cortez."

*****

He ignored the comment, saying instead, "I would think you'd keep better company than a Movement member barely tolerated because she's one step away from a freak herself."

Angelina spun around to face Tigershark, who had moved away from the wall and was approaching the stout man with murder in his eyes. "David!" she said in exasperation.

He swept his gaze to her and blinked, stopping his advance, and she shook her head. He slowly resumed his spot, still glaring at the corporate figurehead. Angelina returned her attention to her uncle, who was currently gazing from her to Tigershark.

"David, is it?" Cortez queried, his eyes lighting again on Tigershark. He flashed a broad and malevolent smile. "So your memories have been restored," he stated, and Angelina caught the slight grimace on her uncle's face before he wiped his expression clean. He again pinned Angelina. "So, why exactly are you here?" he sighed.

"I wanted to hear from you . . . why you did what you did to us."

"We have strict rules regarding spies in my company. It has been mandated, anyone caught using information against the company is to be 'volunteered' for genetic experimentation. After all, not too many people these days willingly become gemue trash. It doesn't matter who you are, even if you are the company president's niece."

"I'm not surprised," Angelina replied sourly. "I'm glad I was able to escape!"

Angelina glanced in Tigershark's direction, and saw him standing tensely, arms folded and head down. His eyes were taking in all the details of this conversation, though. It was obvious without her telepathy that the gemue was pained, angered, and humiliated to be the center of their discussion, and to be reminded of his part in this whole mess. His face showed no emotion, and he was very still, which told her as much as if he'd been tearing the place apart.

"Escape?" Marlin laughed, returning her attention to him. "My dear, I let you go. If I had wanted to keep you, there would have been no breaking those bonds. You would have been as much a freak as your boyfriend there," he emphasized with a wave toward Tigershark, whose head had come up sharply at the mention of his circumstance. His lip was curled slightly, showing several of his serrated teeth, but he stayed anchored to his post.

"Why?" Angelina inquired.

"I felt pity for you, child. You are still a blood relation. I just wanted to be sure that the lesson had been learned. You understand don't you?"

"No . . . No I don't. If that were true, you never would have tried to have me killed. You subjected David to an accelerated transformation process against his will, mindwiped his entire existence, fed him a new persona, and then sent him to kill me. That is as far from pity as I have ever heard."

"A simple mistake," Cortez placated. "Miscommunication, I assure you."

"A . . . MISTAKE!" Tigershark bellowed, coming away from the wall, bearing no more patience with Cortez's smug attitude. He passed by Angelina, not seeing her. Angelina grabbed for him but found no purchase on his sandpaper skin. "What kind of fools do you take us for, Cortez!" Angelina watched helplessly as Tigershark lifted her uncle bodily off the ground and pinned him to the wall behind his elaborate desk. "You gave the order personally to track her and kill her, I remember that! The whole fucking procedure on me was your twisted idea. You let her go," he motioned toward her with his free arm, "to see if your memory cell would hold under pressure. You called it 'the ultimate test of a new biological weapon.'"

"Put me down. You're not going to hurt me," Cortez said smugly, dropping his hand from the grip on Tigershark's wrist.

"What makes you say that?" Tigershark returned darkly.

He lowered his voice so that only Tigershark could hear him. "Because, David Scott, you're an uptown brat, raised with too many scruples to kill of your own free will. You don't have the instinct. That edge was all Tigershark and has been softened for remembering your past."

Tigershark smiled wickedly, lashing out without warning and leaving four furrows across Cortez's left cheek. "You obviously ignored a little of my history, didn't you? I had a record of violent temper, long before I tangled with you." For the first time since entering the room there was uncontrolled fear to be seen on Marlin Cortez's face. "And something else you've yet to grasp is that I am no longer wholly David. Tigershark is well melded into my consciousness. We are a conglomerate personality now, and you, you lucky bastard, created me! I hope that you're pleased with your new product, because you're going to die knowing just how efficient your gemue is!" He drew a stiff fingered hand back, and Angelina rushed in, trying to stop the inevitability. She couldn't let it happen.

"You promised me you wouldn't do this!" she screamed, but Tigershark was well beyond reason at that moment.

*****

"Is the boss in?" Tony asked at the receptionist's desk. He was headed for the door before she could respond. Luckily, he missed her look of disgust at his appearance. His still healing face was covered in rows upon rows of stitches repairing the damage done at his quarry's hands. He was the last person she wanted to deal with, yet he came on a daily basis to confer with her boss.

"He has a visitor, Mr. Karr," she said loudly at his retreating form. "If you'll have a seat."

He squinted back at her. "Who? He doesn't usually have visitors at this hour."

"His niece, Angelina, came by to see him," she said cheerily.

"What!" he bellowed, this time storming toward the door. "You stupid bitch!"

"You can't go in there!" she admonished him.

He pulled his spear gun from its holster, spinning to face her. "Believe me, he's gonna want me in there." He then opened the door and slid inside.

*****

Angelina heard the whistle even as Tigershark's grunt echoed in her ears. She glanced up into what she could see of his features, finding a shocked expression on his face. His mouth had fallen open, a breath escaping from between his slack jaws coming out noisily as he exhaled. She watched in confusion as he relaxed his hold on Cortez and sank gradually to his hands and knees, dragging her down as he went. She swiveled to find her uncle skittering out one of his secret doors to the cavern below, like a crab searching for a protective rock. She glanced back at Tiger and again to the neatly concealed secret door that Cortez had gone through, torn between tailing her uncle and finding out what was wrong with Tigershark. She returned her attention to the gemue at her feet.

"David? Are you all right?" she asked, her decision made. She leaned over further, trying to get a glimpse of his face, nearly hidden by his long shock of hair.

Tigershark blinked finally and slowly met her eyes. "Fine," he exhaled. His eyes were watery and, as she watched, blood began trickling out of his nose and from the corners of his mouth. He coughed violently and more blood dribbled down his chin to the waxed floor.

"Jesus! What hap . . ." She trailed off as he laid a split fingered hand on a spot on his chest and leaned back on his haunches. It gave Angelina a good view of the jointed tip of a spear gun shaft sticking out just under his left breast. He gingerly touched the, tip scarlet with his blood. "This is gonna hurt any second now," he stated flatly. Angelina stood up to find the entry wound, seeing the chrome shaft protruded from his back near his largest dorsal fin. There was a cord clipped to it and Angelina traced the rope to its origin and gasped.

With an expression of triumph on his mangled face and his dead eye staring blindly at them, stood Cortez's right hand. He was braced with his legs slightly apart, one hand on the stock of a very expensive speargun and the other hand wrapped tightly about the slack rope that was tethered via the spear to Tigershark.

Tigershark attempted to see what had caused Angelina's outburst, even as Angelina reached for the rope, knife in hand, to cut it. Neither accomplished what they were doing. Tony yanked hard on the rope, drawing the spear tip against Tigershark's chest with a smack. The action toppled both Angelina and Tigershark. Angelina landed hard on her butt, gathering her wits just in time to see Tigershark use the momentum to his advantage. He managed somehow to roll over one shoulder backward without falling on the shaft still protruding out of his back. He came to his feet, twisting to face Tony, but he overbalanced himself and nearly tumbled forward into Tony's waiting hands. Then she knew he was really in a bad way. He recovered fast though, grabbing up the now slack rope and severing it with one bite of his powerful jaws. Tigershark faced the man, growling in a low feral way. He crouched down low, claws out, ready to rend the flesh from the bigot's bones.

Tony dropped the speargun, now useless to him, and drew a bowie knife. He was motioning Tigershark forward. Tigershark obliged, closing the gap between them. Tony sidestepped, easily avoiding Tigershark's charge. They faced each other and began circling, like two male wolves fighting for dominance of the pack.

"Tony," Tigershark coughed, blood dribbling off his lips, "so good to see you again."

"Humph," Tony grunted. "Wish I could say the same, gemue. But at least I can finish it now."

"I see my going away present improved your good looks," Tigershark taunted. His bravado was admirable, Angelina thought, but he was hurt, badly. She knew he wasn't up to the knock down drag out this was going to be. "At least you're consistent in your prejudices, Tony, I will give you that. And to think, I once looked up to you, considered you a friend."

"What are you talking about?" Tony said with a laugh, as if expecting Tigershark's attempt at distraction. "I don't hang out with no stinkin' gemues."

"Oh, you're right, of course, but I was human then," Tigershark commented snidely. "Daddy paid you really well for your services, didn't he? I never knew what your hunts involved. Big game surely, but never did I suspect my father of hunting other sentient beings! Took getting my humanity stripped from me to find out how you really were." Tigershark's tactic confused Angelina; she didn't understand what he was talking about.

Evidentially, it had the same effect on Tony. Tigershark went on, "You were so open with your hunting log. Too bad I didn't realize it earlier. I'd have killed you back at the aquarium. But now I remember . . . and this time I'm not leaving you alive."

"Who are you?" Tony asked in exasperation.

"Cortez never told you? Tsk. And I thought you resided in his hip pocket. I was the young man who used to listen to all your poison as I was going through college about how evil gemues were, how they were nothing but scum to scrape off your boot heels. Took being one to realize how wrong you, my father, and I had all been. Gemues are humans, not the dumb animals the rest of humanity would portray them as." He nodded and smiled knowingly as he saw the light dawn behind Tony's good eye.

"You're the Scott's boy, David," Tony said in realization.

"That's right," Tigershark said tersely.

Tony laughed hoarsely. "You know, your father was very mad when you joined The Movement, David. Must be the reason he went to an early grave." He grinned, stretching his stitched lips. "Ironic, isn't it, that someone as gemuephobic as you … transformed into not only the ugliest gemue on Earth, but a killer besides."

"Better that than a lackey for a megaglomerate asshole whose whole purpose in life is to strip mine the Earth."

"Shut up, you ungrateful son of a bitch!" Tony spit and lunged forward, feigning left hastily to avoid Tigershark's suddenly slashing claws. Tony grabbed the spear shaft as Tigershark passed by, and wrenched it hard to the side.

Angelina heard the audible crack as his ribs fractured.

Tigershark howled in pain as he was spun around, landing heavily on the floor. He was slow to recover from it, his face twisted in agony, and Tony descended on him swiftly.

"Look out!" Angelina shouted a warning as Tony neared her crippled beau. Tigershark swung with a backhand, catching Tony square and knocking him back several feet. Tigershark pushed painfully to his feet, turning to face his adversary. He was bleeding around the entry and exit points of the bolt in his chest, now showing ugly tears.

"Your dad was megaglomerate!" Tony spit at the injured gemue. He lunged toward Tigershark, slashing, parrying, and stabbing. Several times Tony connected, drawing new blood, causing Tigershark to stagger back.

"That doesn't mean I had to be as blind as he was," Tigershark panted. He stood motionless, weighing his options. He knew he was going to have to end this soon; he could feel his strength starting to slip away. Tony rushed in again and Tigershark held his ground until Tony was nearly on him, and then Tigershark punched him, sending him reeling. He closed the newly opened gap between them before Tony could recover and lashed out several more times, each fist connecting solidly with his scarred face. Tony crumpled then, losing conciousness, unable to take the punishment the Tiger was dishing out to him.

Tigershark stood, doggedly trying to maintain his feet for a moment, waiting as if he expected Tony to get up again. When Tony was still out after several minutes, Tigershark finally turned away and lurched to where Angelina sat, sinking to his knees as he did.

"Let's go," he wheezed. He struggled to regain his feet but was only able to take several steps past her before collapsing to his knees. He attempted to get up once more but was unable to manage it. Angelina came up beside him, studying closely the bolt in his chest. She carefully unclipped the ring holding the several feet of cord still in place, before he seemed to realize what was happening. As she reached to push it through from the back, he flinched away from her. "Don't touch it!" he warned, then winced. "Oh shit," he swore as the pain made him reel.

"But . . ." she began to protest, kneeling beside him.

"But, nothing," he wheezed, staring into her eyes. Tears of pain made white streaks down his bloodied cheeks. "It's the only thing keeping me from bleeding to death, right here."

"Your lungs are going to fill up, though."

"What good are lungs to a fish?" he said, resigned. "They don't work worth a damn anyway. Just get me to some water and I'll be okay."

Before Angelina could protest further, Tony loomed over their crouched forms, knife held high, and Angelina gasped. Tigershark whirled around, rising with a reservoir of strength Angelina was sure that even he didn't know he possessed. Tiger straightened just in time to block the knife aimed at his heart. He caught Tony's wrist in one slender hand as they struggled over possession of the blade. The cutting edge began to descend toward Tiger's collarbone as he grimaced. Tony smiled as he gained the upper hand, the tip now making a dimple in Tiger's tough skin. With great effort, Tigershark raised the knife from his skin and quickly twisted it out and down. He stepped in, biting hard on Tony's biceps, shaking it viciously, causing Tony to drop the knife.

Tigershark spit out Tony's arm and Tony stumbled back, turned away, and gripped the profusely bleeding appendage. Before Tony could recover, Tiger wrapped him up in muscular arms from behind. He pulled Tony forcibly against him, holding back the yelp of pain, sending the point of the spear into Tony's ribcage. Tony struggled again, trying to free himself from Tiger's grip; in doing so, he kicked up and off one of the heavy chairs that was near them. Tiger slammed heavily into the wall behind them, driving the point of the spear through Tony's chest. Tigershark tensed at the burning pain of the shaft moving through his already swollen and tender tissues. Holding his breath, he fought back the abyss that was threatening to consume him to finish Tony off. Tony, like it or not, was stuck to Tiger and he began to thrash about, attempting to rid himself of the tether. Tiger pushed forward, away from the wall, grabbing Tony around the forehead with one hand and slashing his throat with the other one. Tiger then placed both hands on Tony's back and shoved him forcefully away, trying to ignore the white-hot pain as the shaft slid the rest of the way free of his own chest, still stuck in Tony. Slowly, Tony sank to his knees, holding his throat, before he lost consciousness and fell face first to the ground.

"And stay down," Tiger growled as his control over his weak legs vanished and he collapsed. Angelina moved over by him again, laying a hand lightly on his shoulder. She knelt next to him and he blearily gazed up to face her. "Let's try that again. Let's go." he repeated. "There is the entrance we came in." That brought on a fit of coughing in him as he tried shakily to regain his footing.

"No," she replied, pulling him back down.

"What?" he said in exasperation, unsure if he would have the strength to rise once more.

"We're going to go see Doc."

"That's not necc . . ."

226

"To hell it's not! You can't just go to the water. If you do you'll die, and I'm not about to let you do that. All of this is my fault."

"What are you talking about?" he grumbled.

"I should never have let you come with me that day. Then none of this would have happened."

A confused expression moved over his face. "What day? Angelina, what are you talking about?"

Her eyes were watery as she replied, "The day I was sent to Uncle Marlin's to spy."

He laughed airily. "What? So you can look like this?" He shook his head. "No. That was my choice, Angel. There was no way I was going to let you walk into that situation alone. You're not to blame for my current condition, Cortez is. He'll get his." He coughed, spit blood, and returned his gaze to her, trying to be upbeat. "But not right now. If I'm going to get help, it had better be soon. I'm not getting any stronger."

Chapter Eighteen:
Dancing with Death

Angelina nodded tersely, slinging David's arm across her shoulder and assisting him to his feet. Weighted down, she retreated with him out the office doors.

"Where are we going?" he protested. "We can't . . ."

"We don't have time to be stealthy, David. We're taking the quickest way out of here and that's through the front door." Tigershark began to object again but Angelina shot him a look that told him she was above changing her mind about it. As they entered the hall, Angelina placed a call she had hoped not to have to make. "Max, we need you over here. It went badly." She got a positive response and signed off.

They moved as quickly down the hall as Tigershark's failing condition would allow. If they had escaped notice coming in here, everyone noticed their exit. The receptionist stood as the doors clanged open, agape at the sight of Angelina assisting a gemue she didn't remember seeing before. When she witnessed the condition the gemue was in, she ran into Cortez's office, concerned that he might have been visited with trouble. She screamed when she found Tony's bloody carcass on the floor and her employer nowhere to be found. That got the attention of those in the vicinity of Cortez's office and all eyes turned to the albino woman and the injured gemue as they retreated. Many moved after the two, intent on detaining them. Angelina stepped up the pace, causing Tigershark to stumble as he attempted to keep up.

They exited barely ahead of those trying to stop their escape, as a white van screeched to a halt in front of them. The sliding door opened and Max appeared, motioning to them to hurry up. "We gotta go!" he said as Angelina assisted Tigershark awkwardly into the van. He sprawled onto one bench seat as she moved with Max up to the front. Max glanced back a moment at the condition of the gemue she had piled into the vehicle, but didn't comment on it. Instead, he said, "I just heard on the scanner that half of the precinct is on their way here." And with that, he put it in gear and peeled out in the general direction of the hospital. He took several side streets to avoid the approaching force.

Angelina stared at the receding building, and then turned her attention to Tiger, who had not made it fully onto the seat. His knees rested on the floor and he lay on the bench, keeping his chest from contacting the seat with one arm while the other draped over his pain-wracked features. From the sounds that he was making, he had a sucking chest wound. His air exchange was failing fast and it would not be long before they lost him. She then turned her worried eyes to Max.

Max had been released from the hospital several days before from the gunshot wound he had suffered at Tony's hands. She had thought he would refuse her request to back them up should something go wrong, for that very reason. She had noticed that his attitude had seemed to change about the gemue whose life she was now trying to save. He had made no comment on keeping Tigershark in their company. In fact, he had said nothing at all about even that he was a gemue. She wondered what had caused such a change in him. "Thanks for agreeing to help, Max."

"No problem," he said in monotone.

By the time they had reached the hospital, Tigershark could barely walk and Angelina was having a hard time keeping them both upright. She kicked the entrance open, attracting curious and shocked stares from those in the lobby. Without pausing, Angelina headed for the elevator, pushing the button to hail the car. Max had no desire to stay and with thanks she had let him go. Tigershark's raspy breathing seemed amplified by the silence in the room. "C'mon!" she growled, beating on the protective doors of the elevator shaft. One of the security guards gathered enough nerve to approach them. Angelina gave him only a passing glance.

"I'm sorry ma'am, you need to take yourself and your friend here somewhere else," the young man said bluntly, blocking her access to the elevator car.

"Can't you see that this is an emergency? I can't take him somewhere else. He'll die."

"That is not my concern ma'am; your kind isn't allowed in here."

Before Angelina could retort, Tigershark slowly turned his heavy head, glaring menacingly at the guard. He painfully straightened his back to stand at his full seventy-two inch height. His appearance was hellish. Most of his body was streaked dark red with drying blood. A pinkish froth had worked up around his mouth and was dripping from his chin, a result of fighting through blood filled lungs to get every breath.

"Listen, pal, you've got five seconds to back off and leave the lady alone," he grumbled, sounding every bit as bad as he looked.

"You listen, mister. This is a strictly human hospital. You have to go!" The man actually had enough balls to poke Tigershark in the chest.

Tigershark reacted violently, snarling and grabbing the guard by his lapel, then lifting him off the ground; an interesting feat considering his condition. "I am human, asshole, we both are!" he growled with considerable volume, despite his injury. The act nearly cost Tigershark his consciousness and the guard slammed heavily to the floor, Tigershark using the balled fist on the kid's chest to keep himself on his feet. The young security guard was very pale indeed, sure that the gemue above him had calculated that move and had every intention to do him bodily harm. Tigershark slowly pushed himself upright, rubbing a shaky hand across his forehead. When he was a little steadier he glanced back to the guard still on the floor. Tigershark sized him up with that one sweeping gaze. "If you got a problem with us being here, you'd better get some back up. There's no way you're going to take me alone." Tigershark turned away as he heard the chime notifying them that the elevator had arrived. He somehow managed to stumble into the elevator, lean in a corner, and maintain his feet as Angelina joined him, hit the button for the fourth floor, and stared at the guard as the doors shut.

Angelina faced Tigershark once the elevator had started up and he seemed to sense it, for he raised his heavy head. He lifted one hand and laid it on her cheek, his clawed thumb slowly stroking across her pale skin, the webbing between putting light pressure on her skin. A look of sadness and loss was on his face as he said, "I . . . don't . . . think I'm going to make it."

"Don't say that!"

"I . . . can't lie to myself . . . or you anymore." He wiped the blood from his face with one arm. "There's too much blood. I can't breathe . . . I can hardly see. It's gone too far."

Angelina was shaking her head, denying his words. Tigershark clamped her face between his slim hands. In a move so sudden Angelina had no time to react, he smothered her protest, pressing his lips to hers. It was only then that she knew beyond doubt that this changed creature was indeed David. All of the nagging doubts melted away as the warmth, passion, and longing of the kiss took hold of her. It was a moment seemingly suspended in time, and yet when he moved away it seemed to have passed all too soon. As he straightened again, she laid shaky fingers on her lips to retain the warmth of the contact and keep the instant from fading. He peered into her eyes sincerely, saying quietly. "Thank you for bringing me back."

A new round of tears welled up as Angelina desperately embraced Tigershark, and he in turn wrapped an arm around her, burying his muzzle into her neck. "Please, David, don't leave me again," she whispered hoarsely.

"I can't make that promise," he breathed, wavering unsteadily in her embrace. Tenderly he smiled at her, the pain, and loss clear to read on his face, and then, with a weary sigh, he leaned against the near wall and closed his eyes. All Angelina could do was nod and try to keep from breaking down on the spot. He appeared to be making peace with himself as if he knew death was near.

*****

By the time they had reached their floor, Tigershark was coughing uncontrollably, unable to even get a breath. "Stay with me, David!" she said in panic, stomping on the floor as if that would make the thing move faster. The doors gave the impression of opening in slow motion; Angelina slung his arm around her shoulders and did her best to haul him to his feet. She practically dragged him from the elevator to the doctor's waiting room, too panicked to recognize the terrified and appalled glares they were receiving, attempting to hurry before her strength wore out   or David lost consciousness. As they got about five feet into the waiting room, Tigershark went into shock, convulsing and falling in a quivering heap on the floor. She left him for the moment, running to the reception desk.

The receptionist stared angrily at her and then the gemue, beginning to protest their presence. "Don't start, lady," Angelina barked. "He's dying and I need the Doc's help to save him. Doc's a friend, please!"

Her features softened. "All right." She pushed a button on her desk, and it was only seconds before the doctor stepped into the hall. There was a second nurse with him, who barely held back her scream of horror. The doctor glared at her meaningfully and she immediately quieted.

"Jesus, Angel, what happened?" he said, kneeling quickly next to the shuddering body of her companion and assessing Tigershark's condition.

"Tony caught up with him," Angelina replied, leaning back to give the doctor more room to work.

"Monica, get me 10 cc's of adrenaline." He hadn't even looked at her, but she was quick to return with it. Aerating the syringe, he injected it directly into the soft tissue of his gills. "It's going to take a little longer to work so far from the heart, but I don't have time to take a scalpel to his hide. Okay, let's get him in the other room. Clarice, set up one of those burn beds. I want only the forward third filled and aerated; can you come up with something?"

"Yes, doctor."

"Monica, type and cross ten units of blood, and get me the holograph machine. I want to see what kind of damage we're dealing with."

Somehow, they managed to get Tigershark's now limp form into the burn bed. Doc Thomas sat him upright. "Clarice, hold him a second." He secured a piece of plastic over each hole in Tigershark's skin, taping it down to prevent any more air from escaping out of the sucking chest wounds that the speargun bolt had created. He then laid him on his side in the burn bed. Clarice had brought a yard sized trash bag, which she stretched over the head of the unit. As they lay Tigershark down, she tied the other side around his neck just below his gills. She filled it quickly with water and draped a hose from an oxygen bottle into the water and turned it on.

Doctor Thomas set up an EKG and IV lines that would provide Tigershark with lifesaving blood and fluids. He then positioned the holograph machine around Tigershark's chest and shot images at several angles to get the best view of the damages caused by the spear.

It was the next afternoon before the damage from his wounds was corrected. The remaining tissue in his left lung had collapsed and had required inflation. Two tubes were connected to one side of his chest; one provided negative pressure to draw the air out of the chest cavity, and the other provided positive pressure in the lung to keep in inflated while the damage healed. The shaft had also barely missed both his aorta and his heart, and only because of the angle at which he had been positioned when the bolt had struck him. He was lucky; had he been standing straight and not stretched up with the weight of Cortez's body against the wall, it would have been a killing shot.

Surgery had been further hampered by both Tigershark's need for oxygenated water to stay alive and the fact that placing him on his back on conventional bedding was out of the question. They had strapped two gurneys together with just enough space between them to accommodate

Tigershark's dorsal fins, as well as rigging an aerated fishbowl.

By the time it was over, Angelina was a nervous wreck. She practically leapt at the doctor when he appeared from the operating room. "David?" she queried, glancing at the burn bed as it was wheeled to a private room. "Is he . . ."

"We've done what we can to restore his systems. The rest is going to be up to him. His own physiology may complicate matters. His blood is no longer wholly human."

"Oh," she said quietly.

"But . . . if it's any consolation, if he'd been human he would have been dead before he had reached the hospital."

"When will we know for sure if he'll make it?"

The doctor just shrugged. "Hard to say. Like I said, he's not physically human. Nothing's going to be textbook about this recovery."

"Can I see him?" she asked reluctantly.

"You can go in, but don't disturb his rest."

"I won't," Angelina replied, moving down the hall to Tigershark's recovery room. Angelina opened the door and quietly stepped inside. They had replaced the makeshift surgery bed with a more elaborate set up. They had cropped Tigershark's hair very short and fitted him with something that resembled an oversized and upended fishbowl, into which was fed a combination of water and oxygen. Two other tubes emerged from it to direct the overflow into two buckets on either side of the gurney. They had laid him face down on the gurney and left his arms to dangle over each side. They had propped his chest up to counteract the height at which the apparatus put his head.

Angelina pulled a chair to the head of the bed and cast her eyes over him. He appeared to be dreaming, his eyes half-open, exposing the odd opaque inner lids he now possessed. The eyes twitched back and forth, evident even through the distortion of glass and water.

Angelina picked up one of his elongated hands and set it gently in her lap. She began tracing the features of it languidly with a fingertip, marveling at the fine details that gave him such prowess as a swimmer. She glanced over David's body, noticing the well-toned muscle and trim appearance his new life had given him. He was very handsome, even in his current form. It was funny, but she had thought him a handsome gemue from the first time she had laid eyes on him in the Bar Topical. Her uncle had outdone himself. The only good thing she could say about the man was that he never skimped on anything.

Once again her eyes traveled over him and she smiled. She had hazarded a lot to get David back and was happy the ordeal was nearly over. They could start again to build their life together. That thought drifted lazily through her brain as she continued to stare, unfocused now, at him. She leaned closer as something grabbed her attention.

Just below his upturned ear, Angelina again noticed that odd jagged scar and her memory skipped once more back to after the assault that had given him the blemish. She had never really noted before how aggressive David had been in those days, but reviewing those years, she could pinpoint all of the instances that anger had gotten away with him.

And now she knew the reason for everything . . . from his temper tantrums, for the general way that people had usually avoided him when he was drinking, to his way of bullying his way through any debate in class. A history of violence shadowed his past, tainting her previously rose-colored view of him, and suddenly a shiver ran through her. He had been right also in the admonition he had made to her . . . he was the perfect specimen for her uncle's experiments; David's own violent bend was what had made him such a good mercenary as Tigershark.

That brought her to a dilemma. Did she really want to spend her life with him? His newly revealed history was only one part of it.

Then there was the fact that David was now restricted to living in the water for the rest of his life. There was no dryworld existence for him, only teases of hours that he could come ashore to mingle with the human populace, and that group didn't want him around. He could not go back to his family even if he had the desire to. His friends from home would scorn and reject him. His mother? She had met his mother, a nice woman but highly prejudiced against just about everyone, based on their wealth more than anything. However, her regard of gemues was probably about as low as it could get. His dad, before he had died, had hunted gemues for sport, considering them only slightly more intelligent animals, enough to make them sporting in the hunt.

All the friends and family he knew were generally of the same ilk, all of them gemuephobes, and it would hurt David's pride to be treated as an animal by them. To be with David then meant that Angelina would have to move to Old Fresno and probably in one of the subterranean caverns he was adamant about residing in. She was not ready for that in the least. A future as an outcast was not the way she wanted to spend the rest of her days. A pang of anxiety hit her, and she found herself chewing her lip, trying to resolve the dilemma.

Angelina blinked hard, realizing there were tears in her eyes. She felt guilty for questioning her love for David, for allowing herself the consider leaving him here alone in his duplicity for nothing more than his appearance. But he had said it himself: he was not wholly David anymore, and even though Tigershark had been based on David's own belligerent traits, that personality had changed him. He was darker now, more antagonistic and bitter, both for it and for everything he had suffered through. She wondered more and more often how far he would revert. Would he begin to enjoy killing again as he had when he was in high school? As he had when she had first encountered him in this form?

But he had showed such restraint both in college and in the recent month when they had been on the run. She glanced down at his hand again, biting her lip. Shakily, she removed his hand and gently allowed it to dangle again. She rose quickly, wiping the tears away. "I'm sorry," she whispered and turned to leave.

*****

Above me glared a bright florescent light, burning halos into my retinas even through my closed eyelids. I opened watery eyes, peering about me, but there wasn't much to see. To either side of me were thick panes of glass reinforced by heavy beams of metal. The illumination above me kept everything but my peripheral blotted out and all else was shadowed. I attempted to sit up but was hindered by a band of metal that cut into my forehead. I slowly became aware of the bands about my wrists and others around my thighs, ankles, chest, and waist. The combined effect kept me from anything but minor movement.

My stomach fluttered in anxiety, as I realized that Cortez's doctors had something planned for me and it wasn't a good thing. My heart began to race at the gambit of sick possibilities these mad doctors may have had in mind.

I caught a glimpse of movement, a blur of dark against light off to my left, and I strained my eyes until they ached, endeavoring to get a glimpse of who was now in the room with me. There was the hope that it could give me a clue as to what exactly was going on. I was only able to see his form, silhouetted as he was by the florescent glow. The man leaned over the edge of the tank, attaching a clamp, and some of the brightness reflected off the glass to illuminate his features. He was wearing doctor's scrubs and a contamination mask over his mouth and nose, and his eyes were overshadowed such that I could not see them.

The man moved deliberately, not even glancing my direction as he prepared the equipment currently hanging on the edge of the tank. The man draped a two-inch hose into the tank and secured it to the equipment. He paused then and I could feel his eyes on me.

"You unlucky bastard . . ." I heard him whisper, and I thought I saw a shiver run through him. Then he hurriedly turned and disappeared from my view. I listened anxiously as the footsteps receded into the distance. A door opened and then shut, then all was silence, save for my own labored breathing. That was all that could be heard for long moments until another sound started to insinuate itself into the silence. It started as more of a feeling, a vibration, followed by a low whine. My eyes moved to the hose, as it seemed to gain life of its own, shuddering and shaking, suddenly spewing an orange-ish liquid into the space around me. It was just a trickle at first but the flow soon grew heavier. I shuddered involuntarily as the cold liquid splashed against me, raising gooseflesh on my bare skin as it climbed higher, swiftly filling the tank...

My eyes darted back and forth, my brain frantically thinking of a possible escape from this. I tried to control my ragged breathing but my autonomic functions would have none of it. The tension and anxiety rose up inside me as the volume in the tank increased. I began to thrash against the restraints as the liquid reached my chin and seeped into my ears. It wrapped its cold embrace around my cheeks and spilled into my eye sockets and I took one last desperate breath as the liquid engulfed me.

I could feel and hear my own rapid heartbeat as it desperately tried to keep my body oxygenated. What little

I had was burning off quickly and my vision began to gray out as I refused to draw in whatever it was they were intent on drowning me with. It didn't make sense! Why would they do all that they had done to me to this point only to drown me now? That thought slipped away as the gray became black.

I started awake, held by the power of that dream; my eyes flit about the room as my racing heart started to slow. It took me several moments to correlate just were I was and what had happened to get me here. Upon review of the recent events in my life, I realized I was lucky to be alive.

My sight was oddly distorted and I raised a hand to try and rid my eyes of the illusion. The move was solidly blocked, and the same hand explored the blockage to find it covered the entirety of my head. I also realized at that point that the bowl was filled with water, and I panicked. I pushed up sharply, receiving a stab of pain in protest. I ignored the pain, under the impression that someone was trying to kill me by sticking my head in a bowl of water. Straightening further, I was stopped with a jerk by the hoses that were attached to the bowl. Pulling harder in my panic, the hoses separated from the bowl, spilling its contents over the bed and the floor. I grabbed frantically at the sealing material and detached the bowl from my head. I flung the bowl across the room, listening to it thunk dully on the tile, vaguely surprised it didn't break.

I took in a deep breath of air to be rewarded with a tearing pain rippling through my chest, which in turn got sympathy pains from the rest of my body. "Holy shit!" I exclaimed in pained surprise. Talking brought on a wracking cough, only aggravating the problem. The intensity was more than my programmed pain tolerance could stand. I closed my eyes, as the pain slowly subsided.

That had been no dream that had awakened me; it was another memory my brain had finally deciphered. I remembered waking up after god knows how long, looking up through that pinkish orange liquid and realizing with some astonishment that I was still alive. It had been a fluorocarbon infusion in which they force grew my gills, giving them a supplemented oxygen supply in order to test their ability to seine the gas from liquid. I remember just breathing the stuff in through my lungs, like drawing a shake through a straw, tough but not impossible. The action made my chest muscles sore for many days, as they were forced to work harder than they ever had to keep me from dying. Just about the time I had finally gotten adjusted to it, something changed. I woke in the tank feeling strange; the gills had started to work, utilizing a different set of muscles to draw the water through them, another autonomic response added to the checklist in my brain. My chest didn't move, and I remember that scaring the hell out of me. What I had told Angelina was only a partial truth then. The gills had been tested, just not in water.

Only now did I realize how foolish I had been for taking the bowl off my head. Air was not necessary for me, and that I had to remind myself was an indication of just how far I had to go to get my two identities to jive. I wrapped my arms around my torso, finding a large square of gauze taped to my skin, and I felt the wrinkling of tape on my back that indicated that there was an identical one there. There were two other scars on my left side, sewn with neat stitches, and my fingers traced over them lightly wondering why they were there. I attempted to sit up, wincing at the extreme pain I was in. I ended up in a half-seated position, leaning heavily on my left arm as I took another, clearer peek around the room.

This was no hole in the wall gemue clinic. It was a state of the art ICU, and I wondered by what miracle I had been admitted here. The only thing I could recall was a pain-wracked trip in an elevator and the words I had said to Angelina.

A pang of anxiety went through my stomach, and I began speculateing if she knew that I had been serious. That I didn't see her made me wonder, and I hoped she was just on a break from her vigil. I glanced down at my body, and found that I was covered in all sorts of monitoring devices. EKG leads dangled from my chest, still swinging from my rude removal of them from their parent device, and here was an IV in both arms and, frowning, I stripped them all from my body, disregarding the fact that I began to bleed from the needle holes. I was certain that it would bring the whole floor crashing into my room.

"Good. I want them to know I'm up," I muttered. "Misery loves company."

I was in too much pain to venture out into the hallway, especially when I was not sure of the reception I'd receive. As I predicted, Doc Thomas burst through the door, panting heavily for his exertion, two nurses in tow. I smiled crookedly. "That answers the question of my admission," I said, doubling over in pain, having forgotten my injury yet again. As it was, my breathing was shallow and fast to minimize my pain.

He stopped, his mouth a thin line of displeasure. "You shouldn't be up, David." He forcibly made me sit straight, pulled my hand from the gauze on my chest, and peeked under the wrapping. "You'll make these bleed again."

"She . . . told you . . . who . . . ?" I said of his choice of addresses for me, setting me coughing again.

"Hold still!" The doctor motioned one of the nurses over, then ripped the gauze off my chest. "Yes, she told me everything."

"Great," I said in embarrassment.

"You're lucky to be alive," he added, commenting no further on the previous subject. "That bolt nearly took out your heart. As it was it was tricky surgery to get your lung back in order."

"I'll thank the stars that Tony was a bad shot," I said, which caused me to grimace. "How long . . . ?"

"You can stop talking any time now," the doctor grumbled. I only nodded in response. He swiftly cleaned, dressed, and covered each of the neatly sewn wounds created by the speargun bolt. Once that was finished, he replaced the IV's I had removed, and then looked at me, saying sternly, "You pull those out again, I'll have you taken to those butchers who normally handle gemue patients."

I nodded, knowing better than to press my luck.

"You've been here three weeks," he said, finally answering my earlier question.

I marveled at that for a moment. He had kept my presence a secret for that long?

He injected some painkillers into the IV, as the nurses remade the bed and re-rigged the fishbowl. I allowed them to put the device back over my head, thankful for chance to rest my sore chest.

The doctor moved toward the door, trusting the nurses to finish with me.

"Doc?" I asked before he disappeared.

He reappeared in my limited line of vision. "Yes, David?"

"Angelina? I want to talk to her," I said evenly. There were things that she and I needed to discuss. Being that I was not going anywhere now would be a good time for it.

He frowned adding sadly, "She hasn't been here since right after you came out of surgery."

"What do you mean?" I said in a low voice, hardly audible.

"She visited once after your surgery, but she left here crying and I'm afraid she hasn't been back."

I looked away as I pondered what the doctor had said. Angelina had worked very hard to bring me back, and had lost a great deal in return. Yet she had succeeded, so why was she suddenly avoiding me? I frowned, eyes furrowed as the pit of my stomach sank to my feet. I nodded minutely, and then allowed the nurses to assist me in lying back down. The pain was reasonable and I shortly drifted into an uneasy sleep, wondering in the back of my mind, what had gone wrong.

Chapter Nineteen: Abandoned Again

I lay staring at the walls, trying to ignore the constant unsettled feeling in my muscles. I had been lying prone for much too long and my idle body was protesting the forced sedentary time. I was tethered closely to the life support unit by the apparatus on my head, and was unwilling to risk a new round of pain from my still healing chest wounds, by removing the device. As fast as I healed, this was taking what seemed forever.

My stay to this point has been about a month under constant, if secretive, supervision. Doc Thomas had pulled some serious strings to for me to remain here it seemed, and he wanted to keep the general populace ignorant of my presence. He still had doubts about the severity and therefore the healing time of the damage Tony inflicted on my body, and he was overly cautious about allowing me to breathe air. I was reluctant myself to suffer through the pain I had at my waking, and consequently said nothing. But right now it was the thing I wanted to do most in the world, to gain some mobility, even if it was just around the hospital room. I heard the door open behind me and I glanced best I could though the distortion of the glass to see whom it was. In the back of my mind I was hoping it was Angelina, but knew the reality would be quite different. It was only Doc, and I sighed heavily at the disappointment I felt. Since I had regained consciousness, she had yet to stop by and see me. I was beginning to think that she had either lost interest in me or my appearance bothered her.

"'Morning, David," Thomas said in his usual cheery manner.

"Yeah" I said dejectedly.

He lifted the bandage on my back to examine the healing scar, as was cursory for each of his visits. He unsealed the helmet, careful not to spill too much on the bed or floor, and had me sit up so he could do the same on the front bandage. I had this routine memorized: next, he would take a set of ultrasounds to see how the damage internally was healing and then he would tell me the progress or lack thereof. When that was done he would replace the fishbowl and tell me to lie back down. I was right until the part where he replaced the bowl . . . he didn't. I looked at him strangely for the change in routine.

"Go ahead and take a breath, David," he said finally, as if I should have guessed. Tentatively, I cleared my throat and sinuses, carefully drawing air in through my nose, and was relieved to only receive a dull ache rather than the sharp pain I had experienced the last time. "Is there any pain?"

"A little, but it is dull," I said, waiting to eat my words when I talked, but the pain got no worse.

"Good. The ultrasounds are nearly clear of scarring; you should be able to leave the hospital by next week. I want you to exercise that lung, and that means all the way to the limit of your drytime."

"But," I started to protest, not wanting to jump from the frying pan into the fire.

"To accommodate the request I had this made for you." And, as if on cue, the two nurses trusted to attend me wheeled a draped cart into the room. As it neared the doctor, he pulled the cover from it to expose what struck me as a rebreather. It had an odd collar with two hoses coming off of it, as well as a half mask for the face with another two going into it. There was a narrow space in the housing just wide enough, I guessed, to fit my dorsal fins through

"What are those going to do for me?" I asked.

"This is a water rebreather, David. It will allow you to use your lungs as much as your drytime will allow and then you just slip the mask over your mouth and use it as a diver would use a regulator. The neckband can be worn at all times because your gills go unused when you breathe from the air. The only downside to this is that it is extremely heavy, probably weighing about seventy to a hundred pounds."

"That's going to take some getting used to," I muttered, grimacing at the thought of having to lug that weighty thing around with my still tender body. However, I immediately saw the advantage of having such a device available to me. "But I am more than willing to give it a try."

Doc Thomas nodded as if he expected just that response. "With the added weight there will be a considerable drop in your available drytime until you get used to it. There is a second purpose for this contraption, David."

"And that is?"

"I want to strengthen the lung tissue you have left, to extend the amount of time you can remain drytime. Your limit should be flexible, and is only so short because of disuse. We should be able to bring it up to at least twice that with regular use of your lungs, and with less recovery time in between."

"Sounds good," I said with determination that stemmed in part to my tie to Angelina. "Life restricted to the water is less appealing to me now." A big part of me wanted to rejoin my old life, to pick up where we had left off, even when I knew that my family would never welcome me back into their lives. That door was forever closed to me; I would never want my mother to see me like this.

"I won't lie to you, David. You will be restricted to the water for the rest of your life. Cortez ensured that. You will never be a true land dweller again."

My heart fell to my feet at that statement, though somewhere deep down I already knew that. I glanced down, nodding slowly. "I know, but extended time ashore has to be better than what is before me now."

Doc Thomas worked with me intensely until my release on my drytime stamina. There were times he had me near fainting before allowing me to use the rebreather. As predicted, the weight of the pack shortened my drytime when I first began, cutting my already short margin down to a mere hour before my chest hurt so bad it reminded me of the several wounds I just recovered from. Every week my endurance improved until just before my release from the hospital, and the weight did not seem so heavy anymore. My stamina, however, did not increase much, though even so little was a boon to me.

My stomach convulsed as a thought occurred to me, not for the first time. It had been nearly a month since I had regained consciousness and every day I raised my hopes that Angelina would visit me. I wanted to impress her with the amount of progress I had made toward more available time to spend with her. Each time my desire for her to stop by was squashed, leaving me bitter and depressed.

"Well," Doc said as he escorted me to the door, ignoring the stares of the human patrons, "I will see you again, I hope?"

I nodded. "Under better circumstances, with any luck. I'm tired of being your patient, Doc, no offense."

Doc laughed shortly. "It has been a pleasure, David." He offered a hand.

"Thanks. It's good to have met you finally . . . as myself." I took his hand firmly. "I can see why Angelina's family keeps coming to you. And that bedside manner!" I finished sarcastically.

"Good luck," Doc said, waving as he returned to the building.

I sighed heavily as I departed the hospital, knowing it was going to be a long walk back to the shoreline. I started that direction, hooking my mask to my face to unburden my still tender lungs. I had gotten two blocks, pay no heed to the glares and the rude comments on my presence in the neighborhood. A horn honked behind me, and I disregarded it too, not giving the prick driving the car the satisfaction of getting a free shot in on me. "Tiger!" I heard someone say. I paused and glared toward the source of the voice and saw Angelina peering out at me through the passenger side window of a beat up Chevy Malibu. I scowled, twisted away, and trudged doggedly up the street toward the water.

"David," she said, this time rolling slowly alongside my path.

"Go away," I growled, reluctantly acknowledging her as well as noticing absently that the transmitter in my mask worked.

"Talk to me!" she demanded, and I waved her off, wanting to be alone in my self-pity. She punched the accelerator and wheeled into the next drive, blocking my path. "Damn it, talk to me!"

I stopped by her car and ripped off my rebreather mask, spilling a good deal of water on the sidewalk. "Talk to you?" I said incredulously, stooping to glare into the window. "I languish in a hospital for a month and a half and you couldn't be bothered to come by and talk then. Now . . . now you suddenly abound with the need to converse with me?" I shook my head angrily and, standing, tried to skirt around her car. She read the move and slid the car forward more to block me yet again. I glared at her. "Is this some bullshit ride to get me out of your life faster?"

"No," she said emphatically, starting to sound angry herself. She sighed heavily. "I've been really busy, David, and I'll explain . . . if you'll just get in the car." She reached over and opened the passenger door. "At least let's make it a semiprivate argument," she added as she glanced over my shoulder. I followed her gaze to see a crowd starting to gather. "I can even get you to the water before dark . . ."

I relented, not willing to air out my dirty laundry in this part of town. I was risking a mob beating as it was. I crouched down, adjusted the seat to accommodate my abnormal features, and climbed slowly in. As I closed the door, Angelina backed into traffic and started toward the water. We drove in silence for long moments before I had to ask the question that had been eating at me for the last month. "Where have you been? I could really have used your company in the hospital. I was starting to go mad."

"I'm sorry. I really have been busy," she said in what I knew was a half-truth.

"Doing what? What was so important that you could spare no time to come and visit?"

"I've . . . been in court."

"Right," I scoffed.

"Really, I have been motioning for criminal and civil proceedings against Uncle Marlin. Our lawyer says our chances are excellent of coming way with big money for what they did to us; Marlin could go away for life. The criminal trial is set to start next week."

"Our lawyers?" I said, angry and curious at the same time.

She nodded. "Your name is on the suit too."

"Don't expect me to come and testify," I said tersely. "They get one look at me and your case'll be lost."

"Not necessary," she said, pursing her lips. I wondered whether it was that she agreed to me or she already had evidence that ensured a win.

I shook my head, that same thought rattling around in my skull. "That still doesn't explain why you haven't visited, Angelina," I growled as we pulled up to the wharf nearest my new home. "Last I heard, there were no felony courts running at night."

She applied the brakes, the car lurching to a stop, unable to meet my gaze. "I," she started. "To put it bluntly, I'm not sure that we are going to work out."

"What?" I asked incredulously, taken aback at her words.

She said softly, "I thought I would be so happy with you back in my life . . . I was happy that we could be together just as we were before. But we cannot deny that things will never be the same between us. We've changed." She trailed off, as the harshness of what she was saying to me sank into her own thoughts. Angelina tried to regroup, to soften the blow by saying, "This has been such a major transition and I'm just not sure if I feel the same anymore."

I felt my jaw hang slack at her words, and it was loathe closing. I wanted to be mad at her for putting me through all this only to say essentially, "Let's just be friends," but the only thing that filtered through was disappointment. Part of me didn't even blame her; I'd leave this body behind too, if I could. Without another word, I opened the door and stepped out, looking over the water the direction of my home. I suddenly felt as if I was meant to be a recluse, that God had chosen the harder path for me. I smirked at the irony of it, me blaming God for my problems, but the humor faded and left me feeling empty inside. Sighing, I moved toward the only sanctuary I had left.

"David?" I heard Angelina say. I stopped but did not face her immediately, for I did not want her to see the pain in my eyes. "I'm sorry. I didn't want it to be this way."

I finally did twist around to face her silently. I stared at her a long while, trying to figure out in my head why she had come to the conclusion that we wouldn't work out, what the real motivation behind her decision was. After a moment, I nodded slightly, smiling a smile that went no further than my mouth. My brain rattled out, "Then why didn't you just leave me alone, just leave me as Tigershark?" but I didn't say it and was more than glad that she no longer had the ability to read that thought. Instead, I said, "Let me know how the proceedings go." And, unhooking my rebreather, I slipped into the cold waters of the San Joaquin.

Epilogue:
Old and New

I lay in my shallow depression, attempting fitfully to fall asleep.

My chest still ached from my exercises to strengthen my lungs and there was a dull pounding down deep from internal scars that wanted my attention. I stretched again in the warm brackish water, hoping to get them to stop talking. Eventually, they silenced, and I closed my eyes, once more drifting into sleep. I had moved back into the cavern that I had occupied during my time as Cortez's mercenary, if for nothing else than because I had found nothing better in the way of dwellings. I had only abandoned it because I did not want it to be found in the search that they conducted to retrieve me.

When I had gone back, I had been happy to find it undisturbed.

I guess they never credited me with enough brains to consider such a well-set up hideaway. Setting back up had been easy, and I retrieved as many supplies as possible from my previous flight from the area. Unfortunately, the army had ransacked the plant that Angelina and I had used for a temporary hideout; most of what had been left behind had been trashed or taken.

But it was home again, the lights were working and the pool of brackish water had called my name. That did not mean, however, my body was ready to rest, and it was warring heavily with my weary brain.

Images began running across the backs of my eyes, strange visions of things I had never seen, never participated in, like characters from a movie, and a smile twitched at the edges of my mouth. Relaxation finally began to overtake consciousness. I was bordering on the cusp of sleep, when someone laid a hand on my shoulder. I started, my eyes flashing open, and I exploded from the pool, pinning my would-be assailant. I raised a clawed hand, ready to strike when I comprehended just who it was who had invaded my privacy. She seemed as scared as I was angry.

"Angelina?" I said in surprise.

"Hello to you too," she said, smiling crookedly under my shadow.

I pushed off her, rolling over and sitting down. The pain I had ignored in my defense came back suddenly and I was forced to press a hand into my side to get it to subside. "Damn it, Angelina, don't sneak in on me like that!"

I glanced at her, become conscious for the first time that she was without any kind of dive gear. In fact, she was wearing a white button down shirt that was now completely soaked. It left little to the imagination as to how well built she was. I tore my eyes from her before she noticed. "How did you get in here?"

"The back door. I found it about a month ago," she said blithely, rising to peer down at me. She extended me a hand and I gratefully took it to help myself up.

"Great," I said, wondering whom else had found it during my absence, as I gained my feet. "So what brings you to my little hovel?"

"I felt kinda shitty about the way I acted the other day. I wanted to apologize," she replied, unable to meet my eyes. "I've been having a hard time dealing with my own doubts and I'm afraid I transferred them onto you."

Slowly, I nodded, not sure what to say. She sounded sincere, but I was still suffering from being singed before.

"Accepted," I decided finally.

"I also have some other news that I thought you would be interested in hearing," she added. "We won our cases."

"Good," I said agreeably. "How much time did they put Cortez away for?"

She frowned. "Not enough. That man has some damn good lawyers. He's only going to be out of the picture for a year and a half, and that's if he doesn't get off for good behavior."

"That's not nearly enough," I said disdainfully, and finished darkly with, "You should have just let me kill him."

Angelina shook her head, paling a bit. "No . . . If you had, we would have never gotten this." She produced a document for me to see, which, when translated from Legalese, said that we were to get paid, lump sum, $100 million credits. That was a lot of change.

I whistled appreciatively. "Evidently, your lawyers weren't too bad either." She just shrugged demurely, averting her eyes at my inference to her substantial finances. "So what are you going to do with your share?"

"I'm closing escrow today on a house at the outskirts of the city. In fact . . . that's why I'm here. I'm having a housewarming party next Friday and I would like you to come."

"I don't know, Angelina," I answered, turning away as a pang of anxiety coursed through my gut. "I'm not sure I'm ready for socializing."

She spun me back around with a touch on my arm. "C'mon, David, I want you to be there. We both need a good time. We deserve it."

I contemplated for a long time before giving her an answer. "A . . . all right."

"Great." She beamed. "I'll pick you up around six, next Friday."

"With what?" I asked, having been sure I would have to swim my way there.

"My boat, of course," she stated. "Another indirect gift from my uncle."

I nodded slowly, realizing that she was beginning to slide back into her old lifestyle. That did not instill me with much confidence.

*****

Angelina pulled up in a nice nineteen-foot speedboat, throttling to a stop perfectly alongside the spot where I floated in the water. She had always been excellent at piloting boats. I could still recall that fact from all the times that we had gone diving before the unfortunate circumstances I currently found myself in. I paddled the two strokes to the vessel and slung a bag over the side, before easily pulling myself aboard. I landed lightly on the deck and immediately stripped out of my wet pants. That done, I opened the bag and dumped out the contents on the deck of the boat.

Toweling off quickly, I glanced up to see Angelina staring at me in shock. Smiling, I straightened enough to draw on a pair of black jeans on, though I paused again when she continued to goggle at my audacity. My smile broadened. She had seen that view before, granted it had been a while, and I wondered just what she was thinking. Somehow, it seemed that she hadn't expected the equipment to still be there, or something silly like that.

"You didn't expect me to go to a party in my skins, did you?" I said aloud, avoiding the more crass comment that cropped up in my mind.

That drew her out of her lingering gaze as she shook her head emphatically in the negative. She turned away, smiling in embarrassment, starting the boat and heading south along the San Joaquin. As we sped off, I next donned a long sleeved shirt that I had modified to fit me and put it on, wincing slightly at the tearing sensation it created in my chest. I then pushed up the sleeves to make myself more comfortable. Emerging from the bag was a pair of black combat boots, which I slipped cautiously over my oversized feet. They felt strange, awkward and heavy after so long of wearing no foot covering at all. Making quick work of it, I tied the laces and pulled the cuff of the jeans down over the top of them. Straightening, I ran my hand reflexively through the ungodly short hair on my head, feeling strange after it being so long prior to my hospital stay. Out of the bag then came a pair of custom made sheaths designed to provide me better dexterity and to cause less damage to anything I was handling.

I was actually looking forward to this party. There was something I needed to prove to myself even if I could not at the moment pin down just what that reason was.

About ten minutes later, we docked at a small pier. Following the stairs leading up the side of the hill with my eyes, I vaguely made out a small but well laid out house perched with a view of the sea.

I whistled appreciatively. "That is one hell of a house."

It was only about 1600 square feet, probably just two bedrooms, but Angelina's choice of locations was absolutely stunning. It was painted a dark red with white trim around the window and doorframes. Angelina and I discussed the details of the purchase of the house and other quaint small talk that lightened my spirits.

It lasted only until I walked in the door, then the feeling was doused like a flame under a deluge of water. I realized then, quite vividly, that coming here had been a mistake. Everyone was already in attendance and my tardy entrance only served to make me the center of attention . . . activity stopped as all eyes fixed on me. My rebreather thudded loudly to the ground as I stared in shock at the brimming room full of people. I shot a nervous glance around and then at Angelina, who smiled and motioned for me to mingle with those gathered. There were a lot of familiar faces in the crowd and a thought occurred to me that dropped like lead into the pit of my stomach. I turned back to Angelina. "D . . . do they . . . know?"

"Yes," she said blithely, as if there was going to be no problem with my appearance. I felt my face flush hot and wondered if the color showed. I swallowed hard, moving away from Angelina like a first time swimmer letting go of the edge. Yet I dared not stay by her side either, for fear of exploding at her for this not so pleasant surprise.

*****

Angelina smiled warmly as David walked away and disappeared into the crowd. She kept tabs on him for the next half-hour to see how he was fairing. She watched as he made uncomfortable attempts to introduce himself to some friends he had known before. Each time he tried, however, he was brushed off as if he didn't exist, or they said a few words and then ignored him . He skulked away, understandably frustrated. After three repeats of the same scenario, Angelina decided it was time to intervene. As nonchalantly as she could, she walked up to the latest aborted attempt at conversation to find out just why everyone was treating her invited guest so badly.

"Hey, Eric."

"Angelina!" he said warmly. "You are looking so fine! The bleaching does nothing to detract from your beauty. Great party by the way."

"Thanks," she replied, smiling with embarrassment. "Hey, I noticed David found you."

His look turned dour. "Mmmph," was his only reply.

Angelina narrowed her eyes. "I figured you and he would have a lot to talk about, being that he's been gone for so long."

"No, there wasn't much to say." He fell silent for long moments, seeming to have something else on his mind, but was reluctant to mention it. Finally, he broke the silence. "Y'know, there's something I don't understand."

"Oh? What's that?"

"Why you brought him. He's not going to be accepted back into The Movement, and his old friends certainly don't want to talk to him, myself included. If nothing else, you should have left him in his cave just to spare a bit of his pride. I mean, look at him," he finished, in an almost sympathetic voice, pointing to the other end of the room. Tigershark had himself tucked into a corner as if he was ready for an attack.

"Yeah," she said softly. "Talk to you later, Eric."

She didn't believe what she was hearing. To confirm it, she unobtrusively polled those in attendance on their feelings about David's presence and got a unanimously negative response. Some even threatened to leave if the gemue did not. Angelina became angry then, but not at her guests as she had a right to. She instead singled David out to be the blame for all the bad vibes floating about when this was supposed to be a happy time. Partly because there were too many people here she did not want to offend by allowing David to stay, and partly because of her own fears, doubts once more clouded her judgment in the matter. She rationalized that if David had been nicer or more assertive, then the other guests would not react the way that they had. She decided that she had better straighten out his attitude or ask him to leave.

She searched for several minutes to locate him, and discovered that he had finally run into someone who would talk to him, or rather that someone had sought him out. It was Max, to her surprise, but she was too worked up by this point to be deterred by that, and she stormed their direction.

*****

I was frustrated very quickly as I tried to introduce myself into the conversations going on around me. I received one of two responses; I was ignored totally, or the people would be polite enough to return my greeting and excuse themselves to move to conversations that were more comfortable. I soon found myself standing on the sideline, watching the cliques and dialogues change as the night wore on. I looked dejectedly down into my drink and swallowed it fast, trying to dull the anger and frustration I was experiencing at being treated this way. I had expected people to be here, and I had expected to deal with the gemuephobic attitude, but there were too many in attendance, both in numbers and in people I knew. Angelina, either by accident or by design, had chosen not to stay by me and defend my right to be here.

I snagged another drink from one of the catering trays as it skirted by my perch. I practically had to leap for it because the lady came only as close as the crowd forced her to. I spilled part of it in my effort, frowning at my wet hand, and the phrase "alcohol abuse" flared behind my eyes. A moment later, I downed the rest, as quickly as I had the first, ignoring the burning sensation as it slid down my throat.

"David!" someone said enthusiastically from the crowd, catching me by surprise. I gawked up to see Max angling through the ever-shifting mass of bodies toward my position. He had a beautiful brunette on his arm to which he whispered something, and slipped her off before arriving.

I peered around, thinking this was some sort of trick. My shoulders tensed up with my hostility, asking him, "Why are you talking to me?"

He raised his hands in self-defense. "Whoa, calm down. Is that the way you're going to talk to someone who had a major hand in saving your life?" he asked in his high voice as he edged me out of the corner.

"So what? You owed it to Angelina. That doesn't mean you did it out of the goodness of your heart," I growled. "I know you too well, Max, remember that . . . I know you hate gemues. So again I ask, why are you talking to me?"

"David," Max said in admonishment, saying my name easily, not like he was about to choke on the word, "I know what happened to you, everything. I know you didn't have any control over what they did. In my book you are you, no matter your present appearance is. Besides, I began to see what a narrow-minded ass I was being. Angelina opened my eyes to that one." He lowered his eyes, seeming embarrassed.

How ironic, I thought sardonically, *considering how she is acting now.*

Once that thought had run through leaving bile in its wake, I raised an eyebrow at Max's admonition. I was too familiar with his personality to call him a liar on this, and I knew he was being truthful with me. I averted my gaze to the floor, nodding minutely and feeling suddenly bad about my reaction to his show of good will.

"You look a little lost. I just thought that you could use some company," Max added.

My eyes again searched the crowd, my lips thin lines as I admitted, "I didn't know she was going to invite so many people I knew. Had that been the case I wouldn't have thrown myself out here for target practice. They won't talk to me, and Angelina is so busy getting reinstated into her old life she seems to have forgotten I'm here."

"I know. Right now, she's over schmoozing Eric Tannaly from the old wrestling team." He started to laugh, but then sobered when he saw my pain. "I'm sorry, David, this really has to be a bitch for you."

I found myself unable to vocalize.

Max fell silent as well, and it drug out for long moments, when Max began to shuffle his feet as he always did when he had something important to say.

"I never . . . got the chance to thank you," he finally got out.

"For?" I said quizzically, my eyes pinching tighter as I swept the room with mental daggers.

"For saving my life . . . back at the aquarium," Max replied.

My brow furrowed in confusion as I tried to recall exactly what he might be talking about. When it dawned on me, I said, "I didn't do anything, Max, save get you out of harm's way. I wasn't even in time to stop him."

"What you did do was enough." He twiddled his fingers watching them in fascination. "When Angelina first confided in me her belief about your true identity, I didn't believe her, didn't want to. You know how I am." He pursed his lips. "But I knew without a doubt that it was you that day at the aquarium. After I was shot and you came to my aid, I saw it in your eyes. You knew me, recognized me."

I lowered my head as well. "Yes . . . now that I think of it, I did. But at the time it was just an inexplicable feeling of regret . . . honestly, it confused me. If I had only known . . . I would have killed Tony. Instead I left him, and he believes

in the adage 'don't get mad, get even.' He nearly killed me."
I shook my head, rubbing absently with the back of one hand
over the scar just under my left breast as an ache cropped up
and tried to be sympathetic.

We went silent again for some time, watching the people
swirl around us. Without warning, Max stepped out in front
of me, and extended his hand. After a moment I took it in a
firm grip and Max wrapped me up in his other arm, saying
in my ear, "It's good to have you back, bud, even under the
circumstances." He moved away again, grinning warmly at
me.

"Thanks, Max," I answered quietly. "You sure that I'm
not going to cramp your style?" I said seeing several groups
conversing in conspiring tones, their eyes locked on the pair
of us.

"Naw," he replied, waving the comment away. "They
may not like it, but they won't say anything about it. I don't
let them dictate whom I can and can't see. That went out in
seventh grade in my book. You've been a friend longer than
anybody here and I would rather hang with you than them."

I flushed; despite myself. That was probably the biggest
compliment I had received, ever.

Angelina appeared then, beaming falsely our direction
as she plied through the crowd. She stopped next to me,
stringing an arm through mine. "Can I borrow David a
minute, Max?"

He knew as well as I that she was upset about something,
but I signaled to Max over her head. His face broke into a
grin just as false as Angelina's was as he said, "Sure. Talk to
you later, David."

"All right," I said as Angelina practically dragged me to
the kitchen.

When we got there, she was quick to drop the pretense.
"What the hell do you think you're doing?" she started
scathingly.

"Trying to fade into the wallpaper. Why?"

"Do you have any idea what it took for me to get these people here?"

"No, but I'm sure you're about to enlighten me," I replied angrily, folding my arms over my chest.

"I had to convince them that you hadn't changed at all despite your process, and you do this! You were supposed to converse with them, not offend them!"

"Offend them? Angelina, I would offend them if I were on the balcony tied to a leash! I can't convince anybody of anything if they don't acknowledge my presence. I did kind of expect you to stay with me to help me out. Instead you drop me into the meat grinder and go about your own merry conversations."

She paused at the comment, but only for a second. "You're ruining this for me!" she said, redirecting the conversation.

"I am?" I said incredulously. "If you were so all fired worried about their reaction to me, then why did you invite me? You know these people as well as I do. You know they don't like gemues, and I commend you for getting them past that little phobia to look past the color of your skin. I, however, am too much for their small attitudes to take, and you can't make them take me back into their circle. After all, it has to be very disquieting to find that someone whom they used to tell all that gemuephobic crap to, someone who even shared those views in the past is now one of 'them.' You should have known that they would react this way."

She averted her eyes from my face, licking her lips. "I . . ."she started.

I raised a hand angrily to stop her. "Forget it . . . to make you happy, I'll go." I stormed toward the door.

"Wait," she said at my back and I turned around, actually thinking that she might just apologize. I was glad I didn't hold my breath. "Before you do . . . Here." She handed me a slip of paper with a long string of numbers on it.

"What's this?" I asked, still angry.

"Your half of the settlement." She shrugged. "I didn't want you thinking that I had taken what is rightfully yours. That's the account number where your half of the money is. It's in a place that . . . doesn't restrict . . . gemues."

I scowled before shaking my head and handing the slip back to her. "Keep it. I don't want money. Use what it takes to pay Doc for the Wet-Breather, and keep the rest."

"But . . ." she started pushing the slip back toward me.

"I said, 'I don't want money'. It was never about that. I pity you if that is why you thought I came here tonight. I honestly thought you wanted to spend some time with me. I didn't expect to be forcefully reacquainted with my former friends, nor did I want to be subjected to the crap I've put up with tonight. How dare you accuse me of trying to sabotage your party!

"I'm not here to be an easy target. Good night and I hope your party goes well." I hissed, and I left her standing in the kitchen.

I was intent on getting out of this house as soon as I said goodbye to Max. After the support he had given me, and the inferred friendship he had offered, I at least owed him a goodbye. I finally found him on the other end of the house, surrounded by a few familiar Movement members that we both had known when I still worked for them. Without apology, I violated their circle and took Max by the arm saying, "I've got to go. Angelina just broke this camel's back."

"Oh," he said, trying to draw the details out of me.

"I'll tell you about it sometime when it's not so fresh."

Max's mouth thinned, getting the gist. "I'm sorry to hear that." He fished through his pocket a moment and came up with a card. "Here's my vid number. Give me a buzz and we'll get together, preferably somewhere with less people."

"Sure, I'll do that. You take care."

"I will," Max said as he watched me push through the crowd toward the door.

As I stalked off, I could hear them talk about me. "Like you really want to talk to him," one man said.

"Good show at playing nice with the dumb gemue, Max," Sarah said. She was an old college friend, or so I had thought. I stopped just beyond their line of vision, angry for their insults. My jaw worked furiously and I was ready to turn around and defend myself when Max spoke up for me.

"He has more brains than the two of you put together," Max snapped incredulously. "Don't you know who that is? David was your best friend in college, Sarah."

"A) Don't insult us like that," Sarah said indignantly, "and B) he must not have too many brain cells if he let himself get turned into a gemue."

"Even less after they irradiated his ass, eh, Sarah?" the other man said and they both laughed hysterically.

I heard a thump that I knew to be Max putting the guy on the wall. Max didn't look like much but he had learned long ago to handle himself. "You ungrateful son of a bitch! That man sacrificed his humanity to try and get us information . . . can you say that you're willing to do the same to support The Movement?" The man was silent and that was all the answer he needed. "I thought not."

"Thanks, Max," I whispered under my breath as I turned and left.

I made my way to the pier swiftly in the darkness, wishing there were no lights on the dock to give away my retreat. I hated retreats, but found myself with no other choice. All I wanted was to get away from here before my emotions overran my calm. I snatched my bag from the boat and changed back into my skins, not caring if anyone saw me, and glad to be free of the confines of those shoes. I was slower to stow my party clothes back into the waterproof duffle, mulling over the events of the day. All I could do was shake my head as I rose and turned to gaze at Angelina's new place, not quite believing all that had transpired. I clipped the bag of clothes to my waist, conjecturing on why I had bothered coming here. I was still not sure what I had been there to prove. Maybe it was to prove to myself what I had suspected at my release from the hospital - that she really did not feel the same anymore. I sighed heavily and said a mental goodbye to Angelina, and the tie that she had represented to my old life, before slipping into the water.

Time for me to live my new life on my own terms.

*****

Angelina stared out the window, observing as David moved further and further away. She didn't hear the party taking place behind her; all she could do was ponder why she had just excommunicated the only man she had truly loved from her life. She was numb, aghast with herself and how she had let her fear of losing her old friends bring her to do that to David.

Angelina was at war with herself about whether or not to run after him and beg his forgiveness, but her stubborn pride won out. Angelina saw him, as he looked one last time her direction, seemingly straight at her before slipping into the black water of the sea. Slowly, reluctantly, she moved away from the window and back into the swirling eddies of people, trying halfheartedly to forget about him and return to her friends.

The only thing she could think, though, was that these were shallow people, and she had just sunk to their level. She felt dirty somehow for that realization.

Printed in the United States
28749LVS00001BA/47

9 781420 833072